"Why did you leave, Gray? Why did you just disappear from the ranch, from my life, nine years ago?"

His gaze left Catherine's face and focused someplace over her shoulder. "First love, teenage fantasies." He looked at her once again, his eyes dark and unreadable. "What we had was just the lust and the wonder of young love. I did you a favor by leaving here and letting you get on with your adult life."

"It didn't feel like a favor at the time," she said softly, remembering the aching pain he'd left behind. However, there were certainly bigger issues at the moment.

"Water under the bridge, right?" he said. "We can't go backward, Catherine. We need to figure things out here and now. We need to make sure that you're covered at all times. And the only way I can do that is if you marry me."

The Coltons of Wyoming: Stories of true love, high stakes...and family honor.

Dear Reader,

The excitement and dysfunction of the Colton family makes the best kind of reading—addictive and a definite guilty pleasure.

There's also nothing better than a Colton marriage... unless the bride is unwilling and the groom is reluctant. Add in a heavy dose of desire between the two and a kidnapper determined to claim the new bride for ransom and you've got a roller coaster ride!

I hope you enjoy reading *The Colton Bride* as much as I enjoyed writing it.

Keep reading!

Carla Cassidy

THE COLTON BRIDE

Carla Cassidy

PAPL
DISCARDED

◆ **HARLEQUIN**®ROMANTIC SUSPENSE

Special thanks and acknowledgment to Carla Cassidy for her contribution to The Coltons of Wyoming miniseries.

Recycling programs
for this product may
not exist in your area.

ISBN-13: 978-0-373-27842-8

THE COLTON BRIDE

Copyright © 2013 by Harlequin Books S.A.

Printed in U.S.A.

www.Harlequin.com

Books by Carla Cassidy

Harlequin Romantic Suspense

Rancher Under Cover #1676
Cowboy's Triplet Trouble #1681
*Tool Belt Defender #1687
Mercenary's Perfect Mission #1708
**Her Cowboy Distraction #1711 ✓
**The Cowboy's Claim #1723 ✓
**Cowboy with a Cause #1735 ✓
A Profiler's Case for Seduction #1748
**Confessing to the Cowboy #1755 ✓
The Colton Bride #1772

‡Natural-Born Protector #1527
A Hero of Her Own #1548
††The Rancher Bodyguard #1551
5 Minutes to Marriage #1576
The Cowboy's Secret Twins #1584
*His Case, Her Baby #1600
*The Lawman's Nanny Op #1615
*Cowboy Deputy #1639
*Special Agent's Surrender #1648

Silhouette Romantic Suspense

‡Man on a Mission #1077
Born of Passion #1094
‡Once Forbidden... #1115
‡To Wed and Protect #1126
‡Out of Exile #1149
Secrets of a Pregnant Princess #1166
†Last Seen... #1233
†Dead Certain #1250
†Trace Evidence #1261
†Manhunt #1294
††Protecting the Princess #1345
††Defending the Rancher's Daughter #1376
††The Bodyguard's Promise #1419
††The Bodyguard's Return #1447
††Safety in Numbers #1463
††Snowbound with the Bodyguard #1521

‡The Delaney Heirs
†Cherokee Corners
††Wild West Bodyguards
*Lawmen of Black Rock
**Cowboy Café

CARLA CASSIDY

is an award-winning author who has written more than one hundred books for Harlequin Books. In 1995 she won Best Silhouette Romance from *RT Book Reviews* for *Anything for Danny*. In 1998 she also won a Career Achievement Award for Best Innovative Series from *RT Book Reviews*.

Carla believes the only thing better than curling up with a good book to read is sitting down at the computer with a good story to write. She's looking forward to writing many more books and bringing hours of pleasure to readers.

Chapter 1

The three Colton sisters sat in the parlor area of Catherine's bedroom suite, each of them pretending to carry on a casual conversation while ignoring the reason they were gathered together.

The pregnancy test Catherine had just taken was in the adjoining bathroom and none of them had looked at it yet to see the results.

The suite was three rooms: the sitting area, the bedroom and the bath. All were decorated in a splendor of pinks and black with silver accessories. This was Catherine's haven, the place she felt most safe and secure, but at the moment her nerves screamed inside her.

"Jim Radar's bull got himself all tangled up in a mess of barbed wire this morning. It took me hours to get him unwound and cleaned up," Amanda said. At twenty-eight, Amanda had a successful large animal veterinarian practice and a six-month-old daughter, Cheyenne, who was the love of her life. "I gave Jim a lecture about the dangers of barbed wire, but I think it went in one ear and out the other."

"How's the barn project coming along?" Catherine asked her younger sister, Gabriella. Gabby had a dream of turning an old red barn on the property into a center for troubled teens. She was not only devoted to her project but also planning a Christmas wedding with Trevor Garth, head of security here at the Dead River Ranch.

"Slowly," Gabby admitted, her green eyes sparkling with happiness. "I keep getting distracted by wedding plans. It's already October and that doesn't give me much time to have a perfect wedding by December."

"It's going to be a beautiful wedding and hopefully it will bring some joy into this place," Catherine replied.

Amanda sighed with a touch of impatience. "We've only got an hour before dinnertime. Shouldn't somebody go in there and check and find out if the answer is yes or no?"

Once again Catherine's nerves jumped erratically inside her veins, as if attempting to make a hasty escape. How had she gotten herself into the situation where she'd even have to take a pregnancy test? Before the question fully formed in her head, she knew the answer. She'd been such a fool. They'd always been so careful, always had what she assumed was safe sex, but apparently it was possible that at some point a condom hadn't done its job.

She stood from the dainty pink-and-white chair

where she'd been seated, an anxious dread attempting to weigh her back down. "I guess I'll go find out."

Gabby jumped up off the chaise where she and Amanda had been seated. She grabbed hold of Catherine's cold hand. "I'll go with you, Cath."

The whole thing felt surreal. When Catherine had missed her first period she'd chalked it up to all the stress and madness that had been taking place over the past couple of months at the ranch. When she'd missed her second period, she'd finally decided it was time to take the test. And now it was the moment of truth.

She squeezed Gabby's hand tightly as they entered the large, plush bathroom. The plastic test container was on the back of the stool and within five steps of it she could see the result. The positive sign glared up at her.

She was vaguely aware of Gabby's small gasp, but a curious numbness swept over Catherine. Pregnant. She was pregnant. The words went around and around in her head, but she couldn't grasp the concept.

She picked up the test and threw it into the small trash can next to the commode and then she and Gabby returned to the sitting room. Gabby gave a nod to Amanda as Catherine sank back down on her chair.

"So, what are you going to do, Cath?" Amanda asked.

"I don't know. I'm not sure. I need some time to think," Catherine replied. "Neither of you can tell anyone about this. It has to be our secret until I figure things out."

Amanda nodded solemnly. "My lips are sealed."

"Pinky swear," Gabby said. "You know your secret is safe with us."

Catherine did know. She and her sisters had always been a team, confiding in each other, trusting each other, especially lately when there was such tension, such a sense of uncertainty and a faint simmer of danger in the house.

"I need to go check on Cheyenne," Amanda said as she stood.

"And I've got some things to get to before dinner." Gabby gazed at Catherine in concern. "Are you going to be all right?"

"Of course." Catherine forced a smile to her lips.

"Do you need to talk or something?"

Catherine shook her head. "I just need some time to process everything. I think I'll head out to the petting barn for a little while before it's time to eat."

She'd be able to think more clearly there among the little creatures that depended on her for their care. She'd always found peace in the petting barn and she definitely needed some peace at the moment.

Thankfully, as she made her way downstairs and to one of the back doors, she encountered nobody. She didn't want to see anyone right now, didn't want to have to indulge in idle chitchat. She needed to embrace the fact that she was pregnant by a man she'd thought she might be in love with, a man she now abhorred.

The Dead River Ranch was one of the most prosperous spreads in Wyoming. The two-thousand-acre ranch was located in the Laramie Mountains, forty miles from Cheyenne.

The enormous mansion housed not only the three sisters, but also their sickly father, other relatives and staff and ranch hands. It was an entire community unto itself, and for the past three months the community had been folding in on itself, but she couldn't think about all that right now.

Not only was the house huge, but there were outbuildings everywhere and the remains of several that had burned in a horrible fire that had occurred two months before.

Old barns competed with new ones, stables and sheds dotted the landscape against a backdrop of blue endless skies and thick woods of a variety of trees.

As she stepped outside, she drew in a deep breath of the fresh, slightly bracing October air. It smelled of evergreen tinged wind from the mountains and of pastures browning with the cooler air. Cattle were visible in the distance, enjoying the late-afternoon sunshine while they grazed.

She headed toward the miniature barn where the petting area was located next to the huge stables building. The petting barn had been built two years ago when Catherine had found herself the unexpected owner of two friendly ferrets.

The owner of the ferrets, a friend of Catherine's, was getting married and moving and she didn't want to take her little babies to the local animal pound. Catherine had taken them and then had talked her father into building the petting barn.

She'd known her father, Jethro, would like the idea of a place where school and scout groups could come.

He loved the idea of anyone visiting the ranch and admiring all that he'd built here.

The minute she opened the waist-high white gate that surrounded a small outdoor arena, Inky and Dinky, the two miniature donkeys brayed a greeting and competed with two sheep, three pygmy goats and a pot-bellied pig to get her attention.

She laughed as she was nudged and head-butted by the variety of animals all vying for an ear scratch, a belly-rub or the nuggets of grains she often carried with her before coming into the enclosure. "Sorry, kids, nothing for you this afternoon," she said. Her words didn't lessen the enthusiasm of the furry, fluffy creatures who loved her with or without treats.

It took several minutes for her to make sure that each and every one of them got a little special time and then she headed inside the miniature barn that housed the smaller animals. Rabbits ran in a fenced area and ducks quacked their happiness as they swam in a small pool that was continuously fed fresh water. A large cage held Frick and Frack, the two ferrets who were favorites among the school and scout troops that came to visit the hands-on animal barn.

During those visits, Catherine acted as spokeswoman, educating the kids on each type of animal and their natural habitats and origins. It was something she loved to do when she got the opportunity.

There were stalls to house the outdoor animals during the harsh, cold winters and the entire barn was heated to keep everyone toasty while the snow flew outside and the temperatures dropped to subzero.

Today, as she checked food and water containers, petted and stroked each and every animal, her mind was a million miles away.

Pregnant.

She was pregnant.

Catherine admired Amanda her veterinarian business and Gabby for her commitment to troubled teens. At twenty-six years old Catherine hadn't yet figured out what she wanted to do with the rest of her life.

All she'd ever really dreamed of was being a wife and a mother. She'd once believed that would happen with Gray Stark, one of the ranch hands whom she'd loved with every fiber of her being when she'd been a teenager. Then one day she'd awakened to discover that he'd left Dead River Ranch and her behind without a word of explanation.

It had taken her a long time to realize he wasn't coming back, that whatever they'd shared was over and eventually she got on with her life. Thank goodness she hadn't waited around for him. He'd been gone from the ranch for five long years.

She lowered her hand to stroke a small circle across her still-flat lower stomach. Pregnant. Be careful what you wish for, she thought ruefully as she headed back toward the gate. She'd gotten half her wish, but the timing couldn't be worse.

She and the father of the baby had broken up two months ago and nothing and nobody would fix that particular relationship. She didn't want it fixed under any circumstances.

An attempted kidnapping, a couple of murders and

a dozen other crimes had created a houseful of distrust and wariness. Her father was on his deathbed and she and her sisters had been working hard in an attempt to locate their half brother Cole, who had been kidnapped over thirty years ago.

Now wasn't the time for her to be an unwed mother, and yet that's exactly what she intended to be. The minute she had seen the positive sign on the test she'd known she was going to have this baby.

She paused at the gate, nervously twirling a strand of her hair with one hand while the other moved to her stomach once again.

Despite the fact that she'd grown to hate the man she'd been dating, the scoundrel who had fathered the baby, she already loved the life growing inside her. This was her baby and there was no way she'd let Dirk Sinclair know anything about it. He'd shown his true colors and she didn't want him anywhere near her or her baby.

A wave of light-headedness swept over her as she stepped out of the gate. She clung to the fence, waiting for it to pass, but it seemed to get worse.

Stress.

It was all too much.

Her head spun with memories of the night somebody had attempted to kidnap her little niece, Cheyenne, and the unsolved murder of the governess Faye Frick who had tried to intervene. Poor cook's assistant Jenny Burke, murdered in the ranch kitchen pantry and her killer not yet found.

Flashes fired off in her brain of her father in his bed, looking like death as he drifted in and out of comas because of the cancer that ate at him. So much, there was suddenly too much spinning around in her head.

And now, in all the chaos and uncertainty, she was pregnant. Everything whirled faster and faster in her mind and then light-headedness overwhelmed her. She slumped to the ground with her back against the fence. She just needed a minute to rest. She'd be fine if she could just rest a bit, she thought as darkness claimed her.

He smelled her long before he saw her. Ranch foreman Gray Stark had a history with that distinctive fragrance of exotic spices and mysterious flowers. Catherine Colton had worn it for the year and a half he'd loved her, for the five years that he'd hated her and now for the past four years of his cold indifference toward her.

He only had to take a couple of steps out of the stable and he knew she was someplace nearby. The scent eddied in the air, rising above the smell of animals and hay and oiled leather.

She was probably at the petting barn. He glanced at his watch and noted that it was nearing dinnertime. He wondered if she knew how late it was getting.

Although his usual pattern was to avoid being anyplace where he thought she might be, he decided to walk over to the small barn and let her know that it was almost time to eat.

He knew she often lost track of time when she was tending to the ranch's animals. She'd always loved the creatures of the earth and was a natural at nurturing all the ones in her care.

As he ambled toward the small barnlike structure, he steeled himself to see her. He'd believed he'd cast her out of his head, out of his heart in the five years that he'd been away from Dead River Ranch and working on a ranch in Montana.

Four years ago when his father, the former ranch foreman, had become ill, Gray had come back to Dead River Ranch and when his father had passed, Gray had become the new foreman.

In all that time there were moments he almost forgot that he'd once loved Catherine Colton, there were increments of time that he almost forgot the depth of her betrayal. But, seeing her always wrought myriad emotions in him, emotions that he consciously schooled to indifference.

She had no place in his life and he had none in hers. He'd learned that lesson when he'd been eighteen years old, a hard lesson that he was likely never to forget.

Any indifference he might have felt for her fled as he rounded the corner to the petting barn and saw her slumped on the ground against the fence.

Adrenaline roared through him as he raced to her side, his gun pulled and at the ready. Had she been attacked? He hadn't been that far away in the stables and he hadn't heard her cry out, hadn't heard anything that would warrant action or warn of any danger.

It took only a quick assessment to assure him that she didn't appear to have any wounds anywhere. He tucked his gun back into the holster, sat next to her on the ground and pulled her into his arms.

"Catherine?" Everyone around the ranch called her Cath, but when Gray had returned to Dead River Ranch, he'd decided he'd never call her by that affectionate nickname again. He also refused to call her Miss Catherine as all the other staff did. Cath had been a woman he loved. Catherine was just one of his bosses.

He felt the side of her neck, where her pulse was steady and strong. "Catherine," he said louder, as if by the sheer strength of the command in his deep voice alone he could bring her around.

It worked. She drew a deep breath and slowly opened her eyes. For just a moment he was eighteen years old again and she was seventeen. Her indigo-blue eyes held sweet softness and her long blond hair spilled over his arm like a sheet of honey-colored silk. As if in a trance, her lush lips turned up in a smile of such pleasure it ached deep inside him.

Like a time warp, it was as if they were both momentarily trapped in the past, in a time when they'd loved one another more than anyone else in the world, in a time when he'd been foolish enough to believe that a wealthy Colton might really choose a future with a dirt-poor ranch hand.

The moment snapped and she bolted upright at the same time he released her and quickly rose to his feet. "What happened?" he asked. Reluctantly he held out his hand to help her up, unsure if she'd accept his aid or not. They hadn't exactly been on friendly terms for the past few years.

She slipped her small hand into his and he pulled her up, both of them breaking the physical contact instantly once she was on her feet.

She looked around, as if momentarily confused. "I don't know. I guess I fainted." She frowned and her hand went to her stomach. "I got really light-headed and sat down and that's the last thing I remember."

"Why would you faint? You've never been the fainting type before." He looked at her in disbelief.

A new tiny frown danced in the center of her forehead. "I…uh…didn't sleep well last night and I missed lunch."

His disbelief deepened. A night of little sleep and a missed meal wouldn't make somebody as healthy and strong as Catherine faint. There had to be something else going on with her.

"I'm pregnant." The words blurted from her lips. Her eyes widened as she slapped a hand over her mouth. She slowly raised her hand to her hair and twirled a strand of it, a remembered indication to him that she was upset. "I took a test just a little while ago and it was positive. I'm going to have a baby."

A whole new host of emotions flew through Gray. "I'm sure Dirk must be very happy. Is there a wedding planned for the near future?" He knew she'd been seeing society playboy Dirk Sinclair for the past six months or so. Their pictures had graced the society pages more than once in recent months.

"There won't be a wedding," Catherine said as she started walking toward the house. "Dirk and I broke up two months ago when he discovered I wouldn't get my inheritance until I turned thirty years old."

Gray fell into step beside her. Everyone who lived and worked at the ranch knew that Catherine's father, Jethro, had stipulated that all heirs had to live at the ranch until they turned thirty years old and only then would they receive their inheritance, a substantial amount of money.

"Only my sisters know about the baby and I've sworn them all to absolute secrecy. Dirk will never know. He made it obvious to me that he was courting my money, not me, and I don't want him in my life for any reason."

"I'm sorry about you and Dirk," Gray said, only because it was expected of him.

"I'm not." She raised her chin. "I'm just grateful he showed his true colors before I accepted his stupid proposal." Her hand slid down her light blue sweatshirt and lingered on her stomach, her eyes darkening. "This is my baby and nobody else's."

Gray's stomach clenched with an unexpected tightness. He was surprised to discover that it bothered him more than a little bit that she carried another man's baby. It was a stupid reaction that he refused to give weight. He was never meant to be the father of her children. Far better men than him were destined for that particular role in her life.

What her information did do was make him recognize that this would make her a particularly desirable victim to any kidnapper with a brain…two Colton heirs for the price of one.

"If you're smart you'll keep this a secret for as long

as you possibly can. It puts a huge target on your back," he said and then hurriedly added, "not that it's any of my business."

He thought she saw a faint flinch etch across her pretty features. "You're right, it isn't any of your business," she replied coolly, making him wonder if he'd seen the flinch or just imagined it. He couldn't imagine that there was anything he could say to her that would actually hurt her.

Whatever he'd thought they had together years ago had been nothing but an illusion and in the four years that he'd been back at the ranch she'd dated a variety of men befitting a Colton, confirming to him that she'd never really cared about him anyway.

Still, when they reached the back door where she would enter and he would continue on around the mansion to the entryway for staff, he took her by the arm.

He wanted to ask her what in hell was she thinking? There was danger all around them. This was the worst time to let people know a new Colton heir was on the way. It had only been three months since somebody had tried to kidnap the youngest Colton heir, Cheyenne, the first time. A second attempt had been made less than a month before, thankfully both unsuccessful, but the first attempt had left his best friend's mother dead.

At the moment, Catherine and the baby she carried lived in a crazy world, in the house that suddenly felt mad with a simmering sick energy.

"I'm serious, Catherine. You need to be careful and you should keep your pregnancy a secret."

She pulled her arm from his grasp, as if unable to

abide his touch. "I've been taking care of myself for years. I'm sure I can take care of myself now." She didn't wait for a response, but turned on her heels and went inside the door, leaving him only the whisper of her perfume lingering in the air.

He muttered a curse and headed for the employee door. He'd have just enough time to head up to his Spartan room in the male staff housing area, take a quick shower and then get down to the employee dining room for dinner.

Minutes later, he stood beneath a spray of hot water and tried to keep his thoughts away from Catherine, but it was next to impossible.

Holding her in his arms for those brief moments had picked the scabs off scars he'd thought long healed. In the five years that he had been away from Dead River Ranch and working on a ranch in Montana, he'd occasionally dated other women. But none of them had managed to evoke in him the depth of tenderness, the wealth of desire, the overwhelming rush of love that Cath had so many years ago.

Cath. She'd always been his Cath but since his return to the ranch she was Catherine in his heart and mind, the distinction necessary for him to forget what had been, what he knew would never be.

In the four years since he'd been back at the ranch, as if by mutual agreement she and he had steered clear of each other, rarely speaking to one another unless it was absolutely necessary.

She'd stopped being his problem almost nine years ago and there was no reason for anything to change now.

Still, he couldn't help the simmering anxiety that tightened in his chest as he thought of what a perfect target she would make for a kidnapping and ransom scheme.

The crime had been attempted before with the result being the wrong child kidnapped and a beloved governess dead and the second attempt had only intensified the feeling in the house that both crimes were probably inside jobs.

The family was a convoluted mess, with an ex-wife, illegitimate children and sundry other relatives living in the mansion while the patriarch, Jethro, battled leukemia and drifted in and out of consciousness depending on the day. His illegitimate son, Dr. Levi Colton, had come to do what he could for the man who was his father.

He'd not only brought a bag of medical tricks with him, but also the baggage of a child who had never been acknowledged. At least in the past month Levi had found some peace and had fallen in love with pastry chef Katie McCord.

Gray had no idea how well the staff had been vetted. Mathilda Perkins, the head housekeeper, was in charge of the hiring and firing of employees. He'd never had any reason to doubt that Mathilda did adequate background checks on the people she hired and that she had the best interests of the family at heart at all times. She'd been a devoted employee for many years.

As he pulled on a pair of clean jeans and a denim shirt, he reminded himself that Catherine and her situation weren't his problem. All he had to worry about was ordering supplies, overseeing the other ranch hands and keeping the horses and cattle healthy and happy.

Catherine Colton wasn't part of his job, nor was she a part of his life, and he definitely intended to keep it that way.

Chapter 2

Dinner in the Colton family dining room was always a study of pretend civility, underlying tension and slight unpleasant innuendoes. The dining table stretched from nearly one side of the plush, elegant dining room to the other and as Catherine took her seat her gaze automatically went to the empty chair at the head of the table.

Her father had been a stern man with little time for his daughters, but Catherine loved him in spite of all his flaws and she always missed his presence at the evening meal.

When she'd been little he'd command the conversation, talking about how he'd built Dead River Ranch to be the most prosperous ranch in the entire state of Wyoming. He loved his ranch, his money and women and he occasionally remembered that he had three little daughters who were totally dependent on him since their mother had run out on them.

Now his chair was empty because of his illness. At the opposite end of the table was another empty chair, one that stood ready for Cole Colton, Jethro's son who had been kidnapped as a baby thirty years ago.

When their father had first become ill, Catherine, Gabriella and Amanda had hired a private investigator in an attempt to find their missing half brother, hoping that a reunion would buoy Jethro's spirits and give him a reason to fight his illness. There was also a possibility that Cole could be a bone marrow donor and save Jethro's life.

But, while some clues had come to light, there had been nothing so far that pointed them to Jethro's missing son. It was a thirty-year-old cold case that wasn't going to be suddenly solved.

Next to Catherine at the table were Gabby and her fiancé, Trevor Garth, who also served as head of security for the ranch. Amanda sat at the end of the table with six-month-old Cheyenne in a bouncy seat on the floor next to her.

On the opposite side of the table were Levi and Katie, Jethro's third ex-wife, Darla Colton, and her two grown children, Tawny and Trip.

Without Jethro at the table, meals had become noisy, chaotic affairs where people talked over one another while the air shimmered with distrust. Darla, the Botox bottled-blond bitch, as the sisters referred to her, loved the sound of her own voice and if it wasn't her doing the talking, then it was her son, Trip, who often smelled of booze or pot, depending on the day and the time.

A headache began at Catherine's left temple as she declined the traditional glass of wine that was always served with the evening meal.

The conversation that swirled around the table throughout the meal was much like it had been for the past couple of weeks. It revolved around the latest attempted kidnapping of Cheyenne, the intervention by Jagger McKnight, an investigative reporter who had been attacked and left for dead on the ranch property. For a while everyone had believed that Jagger was the long-lost Cole, especially when it was discovered he had a piece of an old blue blanket with distinctive embroidery on it in his pocket, a piece of blanket that had once belonged to the missing Cole.

The truth had come out, that Jagger was a reporter, that the blanket bit had been planted on him while he'd been unconscious and everyone had been left with more questions than answers.

Halfway through the meal Catherine wished she had decided to eat in her room. Gabby touched her arm lightly, her green eyes filled with concern. "Are you all right?" she whispered.

"I'm fine. I just have a touch of a headache," Catherine replied.

"Gee, I wonder why?" Gabby inclined her head toward Trip, who was on his fourth glass of wine and getting louder and louder with each minute that passed. His favorite topic was his prowess with the staff and how every maid who worked in the house had the hots for him.

The sisters had speculated for a long time why Darla and her children were allowed residency in the house. Jethro and Darla had been divorced for years and he'd never shown any interest in her or her two children by a previous marriage, and yet they had their own suite in one of the wings of the house.

They had all decided that Darla knew something about her ex-husband, that she had some piece of information so damning that she'd managed to blackmail herself into a cushy place in the mansion for herself and her children.

Catherine wasn't close to Darla or her two spoiled adult children and with everything that had happened recently, she couldn't help but be suspicious of them.

Everyone was suspicious of everyone else, and the recent months of murder, deceit and chaos had taken a toll on each and every resident in the huge mansion. The only people Catherine truly trusted were her sisters.

When the meal was finished, head housekeeper Mathilda Perkins slid into the room and stood next to the wall as two young women carried silver trays of after-dinner coffee.

Mathilda looked like something from a gothic movie with her silver-blond hair pulled into a severe knot at the nape of her neck. Narrowed blue-gray eyes and a starched gray dress added to the aura of a gothic servant. The only difference was she watched the two new kitchen hires, Lucinda Garcia and Kyla Winters, with benevolent eyes, the same way she gazed at each and every person at the table with a hint of fondness.

Catherine's headache had blossomed from her left temple to chase all the way across her forehead. Caffeine. There was nothing she loved more than her after-dinner shot of leaded coffee.

As Kyla was about to pour her a cup, Catherine suddenly thought about the new life inside her and quickly stopped her. "I'd rather have decaf," she said.

From across the table Darla arched a blond perfectly tweezed brow. "Interesting. No wine before dinner, no caffeine in your coffee. Why one would think that you might have a little secret."

"She's pregnant," Tawny exclaimed with excitement, as if she'd suddenly cured cancer.

It was obviously just a guess on her part, but the expression on Catherine's face must have given her away. Suddenly the conversation ratcheted up in volume as everyone talked about the prospect of a new Colton heir.

Escape! With her head pounding, Catherine needed to escape the table, escape this room and these people. She excused herself and ran for the door, leaving the rest of them to speculate on who the father might be, when the due date would come and whether it would be a boy or a girl.

She'd scarcely found out about her condition herself and already it was gossip fodder around the dining room table. How had Tawny guessed so easily? Drat it all, Catherine should have taken the pregnancy test and buried it in the pasture instead of throwing it into her bathroom trash can. For all she knew Tawny went through everyone's trash to learn whatever secrets somebody might have.

There were only three places where Catherine found peace, the first was her bedroom suite, the second was the petting barn and the third was in her father's suite where she often sat next to his bed and talked to him.

She knew he was in a coma at the moment, but as terrible as it sounded, that was the time she found it easiest to sit with him, to talk to him, to simply love him.

It took her some time to walk the long corridors that led to his suite of rooms. She entered his sitting room, a pleasant area filled with a stone fireplace, bookshelves and decorated in rich greens and golds. The fireplace stood cold and empty, but it wouldn't be long before it would be filled with burning wood to keep the winter chill from invading the area.

To her left was her father's bedroom and as she entered, she nodded to the middle-aged woman in the white uniform. Nurse Linetta Wheeling had been hired several weeks ago to sit with Jethro during the evenings and overnight.

"Good evening, Miss Catherine," she said as she rose from the straight-backed chair near Jethro's bed.

Catherine nodded and then looked at her father, her heart squeezing tight as she took in the sight. Jethro had once been a robust, imposing figure, but now his face was gaunt and he looked tiny beneath the heavy green spread that covered him.

"Any changes?" Catherine asked.

"None." Linetta offered a sympathetic smile. "I'll just step outside and give you a little time alone with him." As quiet as a mouse, Linetta slid out of the room and into the sitting room.

Catherine pulled a green-and-gold patterned chair closer to the side of the bed, ignoring the IV and medical equipment hooked up to the sick man in the bed.

"Hi, Daddy. It's me, Cath." For a moment she merely sat quietly. Jethro Colton was a complicated man and he'd been a difficult man to love, as a man and as a father. He'd always loved the women and women loved him back, a reality that usually placed his daughters on the back burner of his life.

Still, there had been moments in her childhood when she'd seen him be the kind of father she yearned for, the daddy she could love with all her heart, and it was the memory of those rare moments that kept her loving him now.

"I've gone and done something stupid, Daddy," she finally said. "I was hoodwinked by a man I thought I could love but I discovered all he was after was my inheritance. When he found out I wouldn't get it for another four years, he dropped me like a hot potato. Unfortunately, he left a little something of himself behind. I'm pregnant, Daddy. You're going to be a grandfather again and you need to wake up and get well."

Her eyes blurred with tears as she realized the futility of the conversation. The cancer was draining the very life from Jethro. He'd probably never live to see his new grandchild.

If only they could find Cole. Surely being reunited with his firstborn son who'd been kidnapped so many years ago would rally Jethro to aggressively fight the disease that was eating away at him.

Her mind drifted from her father and his missing son to Gray Stark and that moment in front of the petting barn fence when she'd opened her eyes and had been in his strong arms.

His sandy blond hair had gleamed in the dusk light of day creating a halo effect around his head. In the depths of his brown eyes she'd imagined the soft, sweet emotions she'd believed he'd once felt for her.

Reality had slapped her in the face as he'd quickly released her and she realized his eyes were dark, assessing. No illusion of evening sunshine could turn Gray Stark into a loving, caring angel of a man.

The few times they encountered each other all she got from him was dark eyes, fathomless stares and few words. The boy she'd loved was gone, replaced by a man she didn't know, a man who made no pretense that he didn't want to know anything about the woman she had become.

She wondered if he'd loved somebody in the five years he'd been gone from Dead River Ranch. She wondered even more why she cared. In the four years he'd been back she'd never heard any gossip about him and any woman.

What little gossip she had heard about him was that he was all work and little play, a tough but fair taskmaster who kept a keen eye on the wranglers who worked beneath him.

She returned her gaze to the man on the bed. "Daddy, you need to fight this." She gently picked up one of his hands that lay on top of the bedspread. Calloused from hard work, yet thin and cold, it lay lifeless in hers. She rubbed his hand with both of hers, trying to warm his, but it didn't work.

She returned his hand to the top of the spread and then stood, unsure what she was hoping to gain from being here, but knowing she'd gained nothing.

Dinner had just finished up in the employee dining room when kitchen helper Lucinda Garcia reentered the room, her brown eyes sparkling with excitement. "Looks like there is going to be another Colton heir," she announced.

"Miss Gabby going to give the little princess a baby brother or sister?" George Jeffries, one of the ranch hands, asked.

"Nope, it's Miss Catherine," Lucinda replied.

Gray's blood turned cold as he shoved back from the large, rough-hewn wooden table. What in the hell had she done? Made an official announcement over dinner?

Hadn't he warned her to keep the information about her pregnancy to herself for her own safety? Now everyone in the entire house would know…all the family…all the staff and Gray was positive that the evil that had created such havoc in the past couple of months had come from within, not from some outside source.

It was with a head full of steam that he left the employee dining room and went in search of Catherine. He knew her habit was often to visit Jethro's suite right after dinner and that was where he headed.

He stalked the long hallways toward the master suite,

unsure what he intended to say to Catherine, even more uncertain why he felt the need to discuss the matter with her at all.

What he wanted to do was take her by her slender shoulders and shake her for telling everyone. What he wanted to do was forget that for just a moment at the petting barn as he'd held her in his arms and she'd smiled up at him he'd wanted to lower his lips to hers and plant a kiss that would possess her completely. He'd wanted to brand her as his own in a way he'd obviously been unable to do as a teenager.

He clenched his hands into fists at his side. The fact that he'd entertained any notion of kissing her ticked him off. He was now ranch foreman, but that didn't mean he would ever be good enough for Catherine Colton.

This simmering old anger mixed with the aggravation he felt for her over spilling her secret. When he reached Jethro's suite he stood just outside the door, able to hear Catherine's soft voice murmuring from the bedroom.

He leaned against the wall, unwilling to interrupt her time with her dying father, but determined to have his say to her. In the distance he could hear others in the house moving around, going to their own suites or gathering in the great room for some conversation before heading their separate ways. He easily imagined he could hear the whispering of deadly secrets, the plotting of evil, the suppressed air of danger ready to spring at any moment.

The problem was he wasn't sure where the danger

might come from or who it might be directed at, he only knew that Catherine, with her surprising news, had just placed herself in a potential place of extreme vulnerability and she had absolutely nobody to watch her back.

It didn't take long for Catherine to leave the suite and as she turned in the opposite direction of where he'd been waiting for her, he took two long steps forward and reached out to grab her by the arm.

She gasped in alarm and only relaxed a bit when she turned to see him. "Gray, what are you doing lurking around in the shadows of the hallway?" She pulled her arm from his grasp. "What do you want?"

He was momentarily speechless as he gazed at her in the semidarkness of the corridor. She'd changed for dinner from the sweatshirt and jeans into a blue dress cinched at her slender waist, fitted across the bodice and then flaring out in a short fall of silk to her knees, exposing her long, shapely legs.

She looked stunning and the fact that he noticed only raised the level of his anger. "I want to ask you if you have a death wish," he replied, his words clipped, terse with his displeasure.

"What are you talking about?" She frowned.

"I thought we'd agreed that you would keep your pregnancy a secret for as long as possible."

"I don't recall agreeing to anything with you," she replied. Her cheeks dusted with color. "Besides, I didn't actually tell anyone. I just refused wine at dinner and asked for decaffeinated coffee afterward. Darla and Tawny noticed and made a big deal out of it and before I knew it everyone had guessed my secret."

"I told you that this 'secret' puts you at a higher risk for something bad happening to you," he replied.

Her frown deepened. "You're making this into too big a deal."

"Too big a deal?" he asked incredulously. "Have you forgotten that three months ago somebody tried to kidnap Cheyenne and in the process Faye Frick was killed? Have you forgotten that Jenny Burke was found dead in the kitchen pantry? Only a month ago another attempt was made to take Cheyenne?"

"Okay, stop!" Catherine placed her hands over her ears, not wanting to hear anything more. She knew awful things were happening all around her, but she didn't want to hear them listed out loud. She didn't even like to think about them. "I know what's been going on," she said as she lowered her hands to her sides.

"You don't seem to be taking all of it seriously enough," Gray retorted, some of his anger seeping out of him as concern took over. "You need to hire yourself a bodyguard or something."

Catherine looked at him in disbelief. "This is my home, my family. I shouldn't need a bodyguard here. Besides, Gabby doesn't have a bodyguard."

"True, but she's living and sleeping with Trevor, the head of security."

"What about Amanda? She comes and goes as she pleases."

"And also has an ex-marine tough guy playing bodyguard to Cheyenne." He leaned against the wall. "In fact, you've probably done him a favor by taking the target off Cheyenne and putting it right on your back.

Maybe he'll be able to sleep a little better at night now knowing there's a new target to take the heat off him."

"You're just being hateful," Catherine replied, her tone of voice slightly higher than usual.

"I'm being realistic," he countered and pushed himself off the wall as she continued down the hallway. "If you were smart you'd marry that kid's father and move him in here where he could keep an eye on you."

"That's never, ever going to happen." She stopped walking and turned to face him once again. "I wasn't sure I was in love with Dirk before he broke up with me and since then I'm positive that marrying him would have been the absolute worst mistake of my life."

Her eyes flashed with the certainty, with the fury of her emotions and words. She looked absolutely magnificent. Gray was oddly pleased by those words, although they certainly didn't help her situation at all.

"I don't need him and I don't need your help, Gray. I've done just fine without your advice, without your presence in my life for the past nine years. Since you've been back at the ranch for the past four years we've scarcely exchanged ten words with each other, so don't go pretending that you care about my well-being now."

She raised her enchanting delicate pointed chin. "I don't need Dirk. I don't need a bodyguard and I certainly don't need you."

She whirled around and stalked down the hallway as Gray gazed after her, wondering why in the hell after all these years he felt that an obstinate part of his heart was still invested in her.

Chapter 3

Dreams of Gray haunted her sleep, erotic, hot dreams of the time when they were teenagers and meeting secretly in the stables after dark. She'd loved him since she was fifteen and he'd been sixteen, but he'd refused to make love to her for two years, although there had been plenty of snuggling and making out and almost lovemaking in those two years.

When they'd finally allowed themselves the pleasure of going all the way, Gray had been tender and so sweet and after that first time they had shared a passion for each other that had been explosive, magic and insatiable.

There had also been a lot of planning in those teenage years. They'd talked about owning a little ranch not far from here, having a couple of kids to raise and a lifetime of love and happiness together.

Catherine awakened and in that brief limbo between dreams and complete consciousness, her heart was filled with love for Gray. The scent of him lingered in her brain, reminding her of how it had felt to be held in his arms, how his lips had plied hers with such fire. In her vision his whiskey-brown eyes gazed at her with such want, such need, it burned deep inside her soul.

Then full awake slammed into her and the fantasy shattered into a million pieces, leaving her heart aching and empty. She clutched her pillow to her chest and lingered for a few minutes, the dream still far too fresh in her head.

Oh, what fantasies they had spun so many years ago and then one morning she'd gotten up and discovered he was gone. She now released her hold on the pillow and got out of bed. And he'd remain gone from her heart, she told herself as she headed into the adjoining bathroom for her morning shower.

He had some nerve, anyway, acting like he was concerned about her, acting like he cared about her safety. After four years of pretending she didn't even exist, he had no right to be concerned about her now.

She shoved all thoughts of Gray Stark from her head as she stepped beneath the water in the large glass enclosure. She had other things to think about…like the pregnancy test she'd taken that had given her a positive result.

She needed to see a doctor and get confirmation of the test. There were prenatal vitamins to take, instructions to listen to and things to learn. She wanted to do everything she could to ensure that she carried a healthy baby and once she or he was born she'd make sure she was the best mother she could be.

There was really no role model for her to follow. Her own mother had left Jethro and the three girls when they were young and she hadn't been much of a mother before she'd deserted them. Catherine had never seen her mother again and had little interest in ever reconnecting with her.

Catherine didn't really know what it was like to have a mother, but she certainly knew what it was like not to have one.

All the things she had longed for as a little girl, as an insecure teenager would be gifted to her own child. Her child would never spend a second wondering if he or she was wanted and loved.

She'd spent far too much of her life wondering that very fact. Her mother had run out on her. Gray's abandonment in her teens hadn't helped her insecurities, and Dirk's desire to marry her only for her inheritance had just been the icing on the cake.

Catherine had what she wanted, a baby growing inside her, and she didn't need a man to complete her. She could do this all just fine by herself. As she toweled off she realized that the pregnancy had made her decide that she had no intention of ever bringing a man into her life again.

She'd never have to wonder if she was loved for herself or for her enormous inheritance that she'd receive in four years. She never had to go through the dating game again. Love just wasn't in her cards, except the love of her child. And that was more than enough to make her happy for the rest of her life.

By the time she left the bathroom dressed for the day, the young maid Allison Murray was in her room, tidying up and making the bed. "Good morning, Miss Catherine," she said with her usual bright, cheerful smile.

"Good morning, Allison. How are the weekend classes coming along?"

"Great," Allison replied as she fluffed a pillow. "My economics teacher told me I have a natural knack for numbers." She laughed, her green eyes sparkling. "Who would have thought?"

"I think it's wonderful that you're pursuing your education," Catherine said to the pretty young woman.

Allison cast her a sly glance. "And I think it's wonderful that you're pregnant. Have you been to the doctor yet?"

"Not yet. I just found out by taking one of those home pregnancy tests." Catherine sank down in her favorite chair while Allison finished plumping all the pillows on the bed.

"You should get yourself to a doctor. I've heard that sometimes those home pregnancy tests can give you a false positive," she said.

"I'll check in with a doctor as soon as possible," Catherine replied, although she knew the test was right. Even though it was far too early for her to feel anything or for her belly to show any signs of the life inside, Catherine knew with certainty it was there. She felt it in her heart, in her very soul.

She visited with the woman for a few more minutes

and then when Allison went into the bathroom to clean up, Catherine headed for the dining room. She was later than usual and was grateful to find herself alone except for Amanda, who was at the table lingering over a cup of coffee.

"Hey, Cath." She greeted Catherine with a smile and gestured to the chair next to her. "You missed the usual breakfast fracas. Darla spent most of the conversation whining that she wanted their suite redecorated and I swear Trip had already been drinking."

"Gee, sorry I missed the fun," Catherine replied dryly. "I was wondering if you could get me in to see your OB/GYN doctor in Laramie."

"Dr. Kendall? You'll love her, and if I give her a call right now I'll bet she could work you in before the end of the day."

Catherine laughed. "I don't think it's necessary to move that fast."

"That baby of yours is going to be Cheyenne's first cousin, her first real playmate. There's no time like the present to get you in to the doctor and on a regimen of healthy eating and vitamins."

At that moment head cook Agnes Barlow stepped into the room, her short red hair an indication of her fiery disposition with the kitchen staff. "Miss Catherine, would you like something for breakfast?" she asked. There was no hint of warmth or welcome in her voice. She was all work and no-nonsense.

"Thank you, Agnes, maybe just a glass of orange juice and a piece of toast," Catherine said.

"Are you having morning sickness?" Amanda asked.

"No, nothing like that. I'm just not that hungry this morning."

By the time Catherine had finished her glass of juice and toast, Amanda had set her up with a four-thirty appointment with Dr. Victoria Kendall.

The sisters parted then, Amanda heading toward the nursery to check in on Cheyenne and Catherine leaving the house for the petting barn to take care of the morning chores.

She could have hired somebody to do the caretaking of the animals for her, but Catherine didn't mind getting her hands dirty and the work out there gave her a sense of purpose that she needed in her life.

She left the house for the walk to the barn and although she saw several ranch hands out in the pastures, thankfully she didn't see Gray.

With her dreams of him still so fresh in her mind, she wasn't ready to see him anytime soon. It was bad enough that she couldn't get the scent of him out of her head and that he'd invaded her sleep all night long.

He'd stood so close to her when he'd encountered her outside of her father's suite that she'd been able to feel his body heat radiating toward her, smelled the scent of fresh minty soap and shaving cream and a hint of woodsy cologne that was so familiar.

She'd read somewhere that scents easily pulled up specific people and places from memory, and she knew it was true. Gray's scent had brought up times in the past that she'd prefer she never remember.

She was grateful when she reached the little barn with its smells of hay and grain and animal. As she worked to clean the area and replace foul hay with fresh, she thought about all the things that had happened in the past couple of months.

Yes, there had been terrible things going on. It seemed that when the three sisters had put into motion a plan to find their missing brother, Cole, the entire world had gone crazy.

However, good things had happened, too. Mia Sanders, who had worked as a nurse at the ranch infirmary, had left with Jagger McKnight, the investigative reporter who many had initially believed was the missing Cole. They moved away to begin a life of love and happiness together.

Levi, Jethro's illegitimate son, had come home to help doctor the man he'd cut ties with years before and in the process had found love with pastry cook Katie McCord. Even Gabby had found true love with Trevor despite the drama of everything surrounding them.

Catherine preferred to focus on the positive than dwell on all the negative things that had taken place in recent months. Her sisters both accused her of being a Pollyanna, but Catherine didn't care. She couldn't control the bad things happening on and around the ranch, had no idea who was behind them and so chose to try to keep her head buried in the sand as much as possible.

After she'd finished at the barn, she went back to her suite to shower again and get dressed for the thirty-minute drive into Laramie to see the doctor.

She skipped the family lunch, deciding she'd make the drive leisurely and stop at a café for a quiet lunch alone and maybe even do a little shopping before her doctor's appointment.

It was just after noon when she got into her red Jeep and headed toward Laramie. She had gone to Laramie and to the bigger city of Cheyenne often when she'd been dating Dirk and to attend a variety of charity events.

The town of Dead, Wyoming, was located only fifteen miles from the ranch, but offered little other than the basics of a small town.

For any real shopping or dining experience most people drove into Laramie or Cheyenne and it was well worth the drive to Laramie for Catherine to become a patient of the doctor who had seen Amanda through her pregnancy with Cheyenne.

Being away from the ranch eased some of the tension she'd carried with her for the past couple of months, tension she hadn't realized she possessed. At least for the day she didn't intend to think about the things happening at the ranch or her father's health. Today she just intended to relax.

She ate a late lunch at a fashionable bistro and then browsed in a nice boutique that had not only clothing but also shoes and a jewelry counter.

It was at the jewelry counter that she saw it…a necklace that the clerk hooked at the nape of her neck. The aquamarine stone in the center was surrounded by sparkling diamonds and nestled as if it belonged on her between her collarbones. She loved it, bought it and wore it out of the store.

As she left to head to her doctor's appointment, the

necklace felt warm against her skin. She could tell her son or daughter that she'd bought it on the very day she'd officially confirmed her pregnancy.

If she had a little girl then the necklace would be a gift for her when she turned sixteen and if she had a boy, then it would be a gift to his bride on the day of his wedding.

She was pleased with her purchase and equally pleased with Dr. Victoria Kendall. The doctor was middle-aged, broad-faced with round glasses and brown eyes that appeared kind and calm enough to deal with any pregnancy jitters.

They began with a list of questions that Catherine answered, questions about her general health and the date of her last period. Blood was taken and then Catherine was set up for an ultrasound.

"I would guess that your due date is going to be around the first of April," Dr. Kendall said as she squirted cold gel onto Catherine's stomach. As she firmly moved the transducer around Catherine's belly, Catherine watched the screen and gasped in surprise as she saw the little fetus inside her.

"Makes it real, doesn't it?" Dr. Kendall said as she pointed out the head, the facial features that had begun to form and the heart beating strong and sure. "This sonogram confirms that you're about nine weeks along and that would keep your due date correct."

"April. It seems so far away," Catherine said once she was redressed and Dr. Kendall was writing out a script for prenatal vitamins.

Dr. Kendall looked up and smiled. "About March

you'll be thinking April can't get here fast enough for you. I'll see you again in a month and in the meantime if you have any questions or concerns, please don't hesitate to give me a call."

It was just after five-thirty when Catherine got back in her Jeep to head home. She sat for a moment, her fingers gripping the necklace around her throat as the wonder of the new life inside warmed her.

This was real. She'd actually seen the baby growing inside her. She was pregnant and she felt as if she'd been given the best gift in the whole world.

By the time she was halfway home she had to turn on her headlights against the darkness usurping the twilight. At this time of year nighttime came early.

Her head was filled with thoughts of names for a little girl or a boy, of visions of what the baby might look like considering Dirk had dark brown hair and brown eyes. It didn't matter; she knew with certainty that her baby would be beautiful.

She'd filled her prescription for the vitamins and had a handful of pamphlets about pregnancy and she carried with her a sense of rightness, that this was what she was born to be…a mother.

It was completely dark by the time she reached the ranch and drove through the huge ornate gold gates that led onto the Colton property.

She was passing the petting barn when she thought she saw a light shining from within the wooden structure. She slowed and then braked to a halt and cut the engine. Had she turned on a light that morning and forgotten to turn it off? Or was the flicker of illumination just a trick of the moonlight overhead reflecting on one of the little windows in the back of the barn?

Although she was eager to get to the house and into her suite, she decided to check out the barn and see if she'd accidently left on a light. She got out of the car and pulled her jacket closer around her, grateful that she'd worn one since the temperature after sunset dropped considerably.

Usually after dark the animals were already bedded down, but tonight they were restlessly wandering their pen. "Hey, guys, what's going on with you?" She leaned over the fence and petted the donkeys and goats and noted that there was no light shining from the open door of the barn.

Apparently the light she'd seen had simply been the moon, for the overhead lamp in the barn was not on. As she left the gate one of the ranch dogs barked in the distance and an unexpected chill suddenly raced up her spine.

It was definitely time to head inside. She wanted to get to her suite, change into her pajamas, avoid any family drama and focus only on all things baby.

She was about to get back in her Jeep when the faint crunch of dried grass behind her shot a warning off in her head at the same time a hand clasped over her mouth and a strong arm wrapped tight around her waist.

Panic exploded inside her as the person began to drag her away from her vehicle. She didn't have time to wonder who had hold of her or what he wanted. The only thing she knew for sure was that she was in terrible trouble.

The attacker continued to drag her farther and farther away from her car and she tried to dig in her heels to make it more difficult for him. When that didn't work she kicked her feet and violently twisted her body in an attempt to break his grip, but he was strong and obviously determined to get her into the wooded area in the distance.

The person who held her so tight made no sound, except for a faint grunt as he continued to maneuver her across the expanse of land. She knew with a certainty that if he got her to the woods, then there would be no hope and whatever happened after that would be horrible.

With a renewed effort, she twisted and slung her body and managed to bite his hand through the thin gloves he wore. He hissed and for just a single second his hand slipped from her mouth. She managed one sharp, short scream before his hand slapped across her lips once again and he continued to drag her away.

Chapter 4

Gray sat in the small cold office in the stables, paperwork before him on the desk and his favorite ranch dog Blackie, a lab mix, on the floor at his feet. Blackie growled, low and threatening and the hackles on his back raised, but he remained lying down.

"What's the matter, old boy?" Gray asked absently. He leaned over and scratched behind one of Blackie's ears. "One of those old barn cats tormenting you?" There were dozens of cats on the property, mousers who kept the stable and outbuildings as free of rodents as possible.

Most of the time the ranch dogs and cats played nice together, but Blackie had become more than a bit cantankerous in his old age. Blackie growled again and got to his feet and at the same moment a scream split the night.

Shrill yet short, it shot a piercing edge of adrenaline through Gray as he jumped up from his desk and raced for the stable doors. He hit the night air and rounded the side of the stables and in the near-full moonlight casting down saw two things…Catherine's Jeep parked in front of the petting barn and Catherine being dragged away from the vehicle by a man dressed all in black.

"Hey!" Gray shouted, his heart pounding as he took off at a dead run. His hand automatically went for his gun tucked in the holster he wore whenever he was out on the property. "Stop or I'll shoot." Despite the threat, he could do no such thing as he couldn't take a chance at hitting Catherine, who was in front of the man like a shield.

The assailant froze and then dropped his hold on Catherine, who crumpled to the ground in a small heap as the man turned and ran. Gray raced forward and once he reached her, she motioned for him to go on and catch the man who had grabbed her.

"Get in the Jeep and lock the doors," he commanded as he flew by her. She'd be safe there and if somehow the assailant doubled back to her, she could always raise hell with the horn and drive off.

The person had a good head start but Gray was in top physical shape and pumped his legs to achieve a speed he'd never reached before. His heart throbbed painfully in his chest. He had to catch him, he had to find out who had tried to grab Catherine. This man could be the answer to so many things that had happened.

Despite Gray's desperate need and the bright moonlight spilling down, once the attacker hit the dense woods, Gray lost sight of him. He clutched his gun tightly, willing and ready to use it if necessary.

He stopped and listened and heard the crashing of brush and crackling of broken tree limbs someplace in the distance to his left. He took off in that direction, his mind completely focused on catching the man who'd attempted to harm Catherine.

Fury drove him forward, half tripping over unseen roots. Shadowy tree branches slapped him in the face and shoulders as he raced forward.

He ran for only a few minutes and then stopped once again to listen.

Nothing.

The only noise he heard was the faint whisper of the wind through the treetops and his own ragged breathing. He remained frozen for several long minutes, hoping to hear a sound, a breaking branch, a faint footfall, any kind of indication where the man had gone.

Realizing that the attacker had the advantage of dark clothing to meld into the night shadows and that Gray really had no idea in which direction to give chase, he reluctantly turned and headed back out of the woods.

As he emerged into the clearing he was stunned to see Catherine still on the ground, crawling on her hands and knees, the sounds of her quiet sobs filling him with a new terror.

Was she hurt? Had he mistaken her condition as he'd raced by her in an attempt to catch the perpetrator? "Catherine!" He reached her side and crouched down where she was on her hands and knees, tears streaming down her cheeks. "What are you doing? Why aren't you in the Jeep? Are you hurt?"

She shook her head. "No…I'm fine, but it fell off…I have to find it." She frantically raked her fingers back and forth through the grass as she slowly crawled forward.

"What fell off? What are you looking for?" he asked, watching her and then glancing all around to make sure there was no more approaching danger.

"My necklace…I just bought it today…for the baby… to celebrate. It fell off sometime when he had me. I need to find it."

Despite her obvious reluctance, he pulled her up to her feet and grabbed her by her shoulders to keep her upright. Her deep blue eyes gazed at him beseechingly in the moonlight.

"What does the necklace look like?" he asked.

"Aquamarine stone on a gold chain." She punctuated the sentence with a thick sob.

"Get in the car and lock the doors. If you see anyone, honk the horn. I'm going to get a flashlight and see if I can find your necklace." He walked her to the car where he opened the passenger door and placed her inside. "Sit tight. I'll be right back," he said and then hit the button that would lock all of the doors.

He raced back into the stables where he grabbed a high-powered flashlight and quickly returned with Blackie at his heels.

He should have paid more attention the first time the dog had growled, that moment when his hackles had risen. Gray should have known something was amiss when the dog reacted to something he didn't like. He'd obviously smelled the intruder nearby.

Dammit, if Gray had only checked outside seconds earlier he might have been able to catch the attacker. He might now have had some answers. At least he'd gotten outside in time to stop what might have happened to Catherine.

He shined the beam of the light inside the Jeep, assuring himself that she was safe and sound inside, although still crying and then he pointed the light to the ground and began to hunt for her missing necklace.

He knew her tears weren't just for a necklace she'd bought that day, but probably a reaction to what had nearly happened to her. The thought of what might have happened if he hadn't left his desk when he had crunched a tight knot in the pit of his stomach.

This was exactly what he'd been afraid of. It was the reason he'd wanted her to keep her pregnancy a secret for as long as possible.

The attacker hadn't wanted to kill her. He could have done that with a single thrust of a knife into her back, with his hands tightened around her neck right by the side of the Jeep. No, whoever it was hadn't wanted her dead at all. He'd wanted her very much alive and away from the ranch.

Gray's anger grew as he continued to sweep the ground for the missing necklace. What had she been doing out here all alone at the petting barn after dark? Had she not taken his warnings seriously? Was she just that reckless to ignore the obvious dangers after everything that had already happened?

He muttered a sigh of relief when his flashlight beam caught the shimmering blue and gold of the missing necklace on the ground. He plucked it from the grass and headed for the car, ready to get what answers he could from Catherine.

She unlocked the car door and he slid behind the steering wheel and held out her necklace. She took it from him with a trembling sob and pressed it tight against her chest. "Thank you."

"Don't thank me yet," he replied gruffly. "I've got some questions that you need to answer and the first one is what in the hell you thought you were doing out here all alone in the dark?" The adrenaline that had crashed through him lingered as he waited for her reply.

She dropped her hands with the necklace to her lap, her tears slowly halting while she looked at the petting barn. "I had been in Laramie all afternoon and when I finally got back here it was dark and I thought I saw a light in the barn."

She frowned and raised a hand to twirl a strand of her hair. "It must have just been a strange beam of the moonlight against one of the windows because when I got out of the Jeep and went to the fence to check it out there were no lights on anywhere. So, I came back out to get into the Jeep and…" Her voice trailed off and she turned her head to look at him, her eyes huge and as dark blue as he'd ever seen them. "He came out of no-where. I heard a faint footstep in the grass behind me and before I could react, he had me."

"He was obviously waiting for you and he probably shined a flashlight in the barn in hopes that you'd stop and check it out." A lump formed in the back of Gray's throat, a lump of both fear and anger.

"Do you have any idea what would have happened if you hadn't managed to scream? If I hadn't been in the stables to hear you?" His voice betrayed the depth of his fear and he drew a deep breath to gain control.

"I'd be dead." Her voice trembled as her hand released her strand of hair.

"No, I don't think so, but you'd be gone and I imagine a pretty hefty ransom would have been asked for your safe return." Gray grabbed the steering wheel and squeezed it so tight that his knuckles whitened. "This is exactly what I warned you about."

"Who would have thought that a simple trip to a doctor's office in Laramie would have resulted in this?" She worried the necklace in her hands as if it were a magical talisman.

"Who knew you were going to Laramie?" Gray fought his need to vent his anger, an anger that had nowhere to go except in her direction.

He was upset that she hadn't taken his warning about her safety seriously, that the evocative scent of her filled the interior of the car and that he wanted to both yell at her and pull her into his arms at the same time.

"Amanda knew because she set up the doctor's appointment for me. Agnes knew because I told her I wasn't going to be here for lunch or dinner. I don't know who else might have known, but surely you can't think anyone from the house had anything to do with this," she protested.

"I wouldn't put this past Trip. I don't trust him or

Tawny or Darla. We've got ranch hands we know little about, new hires all over the house. Any one of them could see you as a ticket to a new life. Catherine, you need to wake up. Somebody in your house is up to no good. There have already been murders committed and no suspect has been identified in those deaths."

Once again she twirled a strand of her hair. "Everything is happening so fast. I just learned I was pregnant yesterday and now suddenly I'm attacked."

"And there's no doubt in my mind that whoever tried to take you tonight knows that you're pregnant, which makes your kidnapping twice as valuable as taking anyone else."

She released a weary sigh. "Just take me back to the house. At least I know I should be safe in my own private suite."

Gray started the Jeep engine, deciding now wasn't the time to tell her that with her suite on the ground floor it wasn't exactly a tall tower to be breached with great difficulty. There was really no place in the entire house that she was safe. After all, it had only been two months ago that kitchen help Jenny Burke had been found murdered in the pantry.

"Catherine, you've got to take this threat seriously. You can't be out alone after dark. You need to keep yourself surrounded by people all the time and we should probably call the chief of police when we get back to the house."

"Why call him and complicate everything?" she countered. "What's the point? The only description I have of him is that his hands were huge and in thin black

gloves. He felt strong as an ox as he pulled me away."
She shivered. "But, I have no idea what he looked like
and I'm assuming you couldn't tell anything about him,
either."

"Medium height. Medium build." Gray sighed,
knowing she was right. There was really no point in
calling out the chief with nothing more to offer him.
The man would be long gone from the woods by now.

He pulled into the garage in the lower portion of
the mansion and parked her Jeep in its usual spot. He
turned to look at her and noted that her lower lip trembled slightly and fear still darkened her eyes.

"You're safe now, Catherine." He couldn't help but
want to erase that fear.

She nodded. "Thanks to you." She opened her door
and got out and he did the same. As he rounded the car
to where she stood, as if unsure where to go or what to
do, he noted that she still grasped the necklace tightly
in her fingers.

"Is it broken?" he asked.

She looked at the clasp and released an audible sigh
of relief. "No, it must have just come unfastened."

"Do you want me to put that back around your neck
where it belongs?"

For the first time some of the fear left her eyes. "Do
you mind? I bought it today to celebrate. Eventually
it will go to my daughter or my son's wife. I'm just so
grateful that you found it. I thought it was lost for sure."

She handed him the necklace and turned her back to
him. As she swept her hair to one side, baring the back

of her delicate neck, he fought the impulse to press his lips against her soft skin.

Damn her for scaring him. Damn her for reawakening his desire for her despite all the years that had passed, in spite of all the bitterness she evoked in him.

And damn her for his shaking fingers as he tried to clasp the delicate gold chain at the nape of her neck. "You need a husband, somebody who can watch over you through the day and be at your side at night." He finally managed to get the necklace on.

She turned and looked at him. "Thanks for the advice," she said dryly. "Unfortunately I don't seem to have any volunteers for the job at the moment."

"I'd volunteer." The words left his mouth before any thought entered his brain. "You could marry me…of course it would just be a marriage in name only, but nobody else would have to know that. It would give me a reason to keep you close and safe."

Catherine stared at him for a stunned moment and then laughed. "Sure, that makes sense. For the past four years you've made it obvious you don't even like me. A marriage between us for any reason is an absolutely ridiculous idea."

"You're right, of course," he said stiffly, wondering what on earth he'd been thinking when he'd even made the crazy offer. Obviously he hadn't been thinking at all.

Catherine would be more apt to marry the society-page playboy, money-grubbing father of her baby than a lowly ranch foreman. He'd learned that lesson nine years ago and he should have remembered it now.

"Then I'll just say good-night," he said and turned to head toward the garage door.

"Gray?"

He turned back to face her.

"Thank you," she said and for just a split second he thought he saw a yearning in her eyes.

Trick of the light, he told himself. "No problem," he said curtly and then left the garage and went outside into the cool night air. He headed back to the stables, needing to process everything that had just happened, needing to lick the wounds of humiliation that stung like a swallowed wasp inside his chest.

As he walked, he kept his gaze moving, seeking anything or anyone who might be out of place, who might signify danger. Even before the events of tonight, all the ranch hands had suffered from the knowledge that nobody could be trusted.

Two kidnapping attempts of Cheyenne, two murders in the house and even the former chief of police in Dead, Hank Drucker, had not only been discovered to be a dirty cop who got arrested, and was now dead, his death was being investigated as either a suicide or a murder.

Gray had the feeling of danger permeating not only the Dead River Ranch, but also the nearby small town of Dead, as well. Worse, he felt the noose of danger tightening around them all and an imminent explosion of evil about to detonate and there wasn't anything he could do but wait for it to happen.

Chapter 5

"I'm so excited," Gabby said as she and Catherine got into the backseat of the town car with Trevor at the wheel playing chauffeur for the day. "I'm hoping to raise a ton of money this afternoon. Thanks for coming with me, Cath."

"Don't thank me. You're doing me a favor by letting me get out of the house and come along and keep my mind off things," Catherine replied.

They were headed to an afternoon tea and silent auction event that Gabby had put together as a fund-raiser for her red barn project for troubled teens. She'd invited all the movers and shakers of Laramie to the posh hotel where the event would take place.

"Are you doing okay?" Gabby asked as Trevor started the engine and headed away from the mansion. She reached over and grabbed Catherine's hand.

"I'm fine." Catherine gave her sister's hand a reassuring squeeze and then released it.

She had told her sister about the attack at the petting barn the night before and how Gray had saved her from being dragged away to parts known. She hadn't told her sister about Gray's ridiculous idea that he marry her to keep her safe.

And it was a ridiculous idea…wasn't it? She gazed out the passenger window and gave herself a mental shake. Of course it was a stupid idea. He'd made it obvious in a million little ways that he didn't like her and she wasn't at all sure that she liked the man he'd grown up to be.

He'd once laughed so easily, his brown eyes always with a special light and a hint of mischief. There had been a spring to his step, as if he couldn't wait to get wherever he was going. He'd possessed a vitality that had drawn her, an energy that had excited her, but that was all gone now.

Physically the grown-up version of Gray Stark was breathtaking. There was no man on the ranch who wore a pair of worn jeans or filled out the shoulders of a shirt quite so well. More than once she'd found herself watching as he worked shirtless during the summer months, showcasing killer abs as his brown hair bleached with strands of blond.

Still, this adult Gray Stark was a man who rarely smiled…at least not at her. He appeared a loner who needed nobody by his side…and yet he'd offered to play husband to her in an effort to keep her safe.

It had to have been some sort of stupid joke on his

part, or a crazy brain snafu. Besides, she'd learned her lesson with him when he'd disappeared from her life without a backward glance. She'd also learned another lesson and had no intention of being outside after dark all alone again. As long as she was smart, she'd be safe. She didn't need a man to protect her.

"You know I invited the Sinclairs," Gabby said with a worried glance at Catherine. She touched a strand of her red hair. "Cath, I don't know if Dirk will show up or not."

"Who cares?" Catherine replied. She gave her sister a forced smile. "Trust me, seeing Dirk isn't going to bother me a bit." Dirk had basically broken up with her when he found out he'd have to wait to get his hands on her money, but even though she'd been offended on so many levels, she's also felt a surprising relief when he'd walked away from their relationship. Now she felt nothing toward him but disdain.

She would be much more unsettled to see Gray, whom she hadn't seen since their awkward goodbye in the garage the night before.

"I'd like to smack Dirk upside the head for hurting you," Gabby said fervently.

Catherine couldn't stop the giggle that bubbled to her lips. Clad in an elegant emerald-green dress that matched the color of her eyes and with her hair impeccably done in an upsweep, she looked every ounce the society queen and yet she was talking like some street fighter defending her home girl.

"Actually, I'm not hurt at all over Dirk. I mean, there's no question he's a jerk, but honestly since we broke up I've realized how much I wasn't in love with him."

"But you seemed so good together," Gabby replied.

Catherine sighed and thought about the man she'd considered marrying. "We were comfortable together. We came from the same kind of background. We knew the same people, attended the same events. It felt easy being with him, but it was never fireworks and heart thuds."

"You definitely deserve fireworks." Gabby cast a loving smile at the man driving the car. "Trust me, when it is right there should be all kinds of fireworks." Her cheeks filled with a hint of a blush, as if she were remembering special intimate moments with Trevor.

Catherine looked out the window at the passing scenery. There had once been fireworks with Gray. It had been when they were young and crazy about each other, and obviously unrealistic about life and enduring love. Each time they'd come together it had been magic and exciting and heart-stopping.

When Catherine had finally had sex with Dirk and all those things had been missing, she'd just assumed that first love was magic for everyone, that the utter splendor of first love and experiencing the act of making love with that person was never repeated again for the rest of your life. But as she saw her sister with Trevor. she wondered if her thinking was all wrong.

Was it possible to have what she'd once had with Gray again? Of course it would be with a different man. She shook her head as if to tumble out all these thoughts. She was a single woman who was pregnant and potentially a target for kidnapping.

Now wasn't the time to think about romance or falling in love with anyone. It certainly wasn't the time to be thinking about lovemaking. It had only been yesterday that she'd convinced herself she didn't want a man in her life, that she'd be fine alone with just her baby.

By the time they reached the ballroom of the luxury hotel, Catherine sat in an elegantly tufted gold chair and watched as her sister took care of last-minute details.

The room was lovely, the round tables decorated with gold linen cloths and matching cutlery and each boasting a floral arrangement in the center that was an explosion of the red and orange and gold colors of autumn.

Three long tables were set along one side of the room, holding the items that were to be auctioned off. Catherine got up from the chair and wandered over to the table to see what kind of goodies Gabby had managed to talk business owners into donating.

Gabby had done very well. There was a trip for two for four days in a five-star hotel in Hawaii, a beautiful painting from a fairly well-known local artist who Catherine knew personally, extravagant meals at restaurants, designer shoes and a hand-beaded shawl in a copper tone that was positively stunning.

Catherine paused at a lovely diamond necklace and matching earrings set and reached up and touched the necklace with the aquamarine stone that hung beneath her collarbone. Hers was definitely less expensive, but far more valuable to her.

Thank God Gray had found it in the grass after the attack. In the brief time she'd owned it, it had come to represent life and hope and love to her. She would have been sick if the attacker had managed to take that away from her along with her sense of safety.

She returned to her chair and tried not to think about the horror of the night before. She wanted to believe that Gray was wrong, that it hadn't been a kidnapping attempt at all, but maybe just some drifter looking to rob her or some creep wanting to get her into the woods to rape her.

It was easier to believe those scenarios, as horrible as they were, than what he believed, that it had been a kidnapping scheme created by the fact that she now carried the next Colton heir.

She was relatively certain that nobody outside of the family, household staff and perhaps some wranglers who worked for the Colton family knew about her pregnancy. And that meant that either a family member or somebody who worked for them was probably behind the attempt.

That meant she had no idea who could be trusted in the house that she called home.

Gray stood just outside the stable, brushing down the thickening hair on a mare named Molly. His thoughts were far away from the horse, instead inwardly focused on the vision of Catherine he had seen just before she'd stepped into the backseat of the town car an hour earlier.

She'd looked lovely in what was probably a designer blue tea-length dress and black-and-blue high heels. Her hair fell soft and silky down her back, glistening in the overhead sunshine. She'd looked every inch a wealthy socialite on her way to a charity event.

A wealth of humiliation accompanied each stroke of the brush as he thought about his impromptu offer to marry her. Obviously his fear for her safety had driven all rational thought out of his brain. He wasn't sure who'd been more surprised by his suggestion, himself or her.

He'd take it back if he could, but the words had been spoken and now lingered in the universe, along with her small laugh of disdain at the very idea.

"She knows you're just not that into her." The deep voice came from behind him and Gray whirled around, wondering if his best friend, Dylan Frick, had actually read his thoughts.

Dylan smiled and pointed at Molly. "She knows your attention isn't really on her."

Gray dropped the brush into a nearby empty bucket and allowed Molly to amble away toward the rest of the horses in the paddock. He grinned at the man who was like a brother to him.

The two had grown up together on the ranch, Gray the foreman's son and Dylan the child of Faye Frick, the governess who had been murdered in the first kidnapping attempt of Cheyenne only three months before.

Dylan was not only an unofficial animal whisperer, he'd always been good with people and well liked at the ranch. Since his mother's murder, he'd changed. The light in his blue eyes was less bright and he preferred to be out someplace alone on the ranch rather than surrounded by people. The one thing that hadn't changed was the bond that he and Gray shared, a bond forged in childhood that had never wavered through the years.

The past couple of months had been particularly difficult for Dylan, who had not only lost his mother, but most recently had been forced to examine everything his mother had ever told him about her and their past.

"Heard there was some excitement out here last night," Dylan said. "From the gossip I've heard around the ranch this morning thank God you were at the right place at the right time."

A cold knot clenched in Gray's stomach as he thought of that moment when he'd seen Catherine being dragged away by the assailant. "You've got that right. Unfortunately, I couldn't get to the man and there was no way for me to even guess who it might have been."

He frowned. "I have a feeling if I'd managed to grab him maybe we'd have some answers about what the hell has been going on around here." He grabbed the bucket and motioned for Dylan to walk with him into the stables.

"You think it was the same person who tried to take Cheyenne the second time?" Dylan asked.

"Who knows? I can only guess that somebody is desperate to get a Colton heir and hopes for a major payday. I can't help but think everything bad that's happened is tied to somebody in the house."

"I'll second that," Dylan agreed. "I can hardly stand to eat in the employee dining room because of the sick energy that fills the air, and that sick energy seems to be in every nook and cranny in the house."

"You're about the only person I trust in this whole place," Gray said.

Dylan's blue eyes darkened. "Lately I have so many questions about my mother and her life before we landed here on the ranch, maybe you shouldn't be so trusting of me."

Gray slapped Dylan on one of his broad shoulders. "Nothing that comes out about your mother or whatever happened before she got here to Dead River Ranch could ever change my feelings about you. Hell, you and I explored every inch of this ranch together when we were kids. We skinny-dipped in the pond together...."

"And we know each other's secrets," Dylan added with a wry grin. "And speaking of secrets, how did it go last night between you and Cath? You were her hero for the night. Surely that broke some of the ice that has existed between the two of you since you've been back here."

Dylan was the only person who knew the depth of love Gray had once had for Catherine and the only person who knew that it was his love for her that had been the reason he'd left the ranch at the break of dawn nine years ago.

"I told her she should marry me," Gray blurted.

Dylan's eyes widened with stunned surprise. "What the hell, man?"

"I know. What can I tell you, it was a moment of crazy." Gray slicked a hand through his shaggy hair and released a deep sigh. "I'm just so worried about her safety. She needs somebody to protect her twenty-four hours a day. She's a double reward for anyone who might manage to kidnap her right now."

"It might be tough for somebody to get a ransom payment from Jethro now that he's in a coma," Dylan replied.

"He still drifts in and out. According to the kitchen gossip they think he's conscious sometimes and only pretends to be unconscious."

"Even if he was conscious there's no guarantee he'd pay a ransom. He wasn't willing to do it for Trevor's baby girl despite Gabby's pleas." Dylan couldn't hide the disgust that laced his tone.

Had it only been a little over three months ago that Dylan's mother had been murdered trying to save Trevor's baby girl, who'd been kidnapped from Cheyenne's nursery, the kidnapper believing the baby he stole was a Colton heir?

Even when the family knew it wasn't a Colton who had been kidnapped, Gabby, falling in love with Trevor and feeling guilty because she had been the one who had placed little Avery in Cheyenne's bed for a nap, had begged Jethro to pay whatever ransom was demanded, and Jethro had refused.

Thankfully, Avery had been found unharmed and the ranch hand Duke Johnson had been arrested for the kidnapping and murder of Dylan's mother. Unfortunately, his arrest hadn't answered many questions, but had instead created more when it was determined he was just a hired gun and didn't know who the mastermind behind the kidnapping attack had been.

"So, any guesses as to who might have attacked Cath last night? Who might be behind all of this?" Dylan asked. Gray knew that even though the man who had actually killed Dylan's mother was behind bars, Dylan still burned with a frustrated need to get to the head of the wicked snake and cut it off.

Gray motioned him into the tack room. "Suspects abound," he said dryly as he leaned with a hip against a sawhorse that held a saddle astride it. "Trip is definitely toward the top of the list of people I don't trust."

Dylan laughed. "Trip doesn't have the brains that God gave a gnat."

"True, but Darla does and I think Tawny is smarter than she pretends to be and I think there's nothing the three of them would like more than to be millionaires in their own rights, living in their own houses and not beholden to allowances from Jethro."

Dylan nodded. "And then there's Stewie Runyon. I'll be the first to admit he's a hard worker. There isn't much around this place he won't do and without complaint, but he's way too closemouthed for my liking. He's harder to read than a ticked-off bull."

"I've got my eye on several of the ranch hands… Jared Hansen and Cal Clark, to name two."

"Jared reminds me of a young puppy who just wants to please everyone and I don't know that much about Cal Clark except he's a hard worker when he's around."

"Yeah, but he tends to disappear occasionally and never has a believable explanation as to where he's gone," Gray replied.

"So, enough about murder and mayhem, you never told me how Cath reacted when you suggested she marry you."

"Stunned dismissal," Gray replied, the knot in his stomach that always formed when he thought of Catherine tightening.

"She just needs to hire a full-time bodyguard," Dylan replied.

Gray frowned, surprised to discover he didn't like the idea of any other man besides him being around her twenty-four hours a day.

Dylan grinned. "Ah, I can tell by the look on your face that the idea doesn't sit well with you. You don't want her, but you don't want anyone else around her, either." One of his brown eyebrows quirked upward. "Or, maybe you still want her even after all these years."

"Nah, that's not it," Gray said even while his heartbeat stepped up in rhythm. "Nothing about the situation has changed. Besides, she wasn't the woman I thought she was years ago and nothing I've seen of her since I've been back at the ranch convinces me of anything different."

"You don't really know her now," Dylan said. "It's been nine years since you were teenage sweethearts. Both of you are different people than you were then. Maybe you should get to know the woman she is now."

"Why would I want to do that?" Gray asked gruffly. "She means nothing to me."

"So, why aren't you dating some hot honey from

town or one of the maids who watch you with hungry eyes?" Dylan asked, his voice teasing.

"Why aren't you?" Gray countered.

Dylan sighed. "I guess we're just a couple of misfit cowboys more comfortable with the animals on this place than with women." He tapped Gray's shoulder. "Come on, let's grab a couple of mounts and take a ride. It will get our minds off murder and kidnapping and women."

Gray nodded and minutes later the two men were racing across the browning land, the October breeze holding the scents of seasonal transition…the memory of autumn and the promise of winter to come.

What madness might the winter bring to the Coltons and their staff? Would anyone be successful in finding the missing Cole Colton and bringing him home to see Jethro before the old man died?

Who was the mastermind behind the kidnapping attempts and who else might lose their lives in what Gray was beginning to think of as a house cursed?

And then there was Catherine. Maybe it would have been easier on him if he hadn't pulled her into his arms after her collapse at the petting barn, if he hadn't held her and remembered the taste of her lips against his, the feel of her breasts in his palms and the magic of their lovemaking.

He'd almost forgotten that, until he'd held her in his arms again and now it was again emblazoned in his brain. He had a feeling he and Dylan could ride from here to Alaska and still that memory would be fresh and painful in his mind.

* * *

Darla stood at the window of her bedroom in her suite of rooms, a frown attempting to form despite her latest round of Botox shots.

She turned away from the view and instead sank down on the edge of her bed, the dissatisfaction that had been inside her for the past couple of months getting stronger with each day that passed.

When she and Jethro had divorced, she'd had enough blackmail material to use against him to broker a deal that had assured her and her two children a wing in the house and a monthly allowance that would give the three of them an adequate, if not fine, living.

But that was no longer enough. She was tired of being treated like poor relatives whose very presence the rest of the family were forced to endure. She'd been married to the miserable bastard, Jethro, for one long year. She and Trip and Tawny deserved so much more.

Unfortunately if they left the Dead River Ranch they had nowhere else to go and precious little money to take with them. What Darla really wanted was a place like this for herself and her children from a previous marriage, a place where they were in charge and didn't have to kowtow to the true Colton heirs.

Although she played nice, she hated all of them and she didn't even want to think about what might happen to her and her kids if the old man really did kick the bucket. She had no idea what was in his will for her, if anything.

She had a feeling they'd be out on the streets and the very idea of that happening was absolutely untenable.

It was definitely time to up her game, to pull out all the stops to make sure the future she desired for herself was assured.

Chapter 6

Catherine stood in the fenced area of the petting barn, checking food and water supplies and trying not to dwell on the memory of what had happened here almost a week before.

There were several ranch workers in her sights so she felt safe despite the fact that the sun hung low in the sky. She had another half an hour or so before twilight would fall and she planned on being safely inside the house long before that happened.

She'd spent the past week close to the house, spending much of her time in her suite reading the material Dr. Kendall had given her about how to have a happy and healthy pregnancy.

She'd already decided where in the sitting room a crib and whatever else was necessary could be added, having decided not to put her baby in the nursery with Cheyenne.

Maybe she'd feel differently about the nursery when the baby was finally here, but right now she felt the safest place for her child was in her room with her. Perhaps in six months' time the house would once again feel like a haven rather than a war zone.

"Working hard or hardly working?" Gray's deep voice pulled her from her thoughts as he stepped up to the fence.

She'd seen very little of him in the past week and cursed the sudden jump in her heartbeat at the sight of him. "Just wasting some time with my little furry friends until dinner," she replied.

Even at the end of a long day at work, he looked sexy with his jeans hugging his long, lean legs and a brown plaid flannel shirt stretched taut across broad shoulders. The hint of a five-o'clock shadow darkened his jaw, only adding to his rugged handsomeness.

"You have any groups scheduled to come through in the next couple of weeks?" he asked.

"One group from the local grade school, but that's it," she replied, trying to hide her surprise that he was actually talking to her. "I imagine that will be the last one for the season. By the time November arrives it's usually too cold for anyone to want to bring kids out here."

"I've heard that you do a good job with the kids."

Once again she tried to hide her surprise. Was that some kind of a compliment from him? Was he actually attempting a civil conversation with her? "I love interacting with the children," she replied.

"You'll make a terrific mother." Although the words were kind, his eyes remained dark and fathomless, not allowing her a glimpse of his inner emotions.

"Thanks. It's really all I've ever wanted to be." She opened the gate and stepped out of the fenced area. "I never had the drive that Amanda had to become a vet or anything like that and while I greatly admire Gabby's project for troubled teens, I always just wanted to be a wife and mother." She offered him a small smile. "At least I got it half right."

"And you still don't intend to tell Dirk that he'll soon be a father?"

Catherine shook her head. "If and when he finds out about the pregnancy or the baby, I'll figure something out to make sure he believes it isn't his. The only thing the baby would mean to him would be a way to get money, to somehow share in any inheritance that will eventually come my way. Besides, he's not cut out to be a father. He has none of the qualities I'd want for my baby's father. He's nothing but a snake in the grass."

They began to walk toward the house. "So his whole relationship with you was all about the money?"

"Somehow everything is always all about the money, isn't it?" Catherine sighed with a hint of disgust. "Faye was murdered because somebody wanted to get at Cheyenne and demand money. Cheyenne's bodyguard was beaten to a pulp because somebody else tried to kidnap Cheyenne to gain a king's ransom." She gave a slight shake of her head and instead focused back on him. "I never told you how sorry I was about your father's passing. He was a good man."

"Thanks. Yeah, he was," he replied, his gaze shooting off in the distance ahead of them. "I miss him every day."

"I keep telling myself that I'm prepared to say a final goodbye to my father, but I don't know that you're ever really prepared for that," she said.

"I've always believed Jethro was one of those people that Heaven wouldn't want and the devil wouldn't take," he said and a small burst of laughter escaped Catherine.

"He has been known to have more than his share of ornery," she replied.

"He's a cranky, stubborn old coot who might still have plenty of life yet to live," Gray replied, his affection for Jethro unmistakable in his tone. Catherine knew her father had always had a soft spot in his heart for Gray and it was obvious the feeling had been mutual.

"I just hope he lives long enough to be reunited with Cole." She stopped walking, grabbed a strand of her hair and began to twirl it as she thought of the missing heir, the half brother who had been kidnapped as a baby so many years ago.

Gray reached out and gently placed his hand over hers, halting the whirling of her hair. "I would have thought you'd grown out of that habit by now," he said and she thought she heard just a hint of tenderness in his voice.

An illusion, she thought as he quickly drew his hand away. She dropped hers to her side. Still, for just a moment that illusion of caring had warmed her, had made her feel not so alone.

She continued walking slowly, marveling at the fact

that they were having a normal conversation, something that hadn't happened between them in all the years that he'd been back at the ranch. For the rest of the walk to the house they spoke about neutral subjects, the weather, the health of the stock and the new help that had been hired for work both inside and outside of the house.

All too quickly they were at the place where they parted ways, her to go into one of the official entrances of the house and him to go around to the back door for employees.

She lingered, oddly reluctant to halt this new communication between them. It would be nice if after all this time they could put the distant past behind them and at least be friendly with each other.

"I heard that you worked in Montana while you were away. Did you like it there?"

He shrugged. "It was okay. It was a much smaller spread than this one. The owner and the foremen were both decent men, old friends of my father."

"Did you do any bull riding while you were out there?"

His sensual lips turned up into a grin that nearly stole her breath away. She couldn't remember the last time he'd really smiled at her, and she'd forgotten how that smile could make a woman feel as if she were the only person on the face of the planet.

"A little, brought home a couple of big buckles and a few trophies." There was no boast in his voice, only a matter of fact. "But I think my bull riding days are done."

She looked at him in surprise. He'd always entered

the bull riding competitions at rodeos around the area. "Really? Why?"

Once again his broad shoulders moved in a shrug. "I don't have the passion for it like I once did." His gaze moved from her to the land surrounding them. "I don't have any passion for a lot of things anymore."

He glanced back at her. "Are you taking care of yourself?" His gaze slid from her eyes to her stomach and then back up again.

In just that single gaze she once again felt a touch of gentle caring, a hint of the old Gray she'd once thought had hung the moon. "Absolutely. I'm taking my vitamins and eating healthy and getting plenty of sleep and if that's not enough Amanda has been giving me daily tips about what to expect when."

"That's good. We wouldn't want anything happening to the newest Colton heir." A bite of bitterness laced his tone, immediately fracturing what had been until now a pleasant conversation.

His eyes were once again dark and impossible to read. "You'd better get inside so you can clean up for dinner," he said as he took a step back from her.

"Then I guess I'll see you around sometime tomorrow," she replied, wondering what had pulled him back from her, what had changed the tenure of the conversation from pleasant to strained.

"See you," he replied as he turned and walked away.

She slipped into the house and headed for her suite. She'd been so careful not to ask why he'd gone to Montana in the first place, why he'd left her without a single word of explanation. The splendor of loving him and the pain of losing him had happened years ago. It was water under the bridge. But that didn't mean she wasn't interested in hearing some kind of an explanation for what had happened. She just knew it didn't really matter now.

She realized her time in the sun with Gray was over, but she had to admit to herself that he still got to her, that even after all this time, even carrying another man's baby, there was a part of her that had never forgotten what it had been like to be loved by Gray Stark.

Gray stalked around to the employee entrance and headed for the employee dining room. He'd spent the past week thinking about what Dylan had said to him the day they'd ridden the ranch together.

It was true, Gray didn't know the grown-up Catherine and he'd decided today that he'd take a first step toward getting to know the woman she had become.

It bothered him that he had a feeling if he allowed himself, he'd like her…if he permitted it, he'd want her again and that would be a repeat of the nonsense that had driven him away from home nine years ago.

"Be smart, boy. You're nothing more than a ranch hand and she's a Colton. No way this barnyard romance is going anywhere. Get out of it now, before it goes any deeper. Leave her be to find the man who's right for her."

Gray's father's voice hammered in his brain, a memory of the night before Gray had left for Montana. It had been his father who had set up the job that would take Gray away from Catherine. It had been his father who had made Gray realize that loving Catherine would only lead him to ultimate heartbreak and wasn't the best thing for her.

As he walked into the room where the staff all gathered to eat, the first thing he heard was the sound of Allison Murray, Catherine's maid, and one of the new kitchen hires, Lucinda Garcia, in the middle of an argument.

"I heard she doesn't even know who the father of the baby is," Lucinda said as she went around the table filling water glasses from a large pitcher.

"That's not true," Allison replied, her cheeks dusty with the color of high emotion. "Miss Catherine isn't like that. She's a true lady and wouldn't sleep around. You just need to keep your mouth shut and stop implying bad things about Miss Catherine."

Gray was just about to enter the fracas when head cook Agnes Barlow stepped into the dining room, her plump face squashed into an expression of deep displeasure.

"Gossip? Is that what I hear going on?" Her voice was strident, her green eyes narrowed as they glared first at Allison and then at Lucinda. Short and rotund, with her blazing fury she looked like a ticked-off troll. "You all know we have a zero tolerance for gossip around here, especially when it involves the family."

She waved the spatula she held in one hand as if she wanted to pop somebody over the head. "Lucinda, work, don't talk. Allison, eat and don't talk." With these final words she whirled around and disappeared back into the kitchen.

"Never a dull moment," Stewie Runyon muttered under his breath as Gray slid onto the bench next to him. "Who cares who the daddy is? It's still a Colton heir." He clamped his mouth shut and Gray guessed that was probably the last he'd hear from Stewie for the remainder of the meal.

Stewie wasn't a talker and despite the fact that he'd worked as a ranch hand for the past eight months Gray knew very little about the young man. He didn't talk about his past, and he didn't mention any family. He was competent at what he did, but remained a loner who had made no real friends in the months he'd been working at the ranch.

Stewie wasn't the only ranch hand that Gray didn't know well. Cal Clark was another one who kept to himself and had rarely appeared to want the company of others. He worked hard, ate hearty and then disappeared, sometimes off the ranch and sometimes into his room.

Gray had mentioned a distrust of Jared Hansen to Dylan, as well. At the moment the twenty-two-year-old sat across from him on the bench on the opposite side of the table, his features wearing that overeager smile that made Gray want to yell at him to stop trying so hard.

Within minutes the table was full and the din grew as conversations swirled and silverware clinked against plates. Gray nodded to Dylan, who sank down on the bench next to him and although Gray tried to focus on the talk going around the table he found his head filled again and again with thoughts of Catherine.

The walk from the petting barn to the house with

her had been pleasant, until he'd thought of the child she carried, the Colton heir, and once again he was reminded that he hadn't been good enough, that he would never be good enough for a Colton.

His father had done the right thing years ago, basically sending him away from temptation, stopping him from humiliating himself where Catherine was concerned. Coltons didn't marry ranch hands.

He thought it would be nice to get to know her, but the problem was he feared he'd like the woman she'd become, that somehow the aching need he'd once felt for her would reappear and that would be devastating. He didn't want to go through heartache again where she was concerned.

It wasn't just Catherine or everything that had happened recently that had him unsettled. For the past few months there had been a vague dissatisfaction in his life, a knowledge that somewhere along the line he'd lost his passion not just for bull riding, but for ranching itself.

He did his job here and he knew he did it well, but somehow the love of it all had paled. The problem was he didn't know where to find a new job to love, a new mission that would be exciting and fulfilling.

Maybe it was time for him to head to another ranch, find work away from Dead. Working on a ranch in southern Texas would be a good place to spend the winter months and would once again give him some distance from Catherine and all the drama going on with the Coltons.

Even as he thought about it, he knew he wasn't going anywhere. In that moment that he'd walked out of the stables and had seen Catherine being dragged away from her Jeep by an unknown assailant, he'd somehow claimed responsibility for her safety. He was reluctant to walk away from that responsibility now, whether she wanted it or not—whether he wanted it or not.

By the time dinner was over, a mental exhaustion plagued Gray and he decided to head up to his room. As he walked up the back set of stairs that led to the male employee rooms, he withdrew his key ring from his pocket. Other than the men who lived in these Spartan rooms only head housekeeper Mathilda had a master set of keys that could open these doors.

Gray used his key and entered the small room that had been his home for the past four years. Each of the staff rooms were pretty much the same, a single bed, a dresser and a small closet.

Over the past four years Gray had added a compact fridge, a nightstand and a small bookcase that held an array of Western and mystery novels he often read in his spare time.

The walls were decorated with the silver and gold buckles he'd won over the years for bull riding, as the dresser top held trophies for the same thing.

The first thing he did was unfasten his holster and place it with his gun in the single drawer in the nightstand. He then reached down into the small fridge, grabbed a cold beer and sat on the bed with his back against the wall.

He didn't want to think. He didn't want to think about his conflicting emotions where Catherine was concerned, or the fact that he wasn't sure what he wanted to do with the rest of his life. He was twenty-seven years old and felt as if he were suffering some sort of midlife crisis.

He'd been a ranch hand because that's all he'd known. He'd been a ranch hand because it was what his father had expected of him. Gray had never thought about doing anything else until lately.

He hadn't been sitting on the bed long when a knock fell on his door. "Come in," he said, unsurprised to see Dylan enter the room and close the door behind him.

Gray motioned toward the fridge. "Grab a cold one."

"Thanks." Dylan grabbed a beer and then sat on the opposite end of the bed. "You were quiet at dinner," he said as he twisted off the top of the bottle and tossed it into a nearby trash can at the foot of the bed.

"Seemed to me like there was enough noise going around the table without me adding to it," Gray replied. "Besides, I could say the same about you. I didn't notice you starting any stimulating conversations."

Dylan gave him a dry grin. The smile quickly faded from his face and instead his features became serious, his eyes dark. "I've been thinking about a lot of things."

"Like what?"

"Like a lot of questions Mia and Jagger raised before they blew out of town." Dylan paused to take a long pull on his beer and then lowered the bottle and stared at a spot just over Gray's head.

Gray waited for his friend to go on. Not only had Mia and Jagger uncovered the fact that the Dead chief of police was a dirty cop, but they'd also uncovered some troubling inconsistencies in how Faye Frick and her son, Dylan, had come to live at the ranch.

Dylan refocused on Gray. "I don't have a single photo of my mother pregnant with me and none of me as a baby. I don't know who my father was because I'm not sure I really believe the story my mom told me about a brief marriage to a man she barely knew who died from a fall from a horse and had no family. She told me she had no family but as I got older and starting asking more questions, I got the feeling she wasn't telling me the truth about things. Mia and Jagger just made me more curious about my mom and her background and where I really came from."

He tipped the bottle to his lips and took a drink, then released a deep sigh and once again looked at Gray. "I'd like you to do me a favor."

"What?" Gray asked curiously.

"I want you to help me investigate my past…my mother's past. Things just don't add up and I keep wondering how we wound up here at Dead River Ranch. I need to know if my mother told me the truth about my father and where I came from."

Gray sat up and set his empty beer bottle on the nightstand. An edge of excitement fired off inside him as he considered Dylan's words. The idea stimulated him, not just because it might give Dylan some peace, but because the idea of conducting an investigation of sorts intrigued him like nothing had in a long time.

"You know I'll do whatever I can to help you find out the truth," Gray said.

Dylan nodded. "I knew I could count on you, but I'd

like this to stay just between you and me and I think we need to go slow and as quietly as possible in finding out answers. It seems that whenever anyone asks questions about anything around here they wind up threatened or dead."

"Don't worry, I have no intention of being dead," Gray replied. "I can be discreet. You take care of the foreman chores and I'll take care of trying to find out what I can about you and your mother."

Minutes later, after Dylan had left his room, Gray once again leaned back against the wall, his thoughts spinning around in his head.

Definitely Mia and Jagger had brought up some interesting questions about Dylan and his mother before they'd left town, but Gray hadn't realized that those questions were apparently eating away at Dylan.

A half an hour ago he'd been considering taking off for Texas and now he'd committed himself to helping Dylan in discovering the truth about his and his mother's past.

Besides, even without the promise to help Dylan Gray had known deep in his heart that he wasn't going anywhere anytime soon.

No matter how badly he wanted to maintain a healthy distance from Catherine, he knew he couldn't leave her here alone and vulnerable until the evil that had a thumb on the house, on the family, was cut off.

Chapter 7

"Miss Catherine?" Mathilda stopped Catherine before she entered the family dining room. As always the head housekeeper was impeccably groomed and warmed Catherine with a beatific smile. "I don't want to be presumptuous, but I was wondering if perhaps you'd like Allison to start bringing you a cup of hot tea and some toast or crackers in the mornings for when you first wake up."

"Oh, Mathilda, that's so thoughtful of you, but it isn't necessary. At least for right now I'm not suffering from any morning sickness."

Mathilda nodded and placed a hand on Catherine's shoulder. "That's good to hear. Now, if you start getting any, you let me know and we'll arrange for some hot tea and morning crackers to start off your day."

"Thanks, I appreciate your thoughtfulness," Catherine replied.

Mathilda nodded and moved away as Catherine continued on into the dining room. Most of the family was already seated at the table and Catherine slid into her seat with a nod to everyone.

"Any change in Dad?" she asked Levi, who sat across the table next to Katie, who had begun taking the evening meal with the family when Levi had proposed to her.

He shook his head. "He's still in the coma. It's hard to tell if he's going to pull out of this one or not."

"He's a tough old bastard. He'll come around," Trip replied airily as he picked up his wineglass.

There were few people who had passed through Catherine's relatively short life whom she could say she truly disliked, but the glib, fake-tanned, newly bleached blond male across the table fell into that category. He had no specific job on the ranch, didn't appear to be interested in doing anything worthwhile, except attend the parties and events that the Coltons were often invited to.

Half the time he smelled of booze and more than once Catherine was certain the scent of pot clung to him. He bothered the young maids, verging on sexual harassment. He was a waste of air as far as she was concerned.

"I'm thinking about getting a boob job," Tawny exclaimed.

"Really? This is appropriate dinner conversation?" Amanda asked dryly.

"I just thought it would be a good time to get everyone's opinion on the subject," Tawny replied.

"Just shut up, Tawny," Darla said sharply, as if embarrassed by the daughter who was a mini-me to her.

Tawny stiffened at her mother's curt order and instead focused on the plate kitchen server Kyla Winters had just set before her.

As all of them were served Catherine silently bemoaned how different family dinners were now that Jethro didn't sit at the head of the table.

If Jethro were here, there would be no talk of boob jobs or such nonsense. The conversation would revolve around the ranch, the stock and old stories of how he had built his empire. Sometimes he would mention in passing one of his ex-wives.

Brittany Beal had been his first wife and had died in a car crash three months before her son, Cole, was kidnapped. Jethro's second wife had been the sisters' mother, Mandy Brown, who had taken off to parts unknown with a rodeo wrangler over ten years ago.

Darla had been his third wife, but there had been other women during and between his marriages, including Levi's mother. The one thing Jethro never spoke about was his kidnapped son and Catherine knew it was probably because the pain of that loss was simply too great for words.

This meal was eaten in relative silence, Tawny obviously pouting, Trip with a glib half smile on his lips as if he were enjoying a private joke and the rest of them simply attempting to get to the end of the meal.

Catherine was definitely eager to finish eating and

get to her suite. For the first time since she'd found out she was pregnant, an unusual tiredness filled her.

She didn't know if the exhaustion was due to her pregnancy, the tension in the house or her encounter with Gray. She just knew she was mentally and physically tapped out. All she wanted was a long, hot bath, her silky pink nightgown and the comfort of her big bed.

Finally the meal was over, but instead of heading directly to her suite, she went to the nursery to spend a few minutes with her niece and think about the time when little Cheyenne would have her baby as a playmate.

As she entered the beautifully decorated nursery, Tom Brooks, the burly ex-marine bodyguard, stood from a rocking chair to greet her.

"Good evening, Miss Catherine," he said.

"Hi, Tom. I just thought I'd stop in and grab a little loving from Cheyenne." Six-month-old Cheyenne lay on a blanket in the middle of the floor, surrounded by toys. She squeaked a happy greeting at the sight of her Aunt Cath.

He smiled at the little girl fondly. "The little princess is always ready for some loving."

Catherine got down on the floor on the blanket with Cheyenne and for the next few minutes she played with the baby and visited with the man who was responsible for Cheyenne's safety.

The second time that somebody had tried to kidnap Cheyenne, Tom had taken a heck of a beating from the intruder. Ultimately it had been Jagger McKnight who had rushed into the room and not only saved Cheyenne, but had also probably saved Tom's life.

As far as Catherine was concerned, Tom was one of the good guys in the house. He'd been willing to give his life to save Cheyenne.

"I hear there's going to be a new little princess or prince in the family," Tom said as Catherine gave Cheyenne a kiss on her sweet cheek and then rose to her feet.

"You hear right, and I'm hoping you're still around to do double-duty protection with both Cheyenne and my baby."

"It would be my honor," he replied.

With a final goodbye, Catherine left the nursery and headed to her suite. *My baby.* The words rang in her ears and, as always, filled her with a sense of wonder, a sense of joy.

Minutes later she entered her suite to find Allison there doing the turn down on the bed. "Is there anything else I can do for you, Miss Catherine?" Allison asked.

"That's fine, Allison. I'm just going to have a nice hot soak in the tub and then get into bed and read for a while."

"Would you like me to start your bath water?"

"No, thanks, I can take care of it," Catherine replied. Although there were many times Allison had prepared a bath for Catherine, tonight Catherine just wanted to take care of herself and be alone.

"I'll check in on you later and make sure that there's nothing you need before bedtime," Allison replied.

Catherine smiled at the young pretty maid. "That would be fine."

Once Allison had left, Catherine went into the bathroom and started the water running in the deep luxurious jetted tub. It didn't take long for the hot water to steam up the mirrors.

She undressed and when she was completely naked she used a washcloth to wipe the fog off the mirror so she could see her reflection.

Did her breasts look just a little bit bigger? Maybe… maybe not. She turned sidewalks and gasped. She'd always been slender, but there was definitely the beginning of a tiny pooch in her lower abdomen, a pooch that she couldn't suck in no matter how hard she tried.

She laughed out loud at the sight and then ran her hand lightly…lovingly over the area. "My baby," she whispered to her reflection. She smiled as she imagined that bump blowing up into a full nine-month pregnancy. She was going to enjoy each and every day of the next six and a half months.

Her smile faded as she thought of Gray's warnings. She eased down into the warm bath water. While she intended to be smart, she refused to allow fear to rule her life.

She couldn't dwell on the fact that she was a particularly tasty treat for a kidnapper looking for a big ransom. If she did so, she'd make herself a nervous wreck and that wouldn't be healthy for the little one she carried inside her. She needed to stay calm, with as few horrible thoughts drifting around in her head as possible.

Despite the fact that she didn't turn on the jets in the tub, the bath relaxed each and every muscle so that when she finally stood and grabbed a fluffy white towel, she felt almost boneless with exhaustion. After drying off she pulled on the long silky dark pink night-gown and then stepped out of the bathroom.

He grabbed her immediately, his hand firm against her mouth as his other arm wrapped her tight against his body. For an instant her brain refused to work. This shouldn't be happening…not in the house…not in her private suite. This couldn't be happening again. It was like a déjà vu only Gray wasn't right around the corner to rush to her rescue.

The scent of fresh air made her realize one of the windows was open and that's where he was taking her… to the window to drag her outside…to take her some-place where nobody would be able to find her.

Terror tightened her throat as her heart banged the rhythm of terror. The gloves he wore were thick enough she knew she couldn't bite through them like she had the night at the petting barn. She wasn't even sure she could actually scream with her throat closed off in such sheer panic.

She smelled him, a sour scent of sweat and deter-mination. Tears blurred her vision as she attempted to fight against him, to somehow free herself from his viselike grip on her.

But she was afraid that in fighting too hard, she'd somehow hurt the baby, that somehow she'd twist too hard or do something that would force him to tighten his grip around her stomach so hard that he'd harm the little life inside her.

As if in a macabre dance without music, they whirled and turned together, closer and closer to the window,

Catherine screaming against the glove, screaming from every pore of her body, but they were screams that nobody could hear.

Gray had been right. There was danger everywhere. There was no safe place when she was alone, and now it was too late. *Help me,* the words shouted inside her head. *Please, somebody help me.*

But there was nobody to hear her internal cries. Nobody was in her suite except her and the man tugging her closer and closer to the open window and he was far too strong for her to fight.

A faint knock sounded on the door. "Miss Catherine?"

Allison! Catherine wanted to scream to the young maid to run and get help. If Catherine didn't answer would Allison assume she was already asleep and go away? If that happened then Catherine had no chance.

Frantic, mere inches from the open window where darkness yawned, Catherine kicked out a leg and managed to connect with her nightstand. The delicate lamp on the top of the table teetered and then crashed to the floor.

"Miss Catherine?" The door opened and Allison gasped. "No! Stop!" she screamed as she rushed the two in an obvious attempt to save Catherine.

The intruder released his hold on Catherine and Allison barreled toward him. The minute Catherine's mouth was free, she screamed. She knew she screamed out loud, but it was as if she'd gone deaf and time stopped moving as the man clad all in black drew a knife from his pocket and plunged it into Allison's chest just before he turned and disappeared out the window.

Allison slid to the floor and Catherine rushed to her side, but it was obvious she was already dead. Catherine screamed and screamed and even when she was aware of the sound of running footsteps coming toward the room, she kept screaming until her throat was raw and she could finally scream no more.

The screams echoed through every corner of the huge house and the horrible sound, coupled with the pounding of footsteps down the hallway jerked Gray off the bed and to his feet, his heart slamming against his ribs.

Something had happened.

Something bad.

He yanked open his door and nearly collided with Dylan in the hallway. "What's going on?"

"I'm not sure, but somebody said Cath was attacked," Dylan said as he raced down the stairs. Gray's heart skipped a thousand beats as he raced down the hallway behind Dylan.

Cath attacked? It appeared the entire household, family and staff were in motion, running toward Catherine's suite. Gray barreled his way through in an attempt to reach the rooms. Before he could get inside, he heard the wail of one of the housemaids. "Oh, God, she's dead...she's dead."

Gray's blood chilled to arctic ice in his veins. No. No, it couldn't be true. His heart stopped beating as he froze in place, momentarily unaware of the rush and cries of the people around him. His knees threatened to buckle beneath him and he reached out for the wall to steady himself.

He'd known she was in danger, but he'd never thought it would find her here, tucked away in her private suite. His heart pounded once again as emotion swelled up inside him. Dead? She couldn't be dead. His brain refused to accept the possibility.

Once again he pushed and shoved through the people in front of him, needing to see her, desperate to somehow make things right even though his brain screamed that it was too late.

When he reached the door to the suite, he barreled ahead and in an instant his gaze took in the scene before him. Allison Murray lay on the floor beneath the open window, her eyes sightless as they stared up to the ceiling. A knife protruded from her chest, but there was little blood, indicating that the wound had been immediately fatal.

Although filled with horror for Allison, he nearly fell to his knees in relief when he saw Catherine. Mathilda had an arm wrapped around her shoulders as Catherine wept in low, deep sobs.

Outside in the hallway the crowd grew bigger, the chatter louder and yet nobody stepped up to take control. Gabby and Amanda pushed into the room, both of them gasping at the sight of Allison and then running to Catherine's side.

"Mathilda, call the cops and then get everyone, staff and family included gathered in the great room," Gray said, deciding somebody had to take control of the situation and it appeared it was going to be him.

"Come on, Cath. Come to my room and I'll get you a robe," Gabby said.

It was at that moment Gray noticed that Catherine was clad in a pink nightgown that clung to her full breasts and that she shivered uncontrollably. Her eyes were wide, vacant and indicated that she was probably on the verge of shock.

Mathilda left the room to do what Gray had asked and Amanda and Gabby led Catherine out of the room, as well. Even though there was no doubt in his mind that Allison was dead, Gray leaned over her and placed his fingers against her neck, seeking any kind of pulse that might give evidence of life. There was none.

He didn't know all the details yet, but it was easy to discern that somebody had come in through the window and had attacked Catherine. Somehow Allison had gotten into the middle of the fight and had given her life to save the woman she served, the woman she'd loved.

As Mathilda herded the people in the hallway toward the great room, Gray remained in the doorway of the suite. He'd make sure that nobody went into the suite until the police arrived. The last thing he wanted was for anyone to contaminate what was now a murder scene.

He leaned against the doorjamb, closing his eyes and reliving the moment that he'd heard the dreadful words, "She's dead." Even now, his knees threatened to give out as he thought of poor dead Allison and the danger that had come far too close to Catherine.

Whoever wanted her was bold enough to invade the

house. That scared the hell out of him. He turned to stare at the window. The screen was missing, probably thrown to the side on the ground someplace in the dark.

How had this happened? Had Catherine opened the window to get some fresh air? He seriously doubted it. The night air drifting into the room was uncomfortably cold. He couldn't imagine her opening the window for any reason.

And that meant whoever had come in had opened it. The windows were always locked. Gray's eyes narrowed as he considered all scenarios. His heart hardened when he kept landing at the same conclusion. Somebody from inside the house had to have unlocked the window to allow easy access for the person who was now not just a foiled kidnapper, but a cold-blooded murderer.

What he wanted to do was find Catherine, yank her into his arms to assure himself she was alive and well. He wanted to feel the strength of her heart beating against his own. But he knew her sisters would calm her and in any case that wasn't his job.

It took twenty minutes for Chief of Police Harry Peters and a couple of his men to arrive on the scene. His presence was followed quickly by the medical examiner. Gray and Harry stood to the side of the room as the medical examiner did his thing and Harry's men processed what they could before the removal of the body.

"You know what happened here?" Harry asked as the men all went about their business, photos flashing and notes taken.

"Not specifically. I haven't had a chance to talk to Catherine, who was here when it all went down, but it's obvious somebody tried to get in through that window and Allison got in his way." Gray's stomach clenched tight. "It had to be an inside job. The windows on the ground level are always locked. Somebody had to have unlocked that window to allow the intruder access inside."

Harry released the sigh of a tired man. Gray knew the new sheriff had his hands full cleaning up all the mess the former sheriff, Hank Drucker, had left behind. "So, you think the intended victim was Catherine?"

"Definitely." Gray told Harry about the previous attack by the petting barn. "She's pregnant, so I can only assume that somebody sees her as a perfect kidnap victim for a king's ransom. I've had the housekeeper get everyone in the house, both staff and family into the great room so they can be questioned by you and your men."

"That makes my job a little easier," Harry said, and then added dryly, "but not by much."

It took a little over an hour before Allison's body was finally taken out of the room. As Harry's men continued to work the room, seeking some sort of evidence that could be used to find the guilty, Harry and Gray went to the great room where ranch hands, kitchen help, maids and the family were all gathered.

Gray immediately spied Catherine, seated in a chair, clad in her nightgown and a dark blue robe. She looked shell-shocked, her eyes wandering around the room at a frantic pace.

Like a magnet she drew him to her with the need to ease some of the fear that darkened her lovely eyes, the need to stand next to her, to touch her shoulder, whether to reassure her or assure himself, he didn't know.

As he placed his hand on her, she looked up, her eyes tear-filled. "You're safe. You're going to be all right," he said softly.

She shook her head, tears spilling onto her cheeks. "He killed Allison. She tried to help me and he killed her."

Gray realized the tears she shed were not of fear for herself, but rather grief for the young woman who had apparently rushed to her aid. He had no doubt that fear for herself would come later, after she'd processed and grieved Allison's untimely and brutal death.

Harry Peters immediately took control of the room full of people. By simply raising his hands everyone fell silent. "I'd like to speak to Catherine and then my men are going to talk to each and every one of you so I'd appreciate it if you all sit tight." Although he said the words politely there was enough steel in his voice for everyone to understand that nobody was to leave this room.

Harry walked over to where Catherine sat. "Is there someplace we can go to talk?"

"The employee's dining room," Gray replied. He had no intention of leaving Catherine alone with the chief of police or anyone else.

Minutes later the three of them settled at the huge table, Gray seated next to Catherine and Harry across the table from them.

"I noticed several of the ranch hands aren't in the great room," Gray said. "Some of them head into Dead at the end of the day for a little drinking. I imagine one by one they'll be stumbling in sooner or later."

Harry nodded and turned his attention to Catherine. "I need you to tell me exactly what happened," he said.

She gave a curt nod of her head and snaked her fingers into her hair to twirl with anxiety. The action broke a piece of Gray's heart and he reached over and stopped her, capturing her hand in his.

She held tight, as if needing any strength he could give her to get through whatever lay ahead. Slowly, she told Harry about taking her bath, then leaving the bathroom and immediately being grabbed from behind. Throughout her retelling, Gray's blood turned cold.

Each and every word that Catherine said recounting what had occurred in her suite shot myriad emotions through him. Fear and anger battled inside him, along with the burning need to make sure that nothing like this ever happened to Catherine again.

When Harry had gotten what he needed from Catherine he left them alone and returned to the great room to begin questioning the whereabouts of every single person in the house at the time of the attack.

At that moment Stewie Runyon came in the back door and Gray rose from his chair. "Where the hell have you been?"

Stewie frowned. "Out for a walk before bed. Why? What's the problem?"

"The problem is Catherine was attacked and Allison is dead," Gray replied. "You'd better get to the great room. I'm sure the police are going to have plenty of questions to ask you."

Stewie's features gave away no expression as he left the employee kitchen. Gray stared after him, suspicion aroused but unconfirmed. He had a feeling Harry had his work cut out for him in firming up alibis for everyone who lived and worked for the Coltons.

Stewie probably wasn't the only ranch hand who would provide a shaky, unsubstantiated alibi for the time of the attack. Lots of the ranch workers had final chores to do after dinner and before bedtime and those chores weren't team efforts. They were mostly done alone after dark.

Then there were the men who drove into Dead for a few drinks and some interaction with people away from the ranch.

It would be the same with the household staff, there were nooks and crannies in this big mansion where maids went to take a breather, or where the kitchen staff escaped briefly from Agnes's iron fist.

"Maybe we should go back into the great room," Gray suggested as he sank back into the chair next to Catherine.

"Can't we just stay here?" Her eyes were dark pools of agony. "The sheriff will come back in to get us if he needs us. I don't want to go in there with everyone else. It's possible that somebody in there killed Allison or was at least partly responsible for her death."

Her full lips pressed tightly together in an expression that looked more like anger and less like pain. "Somebody unlocked my window. Somebody made it possible for that man to get inside my bedroom and try to kidnap me. You were right. There's nobody I can trust here, nobody except my sisters."

"And me," Gray said firmly. Once again he grabbed her cold, trembling hand, but before he could say anything else to her, Amanda and Gabby came in, fluttering over Catherine with concern.

Gray released his hold on Catherine's hand and stood, his chair immediately filled by Amanda. "Cath, you'll stay in my suite with me," she said. "You are not going to be left alone again."

As the sisters offered their love and support, Gray drifted out of the room and into the great room, where a controlled chaos reigned.

It would take most of the night for the sheriff and his men to do their jobs, to finish processing the scene and interviewing everyone in the room. They'd have to do a check of the house to see who was missing and track down any employees who weren't present.

Gray imagined it would be close to dawn before everyone finally settled down and the cops left, and there was no way he was going to bed until everything that could be done had been done.

Catherine would be safe for the night in Amanda's room, but it was only a temporary solution to a long-term problem. Somehow before morning came, he needed to figure out the best way to keep her safe for as long as necessary.

Chapter 8

Catherine awoke to find herself alone in the bed. Amanda had left the suite near the crack of dawn, having received a call of a sick horse that needed tending.

A glance at the window let her know she'd certainly missed breakfast. The light drifting through the glass was pre-lunch. At least she didn't have to worry about anyone coming through the window of this second-floor suite.

As she thought of the horror of the night before she fought against rising emotions…fear, disbelief and grief. If she hadn't knocked over the lamp on her nightstand would Amanda have simply gone away? Would she be alive now? Why, when she had come into the room did she attack the man instead of screaming for help? Instead of running toward him she should have run away.

Catherine shoved these thoughts away. She couldn't

dwell on the crushing guilt she felt about Amanda. It was too late to change things now.

Somehow she had to put one step in front of the other and move forward. She just wasn't sure how she was going to do that. She got out of bed, definitely knowing she couldn't move forward by sleeping the day away.

Noticing that Amanda had apparently gone to Catherine's room and brought some of Catherine's clothing in, she grabbed a pair of jeans and a navy long-sleeved blouse and then went into the bathroom for a shower.

As she stood beneath the water, the events of the night before played and replayed in her head. She wished she'd been able to tell Chief Peters something about the attacker, anything that might have pointed a finger to somebody in particular. But, like the night at the petting barn, she'd only gotten a vague impression of a strong, medium-built male clad in black.

She wondered if this was the same person who had tried to kidnap Cheyenne. Was her value as a pregnant Colton far greater than that of a six-month-old heir? She'd certainly rather have the target on her own back than on precious little Cheyenne's, but more than anything she wished Harry Peters could find out who was behind these attempts and stop the danger to everyone.

She couldn't think about what had happened the night before without thinking about Gray. He'd stood beside her, silently offering her his support throughout the entire ordeal. The warmth of his hand surrounding hers had calmed her, the familiar scent of him so near had eased some of the terror that had continued to rise and fall inside her until she'd finally fallen asleep with her sister by her side.

She got out of the shower, dried and dressed and then left Amanda's suite to head for the dining room where, if her nose served her right, lunch would soon be served.

Lunch was always informal, served to whoever happened to be in the house at the time. Amanda was rarely in, nor was Gabby. Darla, Tawny and Trip never missed a meal and often Levi was in and out at the noon meal.

Thankfully, the dining room was empty when Catherine entered, but obviously Mathilda had been waiting for her presence. The housekeeper immediately appeared at Catherine's side, her features tortured in dismay.

She wrung her hands in obvious torment. "Oh, Miss Catherine, I'm so sorry. I can't imagine how horrible it was for you and poor dear Allison last night. I feel so responsible for everything that happened."

"Nonsense," Catherine replied and patted the woman's shoulder. "Nobody blames you for anything that's happened. I'm sure Chief Peters is going to get to the bottom of everything," she assured the older woman.

"I certainly hope so. I don't know what to think about everything that has happened in the past couple of months. So much death…so much evil." She shook her head with a tortured expression.

"You do a great job around here, Mathilda. Everything is going to be just fine."

Mathilda nodded and then swept her hands down her skirt as if to smooth any imaginary wrinkles. "I just wanted a moment with you, to tell you how sorry

I am by what you've suffered, and now I'd better get back to work."

Mathilda hurried away to do her duties and Catherine went to get something to eat. She had just finished a light lunch of cold cuts and fruit salad and was exiting the dining room when Gray found her.

"Good afternoon," he said, his eyes dark and his expression serious. "How are you feeling?"

She hesitated a moment. "Sad…scared and a hundred different emotions," she finally answered truthfully.

He nodded, as if expecting nothing else. "Want to take a walk with me? I'll help you with any chores that need to be done out at the petting barn."

"I just need to check the feed and water and I appreciate your offer," she replied. As usual, he was dressed in jeans and a flannel shirt. What was unusual was that his jaw sported more than a five-o'clock shadow and the lines in his lean face appeared deeper than usual.

"Not a problem. You might want to grab a jacket. It's cool out there today."

"I'll grab one on the way out." They went out the employee entrance where there was a rack for jackets on the wall. Catherine grabbed her denim work jacket as he pulled down his worn brown leather coat. They put them on and walked into the early-afternoon sunshine.

"You look like you were up all night," she said once they fell into step, side by side.

"I was. Chief Peters and his men didn't leave here until near dawn so I just decided to help Dylan get the morning chores done after they left. Did you sleep all right?"

"As scared as I was, as sick as I was about Allison, I'm ashamed to admit I went right to sleep and slept without dreams."

"Nothing to be ashamed of," he replied. "You were obviously exhausted by everything."

She nodded and they walked in silence toward the stables and the petting barn. It wasn't a tense silence, rather it felt companionable, as if neither had the need to fill an uncomfortable emptiness.

"I'm cancelling the school class that was scheduled to come out here next week," she said, finally breaking the quiet between them. They continued in a leisurely walk. "There's just too much going on here for me to feel comfortable having little children around."

He nodded, as if to assure her that he agreed with her decision. "That's what I want to talk about, what happened last night and the certainty that something like that is probably going to happen again."

"Gosh, are you trying to cheer me up?" she asked dryly, looking up at him.

"I'm trying to be realistic. Two attempts have been made in the past week or so and I'm fairly certain there's somebody on the inside who is working with the kidnapper. Catherine, it's time for you to face the facts. You aren't safe anywhere alone right now."

The chill of the day invaded her body. Even though he was at her side and she knew she could always depend on her sisters, she'd never felt so all alone. "I know," she replied softly.

She couldn't help but notice that Gray's gaze shot from the left to the right often and his jacket was open as if to allow easy access to his gun. It was a definite reminder that they had no idea when danger might come close again.

For the remainder of the walk to the barn they were silent. It was a silence suddenly laced with tension, and she knew Gray wasn't finished talking about her precarious situation.

He stood just outside the fence as she tended to the animals. His back was to the barn and he appeared to survey the surroundings.

Despite all of the old history between them, he made her feel safe. He was one of the few people she trusted right now and she trusted him without question.

It didn't take her long to take care of all her little creatures. She petted and praised, and even laughed as one of the friendly ferrets managed to grab a strand of her hair through the cage wires in an effort to get more attention.

Finally finished with the chores, she rejoined Gray outside the fence. "Come into the stables," he said. "We really need to talk."

With heavy footsteps she walked next to him. She didn't want to talk any more about what had happened the night before. She didn't want to think about poor Allison, who had given her life in an attempt to save Catherine.

Still, she also knew she couldn't just ignore the danger she was in. She couldn't paint a pretty smile on her face and pretend that nothing bad was happening. She'd done that for too long already.

Most of the horses were out in the pasture, leaving

the stable in unusual silence. But the scent of horse and leather, of hay and male was familiar and comforting to her as she remembered the times she'd spent in here with her father or sisters.

Gray led her to the small office he used as foreman, a tiny room with a single chair and a desk. He motioned her to the chair and she sat while he propped a hip against the desk and stared at her for a long, unsettling moment.

"I have a plan to assure your safety, and I just want you to hear me out until I'm finished," he finally said.

She nodded, the muscles in her stomach tightening with a new kind of tension.

"As far as I'm concerned you have two choices that will help keep you safe from harm. The first is that you go away from here. You leave and go someplace where nobody can find you, where nobody knows your name. It would be like you were in the Witness Protection Program. Nobody could know where you were, not even your sisters. You just disappear until somebody gets to the bottom of everything that has been going on here and it's safe for you to return."

"That's not happening," she replied firmly. There was no way she was leaving her home, leaving her sisters and being all alone for the duration of however long it took to clean up the mess of crimes that had taken place here at the ranch.

Besides, she wasn't going anywhere as long as her father was on his deathbed. She didn't want to be holed away someplace without being able to tell him a final goodbye if and when his time came.

"No," she said. "There has to be another way. Did Chief Peters and his men get anything from my room last night? Anything he can use to find out who came in to get me?"

Gray hesitated a moment and then shook his head, his sensual lips pressed together in a grim line. "No hair, no fibers, not a single fingerprint on or around the window."

"Well, you can take the option of me going under-cover someplace off the table. I'm not going anywhere."

"That's what I thought you would say. And that brings me to the second option, which I've already mentioned to you before and you blew me off." He hesitated a moment and then continued, "Marry me."

He held up a hand to stop her instant protest. "Hear me out, Catherine. It would be a marriage in name only, a temporary marriage until we both feel any danger to you has passed and then we get a simple divorce and move on with our lives. We stick together like glue. A marriage will allow me to sleep in your suite, and I'll go with you wherever you need to go and you go with me when I do chores or whatever. It's the only way to assure you and your baby are safe. You need me to be by your side every minute of the day and night."

His eyes narrowed with a dangerous glint. "Nobody will get close to you without coming through me, and I'll make sure that doesn't happen."

Catherine's head reeled with his proposition. "But nobody would believe that it's a real marriage."

"We can make everyone believe that it's real," he replied. "We just tell people that for the past six months we've been carrying on a secret affair and now we've decided to make it public and legal. There are plenty of folks around here who would remember that we had something going together years ago, it's not such a stretch that we would get together again, and we just have to be good actors to make people believe that's what happened."

She gazed at him for a long moment, wondering why she was even thinking about agreeing to his incredible proposition.

"Why did you leave, Gray? Why did you just disappear from the ranch, from my life nine years ago?" It was a question that had burned inside her for a long time and she realized she couldn't seriously consider this proposal of his without knowing what had happened in their past.

"We were just a couple of kids, still wet behind the ears." His gaze left her face and focused someplace over her shoulder. "First love, teenage fantasies." He looked at her once again, his eyes dark and unreadable. "What we had wasn't real or lasting. It was just the lust and the wonder of young love. I did you a favor by leaving here and letting you get on with your adult life."

"It didn't feel like a favor at the time," she said softly, remembering the aching pain he'd left behind. She wasn't completely satisfied with his answer. However, there were certainly bigger issues at the moment.

"Water under the bridge, right?" he said. "We can't go backward, Catherine. We need to figure things out here and now. We need to make sure that you're covered at all times and the only way I can do that is if you marry me and I have a legitimate reason to be at your side 24/7. We can have a ceremony Saturday at the little chapel. Mr. Black can do the honors and since it's not a genuine marriage of love, we don't need all the bells and whistles."

Even though she knew everything he said was true, for some reason his words created both a twinge of pain and a wistful yearning inside her.

This wasn't the way it was supposed to be for her. She'd always dreamed of a beautiful wedding with a man she loved more than life itself. Instead she was pregnant by a man she never intended to invite back into her life and being offered a marriage of convenience to a man she'd once loved in order to save her life.

She felt trapped, as if no matter what choice she made it would be the wrong thing to do. As crazy as it sounded, this scheme of Gray's felt like the sanest option she had at the moment.

Gray remained silent, allowing her to process all the pros and cons of his suggestion and any alternative plans she might come up with on her own.

She had no plans of her own and she knew something had to change. She could hire a full-time bodyguard, but she'd never completely trust that whoever she hired couldn't be bought off or swayed by the temptation of a cut in a ransom reward.

"Okay," she finally said tremulously. "We'll do it your way." Her heart thumped unsteadily because she wasn't sure if this mock marriage was her salvation or the absolute worst mistake she would ever make in her life.

* * *

Allison's funeral was on Wednesday in the small cemetery in Dead. Although most of the Coltons and staff attended, along with several members of the police force of Dead, it was a sad affair.

Allison had no family to attend. She'd never known her father and her mother had passed away a year before. The people she worked for, the people she worked with at the ranch, had become her family.

Horace Black, an ordained minister who lived with his wife in a small log cabin on the Colton property, would be performing the solemn ceremony. His wife, Bernice, stood beside him. She worked as a laundress at the ranch, her domain the lowest level of the house. She was rarely seen and Gray didn't think he'd heard her say more than ten words in all the years he'd spent at the ranch.

Bernice might be rarely seen or heard, but that didn't keep the rest of the staff from occasionally gossiping about the solidly built woman with the long gray ponytail.

Bernice had one brown eye and one that was milky and opaque. The younger staff believed because of her milky eye she could see spirits and ghostly things and they were spooked whenever they had to go to the basement and interact with Bernice.

As Horace began the ceremony, Gray glanced at Catherine standing by his side. It had been two days since she'd agreed to marry him. The past two nights Catherine had stayed in Amanda's suite, and she would continue to do so until Saturday night when he would officially become her husband.

There was no pleasure at Catherine's capitulation to his plan. This marriage was nothing more than a ploy to keep her safe until the police or somebody could figure out who was behind all the deaths and crimes taking place on the ranch.

He had no illusion about their relationship being anything but what it was now…employer and employee. The little bit of history they shared was long gone and the new relationship they forged would be based on nothing permanent or emotional, and when it was safe, they'd walk away from each other to find their futures separately.

His gaze lingered on her. She was clad in a black dress and a matching overcoat. Most of the time she was stunning in black, but today it wasn't her color.

The darkness leeched all the color from her face, leaving her unusually pale. Her hair was clipped severely at the nape of her neck, and her delicate features were taut with grief as Horace wound down the short ceremony.

When it was finished, everyone milled around despite the cold temperature. As Catherine moved to speak to Gabby and Trevor, Gray made his way toward Chief Peters.

"Chief," he said in greeting to the man who looked as if he hadn't slept in weeks.

"Gray." The dark-haired fortyish man nodded. "Sad affair today, but then you've been through this before with Jenny Burke."

Gray nodded. "I hope you're better at getting to the bottom of things than the former chief of police was."

Harry sighed with obvious disgust. "Drucker left behind false statements, dummied-up reports and a mess of things that all need to be checked out and re-examined. The first thing I did when I took office was fire the two inept officers he had on his payroll. Karen Locke and Pierce Deluca have left the building and have been replaced by a couple of sharp men I'm hoping I can count on to be better than efficient at their jobs."

"And they are?" Gray asked, wanting to know as many players as possible in the small town of Dead who might interact with the people at the ranch.

"Officer Mike Harriman and Patrick Carter. Neither of them is from Dead. I hired them from out of state so that I'd know they came in clean with no ties to anyone at Dead or the Dead River Ranch. Hell, going through the reports of everything that has happened I could use my entire force just out at the ranch to investigate a variety of crimes. Unfortunately I've got a town to protect, as well."

His gaze moved across the cemetery where Catherine stood between her sisters. "I'm assuming you're doing everything possible to keep her safe from another attempt?"

"I'm marrying her on Saturday. From that moment on she won't leave my side." An unexpected emotion rose up inside of him, momentarily catching him off guard as Harry looked at him in surprise.

"I didn't see that coming."

Gray smiled. "A lot of people didn't see it coming,

but Catherine and I have been in love for a long time. We'd planned to eventually get married but after what happened we moved up our plans. Whoever is after her will have to come through me and I won't hesitate to shoot to kill anyone who tries to take her or harm her."

Harry seemed like a decent man, but Gray intended to play his cards close to his chest and wasn't about to admit to anyone that the marriage was nothing more than a scheme in hopes of keeping trouble away from the pretty blonde heiress. The lie to the chief tripped effortlessly off his lips.

Still, Gray needed to build a relationship with Peters as he didn't know when he might need him. Despite everything that had happened in the past four days, Gray hadn't forgotten that he'd promised Dylan to look into all the information Mia and Jagger had discovered about his mother's past.

Mia and Jagger hadn't been the only ones asking questions. Katie McCord, a pastry chef and now Levi's fiancée, had been warned to stop asking questions about Faye Frick, Dylan's mother.

There was no question there were secrets surrounding the woman who had worked for years as governess, secrets that somebody didn't want uncovered. Gray was determined to do what he could to help his friend discover those secrets and finally get answers that would give Dylan some peace.

"Congratulations on the upcoming wedding," Harry said, "and I'm sure we'll be in touch about less pleasant things if history is any indication."

As Sheriff Peters ambled away toward a group of his

officers, Gray walked back to where Catherine stood with her sisters.

"I still can't believe the two of you fooled all of us for so long," Amanda said, her gaze speculative as it lingered on him. "I know the two of you were crazy about each other when you were young, but Cath never said a word about you guys reconnecting." She turned her gaze to Catherine, whose pale cheeks filled with a hint of color.

Gray slung an arm around her slender shoulders and pulled her closer against him. "We just didn't want to tell anyone until we were certain things were going to work out."

"Here I've been spending all this time planning what I thought was the next wedding on the ranch, and Cath is sneaking one in before me," Gabby said.

Gray knew it was difficult for Catherine to lie to her sisters about the truth of their wedding, but he'd insisted that it was vital that nobody know the truth except the two of them. He wanted no gossip to escape, no hint that this was just a ploy in an effort to keep Catherine safe.

"Trust me, you're still going to have the next big wedding at the ranch," Catherine replied. "Gray and I are just having a basic ceremony with just you two and Trevor as witnesses and no guests."

"Are you sure that's what you really want?" Gabby asked as if unable to believe that any woman wouldn't want the crowded church, the elegant wedding gown and the flowers and bows of a big wedding.

Catherine nodded. "It's exactly what I want. I want to be Gray's wife, but it doesn't feel like the right time to have a real celebration." She glanced over at Allison's grave and then back at Gabby. "I just need you two standing with me and Gray beside me and everything will be as fine as it can be at this moment in time."

She looked up at Gray, a deep sadness in her eyes. "Can we go home now? I'm tired."

"I think it's time we all get home," Trevor said as he stepped up to Gabby's side. "There's nothing more we can do here."

Gray led Catherine to his truck, instinctively knowing she didn't want to talk, that she was still immersed in the grief over Allison, who had died trying to save her.

Gray didn't have the words to make her feel better. He knew it would take time for some of this pain to ease. As he started the engine, he smelled the scent of her, that evocative fragrance that pulled forth memories he wanted to forget.

He refused to allow the scent to make him remember loving her. What he had to stay focused on was that the marriage to Catherine was temporary, that love had nothing to do with it and all he needed to do was keep her safe.

Chapter 9

A hundred times…a thousand times over the next three days Catherine alternated between going forward with the marriage to Gray and fighting against the very idea.

Still, when Saturday late afternoon arrived, she'd finally resigned herself completely to the crazy scheme, knowing that there was nobody else she trusted in the entire house more than him.

The idea of having him by her side both during the day and through the long nights was both comforting and unsettling. She didn't want to care about him, she didn't want to think about him as anything but a necessary evil to keep her safe.

She now stood in front of her window, gazing at the low gray clouds that obliterated any sunshine and the rain that freckled the glass of the window.

"Happy is the bride that the sun shines on," she murmured as she turned away from the window and headed for her closet, trying to decide the appropriate attire for a temporary wedding to a man who didn't love her and one she didn't plan to stick around forever.

Of course she didn't love him, either. This whole marriage was just a ruse and the last thing she wanted to do was fall into any fantasy that it would become real or lasting.

The staff had made sure that her room was pristine, with no residual sign of the drama that had occurred in the suite. The window that had been opened had been cleaned of the fingerprint dust, the broken lamp replaced by a similar one. There was no shadow of Allison on the carpeting, nothing to haunt her except for her own memories of that horrible night.

"Are you going to pick a dress or be late for your own wedding?" her sister Amanda asked. She stood nearby, already clad in a beautiful navy dress and heels. "You should have bought a real wedding gown, Cath. It's not every day you get married."

"I didn't want to go to all the trouble. I told you this is just a simple affair." Catherine pulled a long cream-colored Dior from her closet. The bodice sparkled with tiny crystals and it was a gown she'd never worn before. It was perfect for this empty ceremony.

Minutes later as she stood in front of her bathroom mirror clad in the dress, she couldn't help but think of all the fantasies she'd once entertained about her wedding day.

Gray had been in those youthful fantasies as had the

vision of her father walking her down the aisle. The church had been filled with smiling friends and family as the sweet scent of flowers eddied in the air.

Instead of that fantasy, Gray was marrying her under false pretenses, her father was in a coma and everything and almost everyone had taken on the shadow of potential evil.

Gabby flew into the room, also wearing a navy dress. She gasped. "Oh, Cath, you look positively beautiful."

Catherine turned from the mirror and hugged her sister. "Thanks." She released her hold on Gabby and fought the impulse to twirl her hair right off her head. Her anxiety level was through the roof. Was this a wise or completely insane decision? Only time would tell.

"I just came up to tell you that it's raining but Trevor has the car ready to take us to the chapel," Gabby said.

"And it's time to go now," Amanda added with a glance at her wristwatch.

Nerves swelled in Catherine as the three sisters left her suite. They headed for the front door where Trevor had brought a vehicle to carry them all to the small chapel in the distance.

Would he be there? Or had Gray gotten cold feet and run in the middle of the night to the ranch in Montana like he had when they were teenagers.

No, she knew with certainty that he would be there. Rain misted the windshield as Trevor drove toward the chapel. She reached up and touched the necklace hidden beneath the dress. The aquamarine stone served as something blue. Amanda had loaned her a pair of shoes that matched her dress and Gabby had surprised her with a delicate bracelet that had belonged to their mother.

Her bases were all covered...something old, something new, something borrowed, something blue. The only thing she was missing was a groom who loved her and one she could wholeheartedly love back.

Her hand drifted down to her tummy. This was why she was going through with this farce, not just to keep herself safe, but to assure the safety of her baby.

When Trevor pulled up to the chapel entrance, Catherine had a sudden impulse to jump out of the car and run as far and as fast as she could, but ultimately she knew there was nowhere to run.

The chapel was a simple building—one room with wooden pews on either side of a narrow aisle. A small stained-glass window hung high above the altar, but there was no sun streaking through to show off its beauty today.

Her heart swelled as she saw Gray, clad in a black suit, standing next to Horace Black. Gray looked achingly handsome and in that moment when he caught sight of her, his eyes appeared to light up. What appeared to be a genuine smile curved his lips.

It's all make-believe, Catherine reminded herself as Gabby and Amanda walked up the aisle in front of her and got into the positions of bridesmaids.

There was no music except the pounding of her own heartbeat. She walked slowly, solemnly up the aisle. She got halfway to where they all waited for her and her steps slowed. A million thoughts whirled through her head.

She was more accustomed to seeing Horace working on a baling machine or fiddling with some kind of machinery than she was seeing him in his suit and tie, and now twice in one week she'd seen him dressed to perform. A funeral and a wedding in less than seven days—it all just felt so wrong.

Then she looked at Gray once again. In the broadness of his shoulders, in the strength of his arms and the resolution on his face she saw safety in a sea of danger.

She quickened her steps and joined them in front of Horace who smiled at her benevolently. When he wasn't acting as a minister, he was the general handyman who fixed things. He had no idea that what he was about to do was temporarily fix a situation that had nothing to do with abiding love and enduring vows.

The ceremony passed in a haze. It was only when Gray slipped a gold band on her finger that the haze lifted, and as she gazed into Gray's gold-flecked brown eyes and Horace pronounced them husband and wife, it felt too real.

"Kiss your bride," Gabby said as there was an awkward moment of silence.

"Yeah, what are you waiting for?" Amanda added.

The kiss. Catherine hadn't thought about the traditional kiss that always followed the pronouncement of husband and wife. Gray wrapped her in his arms and lowered his lips to hers.

She'd expected a mere peck, but his mouth took possession of hers, kissing her deeply and she found herself responding, melding into him as his tongue danced

erotically with hers. It was just as she remembered…
the heat…the fire.

"Okay, you two. Get a room," Gabby said with a
laugh that quickly halted the kiss.

Catherine straightened, reeling with the sensual pleasure that they'd just shared. She wasn't sure she liked
him, she definitely didn't want to love him, but she had
to admit the lust that he'd always managed to stir in her
hadn't diminished over the years.

"Let's get everyone back to the house before this
misty rain turns into a torrential downpour," Trevor
said. "Reverend Black, I'll be more than happy to drive
you to your place."

Horace smiled, displaying several missing teeth. "I
won't melt in a little rain. You get the family safely back
inside the house and I'll walk home."

Within minutes they were all loaded in the car and
heading back to the house where life as Catherine had
known it would now be different.

Half of her closet already held Gray's clothing. Her
bathroom had his toiletries next to hers beneath the
sink cabinet although his trophies and winning belts
and most of his personal items were still in his employee room upstairs. He intended to keep that room
for when the marriage ended and he went back to being
staff. Still, from this moment on they would be together
at all times.

Trevor parked at the front door where they all got out
of the car, and to Catherine's surprise Gray swooped
her into his arms to carry her over the threshold where

many of the house staff were gathered to congratulate the newlyweds.

Like a reception line, Catherine and Gray were greeted with hearty well wishes from the maids, the kitchen help and at the end of the line Mathilda, who wiped happy tears from her eyes.

Surreal. It all felt incredibly surreal to Catherine. It was as if she'd stepped into somebody else's life and had no idea where it would take her.

Head cook Agnes stepped out of the line to address Gray and Catherine. "An intimate dinner has been prepared for the two of you and will be served in Miss Catherine's suite in half an hour if that's agreeable."

"That sounds lovely," Catherine said. What she wanted to do more than anything was escape this crowd of people who'd been fooled, stop the forced smiles that stretched her lips again and again.

"I think we'll head to the suite now," Gray said. "My bride has already had a long day."

Catherine gazed at him gratefully. He smoothly led her away from the crowd and down the hallway to her suite. Somebody had filled the sitting room with vases of flowers…pink roses mingled with fragrant gardenias and delicate tulips.

"Wow, somebody went to a lot of trouble," Gray said as they entered the room and he closed the door behind him.

"My first guess would be my sisters with the help of a couple of maids," Catherine replied, fighting back emotion that made her want to cry. "I think I'll go change into something more comfortable," she said, needing to escape Gray's presence, needing a few minutes alone.

She walked through the bedroom and carried with her into the bathroom a long lounger gown in soft jewel tones. Once she was alone she sat on the edge of the tub and tried to rein in her crazy emotions.

Maybe it was pregnancy hormones starting to kick in, but she felt like weeping because they'd fooled everyone, because everybody seemed so happy for them.

More than anything she wanted to cry because she felt as if she'd given away a piece of herself in entering into a temporary, loveless marriage for the sake of personal safety.

While Catherine was in the bathroom, Gray changed from the suit and tie he'd worn for the ceremony to a pair of comfortable jeans and a brown sweater. He placed his holster and gun on an end table next to the chaise and then sank down into the cushion.

Never in a million years would he have imagined himself married to Catherine Colton and living in a suite of pink rooms. Never in a million years would he have thought that a mandated kiss could have shaken him up so badly.

He'd just intended to give her a peck, a mere touch of his lips to hers. But the moment he'd drawn her into his arms, the moment their lips had met, there was no way he could pull back his need to drink of her, to kiss her as fully, as deeply as possible.

That had been a mistake because now the taste of her, the feel of her warm in his arms was all he could think about. He stared into the next room where the end of the king-size bed was visible. There was no bed big enough in the world for him to be comfortable in it with her by his side.

She probably wanted him to sleep on the chaise anyway. He frowned, trying to imagine folding his six-foot frame into some form of comfort on the delicate pink-and-black patterned chaise longue.

Despite the floral fragrance of the flower arrangements, her scent filled the air, and that along with the memory of the hot kiss they'd just shared created a sharp edge inside him, an edge that held the slightest hint of irritation with himself…with her.

His irritation crept higher as she came out of the bathroom, a vision of soft colors in a gown that shimmered across her breasts and fell to the floor. She looked like a princess. Actually, she looked like a very nervous princess.

"I suppose you expect me to sleep here on the chaise," he said, his voice more gruff than he intended.

She looked at him and shook her head. "You're too big for that. I'll sleep on the chaise," she replied as she sat in the pink chair next to the furniture in question.

"That's not going to happen." His voice brooked no argument. "You're pregnant. You're going to sleep in your own bed where you'll be most comfortable."

She glanced over at the bedroom and then back at him. "It's a big bed. I suppose we could share it without ever touching each other."

At that moment a knock fell on the door. Gray grabbed his gun and went to answer. As he saw Lucinda pushing a cart laden with food covered by lids, he tucked his gun into the back of his jeans so he wouldn't give the kitchen worker a heart attack.

"Here you are," she said with a bright smile. "A nice, romantic dinner for the two newlyweds." She pulled a lighter from her pocket and lit the candle that stood in a single crystal candle holder in the center of the cart. "I'll just come back to take out the cart in the morning." Her sly smile indicated that she assumed they would be busy with other things for the remainder of the night.

"Thank you, Lucinda," Gray said, and the young woman left the room. Gray locked the door after her and then set his gun back on the end table.

"Are you hungry?" he asked as he maneuvered the cart between the chair where she sat and the chaise. "I'm sure Agnes went to a lot of trouble to fix us something special for our wedding meal."

He began to pull off lids, exposing spinach salad with fresh strawberries and juicy prime rib cooked just to perfection. Baked potatoes and fresh asparagus were side dishes, along with yeasty rolls and a small white cake sporting a plastic bride and groom figurine on top.

"It does look good," she admitted as she pulled a napkin from the cart.

"It's definitely better than anything I've eaten in the employee dining room," Gray replied. "I guess that's one of the perks of being married to a Colton. Better food, nicer sleeping arrangements and the joy of spending time in your company."

"Stop that," Catherine said, her chin shooting up a notch and her eyes glittering with a hint of anger.

"Don't make fun of what we've just done. We've lied to everyone we know and love and you shouldn't feel good about it."

"I was just making a joke, trying to ease some of the tension," he replied. "And I don't feel good about lying to everyone, but nobody will make me believe what we've done is wrong. You and that baby are what are most important and this was the only way I could make sure that you both stay safe."

She lowered her gaze from his and drew a deep breath. "Sorry I snapped. I've been switching between the need to cry or scream all day."

Gray picked up his fork. "Catherine, I know this isn't the way you wanted things to go and I know this is going to be difficult for a while, but we'll get through it together. It's not like it's a permanent thing. You only have to put up with me until somebody figures out who the bad guys are."

"Let's hope that doesn't take too long," she replied. "And now we'd better eat before this all gets cold."

She was quiet through the meal. He tried to keep up a running conversation about his chores and how he'd delegated to some of the men more work and appointed Dylan the official foreman in charge for the time being, but eventually he gave up trying to keep any talk going.

The logistics of this marriage would take some getting used to. Not only did he have things that needed to be done as ranch foreman, but he also knew she had events and activities to attend and the petting barn animals to care for.

They would have to work together, to compromise in

order for them to never be apart from each other. There was no way Gray intended to leave her side or allow her any freedom to leave his.

"What do you usually do in the evenings after dinner?" she asked once they had finished eating and Gray had moved the tray next to the suite doorway.

"Drink a beer, visit with Dylan or read crime procedural books and mysteries."

"Read?" she looked at him in surprise.

"Yeah, this dumb cowboy can actually read," Gray replied with a hint of defensiveness.

She reached a hand up to her hair and began the fast twirl of a strand. "Don't be an ass." She released a frustrated sigh. "We've only been married a couple of hours and I'm already in the mood for a divorce."

"Maybe you need a pickle," Gray said in an attempt to lighten things up once again.

Her brow furrowed. "A pickle?"

"And some ice cream," he added.

Her eyes lightened as her hand dropped from her hair to her tummy. "Oh, I don't think I'll ever crave pickles and ice cream. That sounds totally disgusting."

"You think so now but wait until that little bean really starts working on you. Who knows, you might wind up craving peanut butter and peppermints."

"Or meatballs and marshmallows," she added, her eyes lighting with the shine he remembered from long ago as the silly conversation eased the tension that had been between them.

"What do you normally do after dinner? Besides sit with Jethro?" he asked.

"Sometimes we all gather in the great room and chat. Of course, until a couple of months ago there was Dirk and many evenings I spent my time with him."

Gray fought against a surge of unexpected jealousy as he thought of the man who might have married Catherine, the man who had fathered the child she carried.

"I'm afraid I'm probably going to be a lot more boring than Dirk," he said.

She smiled at him, a genuine smile that shot a ball of heat into the pit of his stomach. "If you were asleep you wouldn't be as boring as Dirk."

"Then why were you dating him?"

She leaned back and frowned thoughtfully. "Dirk and I kept finding ourselves at the same events. Initially I thought he was charming and when he asked me out I accepted and suddenly we were dating. I guess I got caught up in the idea of wife and motherhood and he was there and available."

She shook her head dismissively. "But apparently, Dirk is having some financial issues and thought marrying me would instantly bail him out. Four years was too long for him to wait for that bailout." She rested her hand on her stomach. "I got what I wanted and this baby is all I need to be happy."

"I'm sure eventually you'll find some man you love and who loves you and that will complete your vision of a happily-ever-after kind of family," Gray replied.

He was sure that the man Catherine bound herself to in the future would be something quite different than a ranch foreman with manure on his boots and little money in his pocket.

Their conversation remained fairly pleasant and the mood in the room was relaxed until Catherine said she was exhausted and ready for bed.

Gray followed her into the bedroom where he pulled down the bedspread and tried not to think about the torture to come.

As she disappeared into the bathroom to get into her night clothes and prepare for bed, Gray tried to keep his mind off the kiss they'd shared, off how badly he wanted to touch her soft skin, run his fingers through her silky hair. He had to rid himself of those kinds of thoughts. They had no place in this situation.

She came out of the bathroom clad in a short navy silk nightgown that displayed her long shapely legs and smelling of that provocative scent that was hers alone. A knot formed in Gray's chest, a knot of unwanted desire, of unexpected lust.

He went into the bathroom immediately after she exited and stripped off his clothes and started a cold shower to cool his inappropriate physical attraction to her.

Lust for her definitely hadn't been in this arrangement he'd made with her. There had been other women since her, a waitress who worked in a café near the Montana ranch where he'd worked, a pretty blonde dress shop owner who had captured his attention for a couple of months. But nobody in his life had ever managed to stir such a hunger inside him as Catherine.

Ten minutes beneath the cool spray and he felt controlled and clear on what his role was with Catherine… he was a glorified bodyguard with a marriage license.

He dried off and pulled a clean pair of boxers from where he'd stacked them the day before in a large built-in cabinet. He thought about pulling on a T-shirt, but he'd never slept in one in his entire life and didn't intend to start now.

He came out of the bathroom to find Catherine already in the bed, facing away from him and tucked in a ball as close to the edge as humanly possible.

He moved his gun to the nightstand next to his side of the bed and then turned out the lamp, which plunged the room into darkness.

Easing beneath the sheets on his side, there was an ocean of bed between them. "Catherine, you're so close to the edge that if you sneeze or cough you're going to fall off. There's plenty of room for you to relax."

Her faint sigh and shift of movement let him know she'd moved away from the edge of the bed and closer to the center. He squeezed his eyes closed, trying not to breathe in the scent of her, attempting to banish the vision of her in her navy nightgown that had accentuated the spill of her long blond hair and the fullness of her breasts.

He had to remember his place here. He had to keep in mind that he was nothing more than a hired gun, his job to keep her safe from any evil that attempted to come near her.

When he'd made the suggestion of the marriage of convenience, he hadn't thought about moments like this, about lying next to her in the dark and wanting her despite any rational desire to the contrary.

He hadn't thought about how the roar of old memories would resound in his head, taking him back to the time when he thought she was his forever.

That had all come crashing down when he'd overheard part of a phone conversation she'd had with one of her friends. He'd heard her say exactly what would be expected of her when it came to marriage and nothing she said included her undying love for a ranch hand. Nothing she'd said had indicated that Gray would ever be the man she wanted permanently in her life.

That's when he'd run. Filled with busted dreams and a broken heart, he'd gone to Montana where he'd learned to hate her for toying with him, for pretending he meant anything to her.

Water under the bridge, he reminded himself. Teenage angst and first-love drama, that's all it had been. They'd both survived and grown up without too many scars left behind.

One thing was certain: he'd never let her know that she still held a tiny place in his heart. He'd never let her know that he still desired her.

His job was to keep her safe until the danger to her had been resolved, and then his job was to let her go.

Chapter 10

Warm. She was surrounded by a luxurious warmth that made her want to cuddle into it, reluctant to fully awaken. Instead she tried to return to the dream she'd been having, a dream where she'd been holding a little boy with sandy hair like how Gray's turned in the summer. The child also had blue eyes like hers.

She wanted to go back to the dream, but instead once full consciousness claimed her she realized the warmth that she reveled in was Gray spooned around her backside, one of his arms flung across her waist as if to capture her and hold her prisoner against him.

Frozen in shock, stunned by the pleasure, she remained unmoving. Her body took in the sweet sensations of his intimate nearness. He was obviously sound asleep, his breathing deep and even as it warmed the nape of her neck. She knew she should roll away from him, break the embrace that felt so safe and so right, but she didn't.

She simply existed in the nearness of the man she'd once believed would be with her for the rest of her life. She still didn't know exactly what forces had been at play when he'd left her and the Dead River Ranch so many years ago. What was important was that he was here with her now when she needed his safety and strength.

It was obvious they weren't destined to reclaim the love they had once had. She was aware that they had both grown up and were very different people than they had been as young, fanciful teenagers. She could only appreciate the fact that he must feel something for her in order to step into the role he'd taken on.

The room held the faint light of predawn whispering through the window. She knew normally he'd be awake and outside tending to chores, but he'd arranged for Dylan to take care of the morning duties and supervise the other workers as they went about business as usual.

This was probably one of the first mornings in his life that he was sleeping past dawn. The last thing she wanted to do was stir in any way that might wake him up.

She must have fallen back asleep for when she opened her eyes again she was in the bed alone and the sound of the shower came from the bathroom. The bathroom door was open as if to make sure if she screamed for any reason he'd hear her and rush to the rescue. She tried not to imagine a naked, dripping Gray rushing to save her from harm.

She rolled over on her back and stared at the ceiling where the morning light danced bright imps of sunshine through the dappled curtains.

Who was behind the kidnapping attempts both on her and little Cheyenne? Who had killed Allison? And Jenny Burke in the kitchen pantry?

Initially everyone thought Trip had killed Jenny. They'd had a relationship, and days before her death Jenny had been sporting a large diamond ring. The day after her death the ring was found in Trip's room, instantly putting him at the top of the suspect list.

Trip had said that he and Jenny had broken up and he'd taken the ring back and with no other evidence to tie him to the kitchen that night or the murder itself, the crime remained unsolved.

Was it any wonder she was reluctant to leave her bed? Was it any wonder she was grateful for Gray's crazy marriage proposition that suddenly didn't feel so crazy anymore?

They'd made it through their first night together as a married couple and if the worst thing she had to put up with was waking to find his near-naked body warming hers, then she could deal with that. She just couldn't lose sight of the fact that he was a temporary fix, not a permanent solution.

The sound of the shower stopped and minutes later Gray came out of the bathroom dressed for the day. Catherine sat up and offered him a good-morning smile. "So, what are the plans for the day?" she asked.

He sat on the cushioned bench at the foot of the bed. "Before too long I need to check in with Dylan at the stables and I assume you have things to take care of at the petting barn. After that, I have no idea unless you have something specific on the day's agenda."

She swept a strand of her hair away from her face and shook her head. "Nothing on my agenda for the day."

"Okay, then after we get through the morning chores we'll just hang out here."

"I just need to take a quick shower. We can get some breakfast after we finish the chores." She slid out of bed, acutely conscious of his gaze following her as she went into the bathroom.

She wasn't a high-maintenance kind of woman. She showered, quickly dried her hair and pulled it up into a ponytail. She dressed in jeans and a long-sleeved pink fleece sweatshirt and then with a touch of blush, a whisper of mascara proclaimed herself ready to face the day…the first day of her married life with Gray.

By the time she'd left the bathroom he had moved into the sitting room. He smiled at her appearance. Even though his lips moved up in the appropriate gesture, there was a lack of real emotion behind it. His mouth compressed into a thin slash as he pointed her to the chaise.

"We need to set the ground rules before we leave this room," he said.

She sank down on the chaise, noting that he now wore his holster and gun. She knew when he was outside he always had his gun. Most of the ranch workers carried guns when they were out in the pastures. They never knew when they might encounter a hungry gray wolf or a bear threatening livestock.

But seeing his gun on his hip now was a reminder that he wasn't just anticipating a danger of wildlife, but rather a danger of the human kind.

"We never separate. No matter what happens, no matter who calls either of us away for anything, we don't go alone. We go together," he said.

"I'm all for that," she said as her thoughts drifted back to the nights she'd been attacked, most recently to the night Allison had died right here in this very room.

Her gaze drifted to the place where Allison had fallen dead just inside the window and an icy finger walked up her back at the same time a wealth of grief filled her.

"Catherine."

She looked back at him.

His eyes held a hint of softness. "You can't think about what's already happened. We can't do anything about that. We have to stay focused on the here and now."

"I know."

"The second rule is that if I tell you to do something, no matter how crazy it might sound at the time, you do it," he continued. She eyed him warily. "You have to trust me one hundred percent and know that if I tell you to do something it's for your own protection."

She nodded. "I just can't believe everything that has happened around here over the past couple of months. I can't believe that I no longer know who to trust, that I can't figure out the good guys from the bad ones."

"That makes two of us," he admitted. His eyes narrowed. "But one thing is for sure. No bad guys are going to get to you without killing me first, and I'm a tough man to kill."

"I hope so. The last thing I want on my conscience is somebody else's death." Especially his, she thought. Even though they'd had virtually no relationship for the past nine years, for the past four that he had been back at Dead River Ranch his mere presence here had been strangely comforting to her.

She'd often stand at one of the windows in the house and watch him go about his day, drifting in and out of the stables, heading out on horseback to check on things or standing with a couple of men and giving them instructions.

Although she didn't want to admit it to herself, he still owned a small piece of her heart, a piece that she couldn't allow to grow and flourish.

She got up from the chaise and gave him a teasing smile. "Come on, cowboy, the day is wasting."

He rose from the chair and took her elbow in his hand, guiding her out of the suite door. "Stuck together like glue," he reminded her.

It was early enough in the morning that they managed to sneak out of the house without running into either family or staff.

The dawn air was brisk, invigorating as the sun finally rose above the horizon and shot shimmering golden light across the land and outbuildings.

"It's beautiful this time of morning," Catherine said on their way to the stables. She cast him a sideways glance. "I'm rarely up this early in the morning."

"I know. What woke you? I hope it wasn't me getting out of bed. I tried to be as quiet as possible."

"No, it wasn't you." She tried not to think about those moments of enjoying his warmth cuddled around her. "I guess I was just finished sleeping."

"I imagine you'll be doing more sleeping as that baby grows. I don't know much about pregnancy, but I would guess you're going to tire easier than normal."

"I'll deal with it all as it happens," she replied and then glanced up at him and smiled. "I'll deal with throwing up in the mornings, sleeping until noon and raging hormones as long as my baby is healthy."

"How do you feel about mucking out stalls, mixing grain and grooming horses?" he asked, a light tone in his voice that she hoped stayed there for the remainder of the day.

"I'm game for whatever you need me to do, partner."

He grinned, a real, full smile that warmed her from head to toe.

At that moment Dylan stepped out of the stables to greet them. "Well, well, if it isn't the newlyweds, up and around already at the crack of dawn."

"Hi, Dylan." Catherine had always liked Dylan, who had grown up here on the ranch with all of them. Dylan was the only man other than Jethro who managed to gentle Jethro's temperamental, fiery black stallion, Midnight. He was magic with animals and people, and she knew that he and Gray were good friends.

"Miss Catherine." He clapped a hand on Gray's shoulder. "I hope this dusty old cowboy isn't giving you too hard a time."

She smiled at Gray and then at Dylan. "So far so good," she replied. She had a feeling Dylan knew their marriage was an arrangement rather than a true testimony of love.

Gray and Dylan were close enough that Gray would have shared with his friend if he'd been secretly dating Catherine over the past few months. There was no way that Dylan would believe that Gray and Catherine's marriage was real and based on love. It was okay with her that Dylan knew the truth. She trusted Dylan almost as much as she trusted Gray.

They all stepped inside the stable and as the two men talked about work, Catherine zoned out of the conversation and instead found herself wondering if and when the danger to herself and others on the ranch would ever pass.

Who was behind it all? Who in the house had unlocked her window to allow a kidnapper access to her? Who had killed Faye Frick, Jenny Burke and now Allison Murray?

Would Gray still be around playing husband to her when her belly really began to swell? Would he still be at her side when the baby was finally born?

Surely not, and she shouldn't entertain visions of him next to her in the delivery room, holding a new little being in a blue or pink blanket.

Still, the momentary vision that filled her head of that particular event occurring pulled a softness from deep inside her, a softness toward the man who had broken her heart and now protected her life.

It was a softness she quickly shoved away. A single

night of mock marriage was one thing, a lifetime of a real marriage to Gray was impossible.

"I haven't forgotten what I promised you," Gray told Dylan. "And I plan on getting started digging in the next day or two."

Dylan nodded. "I appreciate it, but I understand you have other things on your hands now."

"I feel like you two are talking in secret code," Catherine said.

Gray looked at Dylan, seeking silent permission to let Catherine know what he'd promised his friend. Dylan nodded without hesitation. "We'll talk about it later," Gray told Catherine. "When we're in the petting barn or back in our suite."

He could see her curiosity piqued by his words, but there were too many people in the stables for him to talk about Dylan's request of help right now.

"There's really nothing for you to do here," Dylan said. "Everyone is doing their chores and it should scare you how easily the morning began without you. If you aren't careful I'll be taking over as foreman permanently."

Gray laughed, knowing that's the last position Dylan wanted. "I'm not too worried as long as you can be my eyes and ears out here for the time being."

"I've got your back," Dylan said. "Now get out of here and take care of those critters in the petting barn."

With goodbyes said, Gray and Catherine headed for the smaller outbuilding next to the huge stables. Gray scanned the area, always on the alert for something or somebody that didn't belong, that might be a threat to the woman beside him.

They had just reached the barn when Gray spied somebody lurking in the nearby woods, the same woods where somebody had tried to take Catherine against her will.

"Catherine, get into the petting barn," he said sharply. She didn't dither or pause to ask questions. She raced inside the gate and got into the small building as he pulled his gun and advanced toward the wooded area.

He'd had only a vague vision of a male in a dark jacket and carrying a rifle. He was relatively certain that whoever was after Catherine didn't intend to hurt her. Still the idea of a rifle anywhere in her vicinity worried him since the deaths of the three women had already occurred.

Tension wired Gray taut as he stalked toward the woods.

He was halfway to the targeted area when he recognized the man who stepped out of the woods and into the clearing. Jared Hansen.

The young wrangler raised a hand in greeting as he approached Gray, the rifle pointed safely down toward the ground. "What in the hell are you doing out here?" Gray asked, his gun still held in his hand.

"Gray, everything okay?" Dylan hollered from the stables.

"Fine," Gray replied, although tension rode his shoulders as he continued to stare at Jared. Had Jared intended to shoot Gray and then grab Catherine, but had been thwarted by Dylan's nearby presence?

"I asked you a question," Gray said to Jared.

"I thought I saw a couple of wolves in the woods and I went after them. You mind pointing that gun in another direction?" Jared looked at him as if he'd lost his mind.

Gray slowly lowered his gun, wondering if he *had* lost his mind. "Forget the wolves and get to work on the fencing in the west pasture. I noticed it needed some repair last time I was out there."

"Got it," Jared said. Gray watched as the young man ambled toward the stable and the adrenaline that had raged inside him slowly dissipated.

As he walked to the petting barn he knew that this was what his life would be as long as he was responsible for Cath's safety. He'd be filled with paranoia and distrust of both the people who worked for him and the people he worked for and that wouldn't change until he knew for certain that the danger to Cath had been neutralized.

When he entered the small barn she was seated on a bale of hay in the corner, a white rabbit in her lap. Her eyes were wide as she gazed up at him. "Everything okay?" She stroked the fur softly and he remembered how her soft hands had once felt against his naked skin.

He holstered his gun and sat next to her. "Jared Hansen was supposedly stalking some wolves in the woods. I just saw him as a figure lurking around with a rifle and got a little freaked out." He reached over and touched the rabbit's soft fur. "I don't know. I might have overreacted."

She smiled at him. "I'd much rather you overreact

than underreact, especially if you see it as a potential threat."

"I'm definitely a bit on edge," he admitted. It wasn't just the possibility of a threat that had him on edge, it was her. When he opened his eyes that morning and found himself curled around her warm feminine curves, he'd wanted nothing more than to wake her with his desire, take her drowsy warmth and turn it into an awakening fire.

He reached out and petted the soft fur of the rabbit in her lap. "Should we get to your chores?"

"Not until you tell me what you and Dylan were talking about in the stables." She picked up the bunny and leaned over to place it in the fenced area where it belonged and then straightened and gazed at him expectantly.

Gray leaned back, the scent of the hay pulling forth memories of her in his arms, gazing up at him as if he were the most important person in her life, in the entire world. He wished he didn't remember their lovemaking. Amnesia of the time they'd been teenagers would have been a welcome relief.

He shoved away these thoughts and instead focused on the promise he'd made his friend. "Dylan wants me to help him find out about his mother's past. Questions were raised when Mia and Jagger did some digging and now Dylan isn't sure what to believe and what not to believe about where he came from and what his mother told him about his father."

"I thought his father was a man Faye married and

then he died in some sort of a horse accident," Cath replied.

"That's what he always believed, but now in retrospect he isn't sure that his mother told him the truth."

Cath gazed into the rabbit pen thoughtfully. "Faye was a beloved presence in the house from the moment she was hired by Mathilda. She was like a fill-in mother when ours wasn't available, and then when Mom left for good, Faye was there for us girls."

"She was there for me, too," he reminded her.

She focused her gaze back at him. He could get lost in those indigo depths if he allowed himself. "I've seen the change in Dylan since his mother's murder and it breaks my heart," she said. "He's always been so outgoing and happy and now there's a lonely sadness that clings to him."

She placed her hand on Gray's thigh and every muscle in his body tensed although she seemed unaware of what her touch did to him. "I'm glad Dylan has you, and I'm glad I have you, too."

At that moment time froze as they gazed at each other. He wanted to kiss her. He wanted to kiss her badly. What he really wanted was to lay her back and caress her slowly, until they were both panting with their need for each other.

She pulled her hand back from his thigh, her cheeks dusty with pink color as if she suddenly realized she was touching him. "So, how do we intend to investigate Faye Frick and get some answers for Dylan?"

"We?" He raised an eyebrow wryly.

"Stuck like glue," she reminded him.

Despite his warring emotions and the testosterone that had risen to huge proportions inside him, he smiled at her. "Stuck like glue," he agreed, and then stood, needing to distance himself from her nearness. "And to be honest, I'm not sure how I'm going to start an investigation into Faye's past."

"We'll figure out our plan tonight." She got up from the hay. "And now I've got critters to feed."

As they stepped outside of the barn Gray automatically took in the scenery around them. Seeing nothing to concern him, he leaned against the fence and watched Cath go about tending to her little stock.

"You want some help?" he asked as she filled a bowl full of grain pellets.

"Thanks, but I've got it," she replied. "I'd much rather you keep an eye on other things."

He knew she meant he should keep his eye out for danger, but it was difficult to keep his eyes off her while she went about her routine of feeding and watering and then taking time to give each animal special loving attention.

She had always been a gentle spirit. That was part of what Gray had fallen in love with so many years ago. She laughed easily, was delighted by the small things in life and had always made him feel bigger, better and brighter than he was.

He'd spent a long time hating her when he'd been gone. But upon coming back to the ranch he'd found it impossible to sustain any true hatred toward her. She was simply too innocent, too sweet and vulnerable to evoke that kind of negative emotion.

He didn't believe she had any enemies on the ranch. Cath didn't make enemies. The person who had tried to kidnap her twice and would probably try again probably didn't hate Cath. Rather it might be somebody who liked her quite well yet knew she was the key to a king's ransom.

Greed could turn good men into thieves, honest men into liars and create killers out of thin air. It was possible that during the day the kidnapper greeted Cath with a friendly smile, that he was somebody she'd believe to be a friend, and that only made it more difficult to find the guilty party.

What worried Gray more than anything was that he didn't think he had to go hunting for the kidnapper. What worried him was that the kidnapper would find them once again. He touched the butt of his gun as if to assure himself.

He just had to make sure if and when that happened he was capable of seeing that nothing bad happened to the woman who still managed to own a part of his heart.

Chapter 11

When he and Catherine left the dining room that evening, Gray had that deer-in-headlights look. Catherine couldn't help but giggle as they walked down the corridor to her suite of rooms. "Welcome to the family." It had been his first experience sitting in the family dining room for the evening meal.

"Is it always like that?" he asked.

"Sometimes it's much worse," she replied. "Tonight you just got Trip talking and Tawny whining. Most nights you can add in Darla sniping and you get a trifecta of unpleasantness to go along with Agnes's excellent meals."

As they reached her suite, Gray pulled his gun and shoved her behind him and then opened the door. This had become routine every time they had entered the suite that day. He cleared the three rooms and she followed close behind him. Once he tucked his gun back into his holster, they relaxed.

The day had been a strange one. They had spent some of the morning in the stables where the two of them worked oiling saddles. After a quick early lunch of just the two of them, they had spent most of the afternoon in the suite playing cards and then had dusted off an old chess game Catherine had tucked away in her closet. They'd matched wits for three games. Unfortunately he had won two of those games, crowing with his victory until she laughed helplessly at his mock arrogance.

This had been the Gray she remembered, the young man with the sparkling golden-brown eyes and laughter spilling from his lips. This was the man she'd once loved with all her heart, the man who'd made her laugh, who'd made her feel so safe, so loved.

But that was then and this was now and while the afternoon had been pleasant the evening brought with it the rising tension of sharing the bed.

At least they had arranged for Dylan to come to the suite to talk about how they intended to go forward with the investigation into his mother's past.

As she sat in her favorite chair, Gray flopped down on the chaise. She could feel a restless energy wafting from him. It kept one of his feet tapping absently against the floor for several minutes. Then he got up to stalk back and forth across the sitting-room area and finally landed at the window to stare outside.

"Maybe you should fill me in on some things that have happened around the ranch in the past couple of

months," she finally said, hoping to get him to settle down.

He turned and looked at her. "You've been living in
this house. You should know more about what's been
happening around here than I do."

"I should, but I've tried not to listen. I've been hiding out from the bad stuff as much as possible and now
it suddenly feels like I need to catch up in order to help
myself, and maybe in going through it all we can figure out some things about Faye. I mean, it seems like
everything bad started with Cheyenne's attempted kidnapping and Faye's murder."

He moved away from the window and once again
sat on the chaise. "Maybe we should wait for Dylan to
talk about it." He looked at the clock on the nightstand.
"He'll be here in about a half an hour. I told him to come
as soon as he finished eating dinner." He hesitated a
moment. "Did you ask Levi if there was anything new
with your father?"

She released a deep sigh and nodded. "I was disap-
pointed that he said there was still no change in Daddy.
I wish he'd find the strength to somehow fight his way
out of the coma."

"He's tough," Gray replied. "That could still happen."

"I wish we could find Cole so that he'd be here when
Daddy regains consciousness." She rubbed her hand
over her tummy. "I can't imagine what it would be like
to have a baby kidnapped and never, ever find out what
happened to him."

"Your father didn't talk about Cole?"

"Never. What little I know about his kidnapping I know from staff rumor and gossip. He was stolen right out of his crib in Daddy's suite. The police at the time thought it was a robbery and that the kidnapping was a crime of opportunity. The bedroom was ransacked and some things were missing from a safe and Cole was gone."

She rubbed her stomach again, thinking of the baby she'd already give her life for, do anything to protect. To love a baby for three months and then have him disappear without a trace would destroy her. "After Cole was kidnapped, everyone waited for a ransom note to come. But one never did. Eventually the case went cold."

"And then Levi found out that Jethro's sister-in-law, Desiree Beal, was seen with a baby weeks after Cole's kidnapping. But she was murdered and there was no baby ever found," Gray said, adding to the story.

"And that's all we really know for sure." Catherine frowned thoughtfully. "Even the private investigator that Gabby, Amanda and I hired to find Cole couldn't come up with information as to what happened to him and where he might be now."

"But I can't imagine Cole's kidnapping so many years ago being tied to all the crimes that have happened here over the past couple of months," Gray said.

"I can't, either. Still, I would have liked to have had the chance to know Cole, to have him as a big brother in the house," she said wistfully.

"You going to give the bean a little brother or sister?" he asked, gesturing toward her stomach.

She smiled at his nickname for the baby, but shook

her head negatively. "I doubt it. When I found out I was pregnant I'd pretty much decided that it was just going to be me and the baby."

"And now there's me," he said. "Temporarily," he added, and she wasn't sure if he was reminding her of their situation or reminding himself.

At that moment a knock sounded on the suite door. Gray got up to open it and Dylan stepped in. He took in the pink-and-black décor and then grinned at Gray. "Sweet," he said.

Gray shrugged. "What can I tell you…the lady likes pink."

"I do, indeed," Catherine said.

He gestured Dylan toward the chaise and Catherine smiled at the handsome cowboy who carried with him a tin box. "Evening, Miss Catherine," Dylan said.

"Hi, Dylan. Please, make yourself comfortable."

As the two men sat on the chaise, shoulders battled for space. Catherine fought the smile that threatened to erupt into laughter. They were both far too masculine, bigger-than-life men to share the dainty chaise, but it was the only place for the two to sit in the sitting room.

"So, how are things around the ranch? You keeping an eye on everyone for me?" Gray asked.

"Work is going on as usual, although I've heard several of the men speculating what your marriage to Catherine means as far as you remaining ranch foreman."

"You can tell them I'm taking a little honeymoon period but that my marriage has changed nothing as far as my work on the ranch," Gray replied.

A honeymoon period. If this had been a real marriage would she and Gray have enjoyed a honeymoon at some romantic, secluded place? She was surprised by the wistful yearning that momentarily swept through her. A real marriage, a real relationship that would include more babies and Gray—she was foolish for even allowing the thought to enter her mind.

"So, what have you got?" Gray gestured to the tin box that Dylan held on his lap.

"This holds pretty much everything I've got from my mother." Sadness lowered his voice as he opened the box lid. "There are pictures of me, but none are of me as a baby or an infant. Most of them are of me around eight years old, then some of me as a teenager, but that's it. There aren't any pictures of her." He pulled out a handful of photos and spread them out on the coffee table in front of them.

Catherine leaned forward and grabbed one, her heart aching as she saw Dylan smiling widely for the camera. There was no question that Faye had adored her son. "She always spoke of you with such love, such pride," she said to Dylan. "You were her entire world."

He nodded and fumbled in the box to withdraw a piece of paper. "Here's her marriage certificate to a man named John Frick. She told me he was a ranch hand who died in a fall from a horse only a few weeks before I was born. There are no pictures of him, either. She was always pretty vague about him whenever I asked about him."

"Did she ever mention what ranch he worked for?" Catherine asked.

Dylan frowned once again, as if searching all the

memories he had in his brain. "I think I remember her mentioning some kind of a dude guest ranch called the Bar None." He laid the marriage certificate on the table with the pictures.

He withdrew another piece of paper that looked old and slightly fragile. "My birth certificate," he said. "It shows I was born in Cody, Wyoming, at the Cody Memorial Hospital."

"Cody?" Catherine hadn't even heard of the town.

"It's a tiny town in northeast Wyoming." Dylan frowned. "I asked her how long she had lived in Cody and she said she was just passing through there when she met my dad and was only there long enough for my birth and then moved on." He snapped the document down on the table.

"I should have pushed her harder for more details about her past, about my father and the time before we got here to the Dead River Ranch." Frustration was obvious in his deep voice.

"Don't beat yourself up, Dylan. You couldn't have guessed that your mother would be murdered and these questions would suddenly become so important to you," Gray said sympathetically.

"I know. It's just that I thought I always knew who I was until Mia and Jagger started asking questions that created such doubts inside me."

Gray clapped Dylan on the shoulder. "We're going to get those answers for you, Dylan. You might not know this, but Cath and I are an investigative team better than Sherlock Holmes and his man, Watson."

"I get to be Sherlock," Catherine said jokingly, but

her heart had taken flight at the sound of Gray calling her Cath. She hadn't heard that name of sweet familiarity fall from his lips since he'd returned to the Dead River Ranch over four years ago.

She'd didn't want to dwell on how wonderful it made her feel now, on how much she'd missed hearing that simple nickname coming from his mouth.

"Can we keep all these things for a while?" Gray asked, gesturing toward the legal documents on the table.

"Sure. What are you going to do?" Dylan asked.

"I'm not sure yet, but you let us take care of the investigation and you take care of my foreman duties while I'm honeymooning," Gray replied. "We'll let you know when we find out something concrete, but we can't promise any results right away."

"I've waited this long, I can wait as long as it takes," Dylan replied.

Minutes later, he had left the room and Catherine picked up the birth certificate. She looked at it and then gazed at Gray curiously. "What is he afraid he'll find out?" she asked.

"I'm not sure, but you and I have some time on our hands and I'd rather find out anything bad and break it to Dylan gently than have him find out something bad on his own and try to deal with it without any support."

"You're a good friend, Gray." She'd always admired that about him.

"Dylan is like a brother to me. We grew up together as best friends and his mother was like a surrogate mother to me." He leaned back against the chaise with his arm stretched across the back. "So, Sherlock, since you are obviously the brains of this operation, exactly where do you suggest we begin?"

The next afternoon Catherine and Gray took off for Laramie where they could find a coffee shop with Wi-Fi capabilities. Internet and cell phone service at the ranch was spotty at best and Gray readily admitted to paranoia when it came to people listening in and spying on anything they might do at the ranch.

The first thing they wanted to check out was the Bar None Ranch where Faye had told her son his father had worked as a ranch hand.

It was a beautiful mid-October day. Once again that morning, Gray had found himself waking to the warmth of Cath. In sleep their bodies had melded together, legs tangled and snuggled together like lovers.

He'd been grateful to slide out of bed first while she still slept and take a long cool shower. He had a feeling she'd be appalled to wake up and find herself in his arms.

While she slept another half an hour and then showered and dressed, he'd sat on the chaise and looked at the photos of Dylan as a boy and as a teenager. Each photo evoked memories of Gray's own childhood with Dylan, and as those memories filled him with the warmth of friendship, of brotherhood, he vowed to find answers to any questions that might haunt Dylan.

"We shouldn't have any problem finding a nice little coffee shop to make our base of operation," Cath said, pulling him from his thoughts.

He smiled inwardly. *Base of operation.* She talked like they were about to breach national security. She held her laptop computer in a bright pink case against her stomach, as if it might hold all the answers they sought to solve every problem in the universe.

She looked cute as a bug with her eyes bright with excitement and clad in a pair of jeans and a pink-and-white sweater. Her hair hung long and silky below her shoulders and he now knew that it smelled of orange blossoms.

He tightened his hands on the steering wheel, refusing to allow the sweet, fresh scent of her hair, the thought of her warm and curvy in his arms to arouse him.

"Wouldn't it be something if we discover that John Frick is actually still alive and working at the ranch?" She didn't give him a chance to reply. "It would be wonderful if Dylan found out his father was alive and well and wanted a relationship with his son."

He gave her a quick glance then directed his attention back to the road. "You're always looking for the happy endings."

"Everyone likes happy endings, and Dylan is a good man. He deserves his own happy ending."

"But if John Frick is alive and well, that means Dylan will have to assume that his mother took him and ran and never allowed him to have a relationship with his father, or his father never wanted anything to do with him. Either way, that sucks. I know how much Dylan missed having a father in his life."

"He was pretty close to your father, wasn't he?"

Gray nodded. "Dad had his hands full trying to father two hooligans running wild on the ranch. Dylan spent a lot of time with me and Dad, and Dad treated him like a second son." As always thoughts of his father brought a sadness streaking through Gray. He missed the old man every day.

"You know it's possible Mia and Jagger brought up questions about Dylan and we'll find out there's nothing to question, that Faye was just a widow woman who brought her baby with her to the Dead River Ranch for a job," Cath said.

"For a little while I think they both wondered if Dylan was Cole," Gray replied, unsurprised when Cath laughed.

"That's ridiculous and doesn't make sense on any number of levels. Besides, they thought everyone who had brown hair and brown eyes might be Cole."

"I agree, but I understand Dylan's need to find out if what his mother told him about her past was true. Don't you ever wonder about your mother? Where she is and what she's doing with her life?"

"I wonder about her occasionally," Cath admitted. "But now that I have a baby growing inside me, now that I feel a motherly love, I can't imagine or excuse what she did when she just up and left us all. It was a selfish, horrid thing to do."

"That's pretty much the way I feel about my mother," Gray replied. He remembered as teenagers how often he and Cath had talked about their missing mothers, wondering what had been better, what had been more wonderful than being mothers to them?

The ride was pleasant as the conversation turned to

Gabby's work with her troubled teens, little Cheyenne's funniest antics and how nice it was to be away from the ranch for the day. She also reminded him about a charity event she had coming up in Cheyenne and that they would need to shop for a tuxedo for him.

Gray couldn't imagine himself in a tux and the last place on earth he wanted to find himself was in a hotel full of wealthy people for an evening. But his promise to her when he'd offered her this marriage of convenience was that she'd go where he went and he'd go wherever she needed to go.

It was just after noon when they found the perfect place, a coffee shop that served hearty sandwiches, gourmet java and Wi-Fi. Cath slid into an empty booth and got out her laptop while Gray went to the counter and ordered sandwiches, chips and one regular and one decaf coffee.

By the time he got back to the table she had her computer powered up and ready to work. "Eat first," he said, sliding across from her with the tray of lunch items. She moved her computer from in front of her, obviously ready for something to eat.

"I got you chicken salad," he said as he placed the paper plate with sandwich and chips in front of her. "It sounded like a girly kind of food."

"What do you have? A whole steer on a bun?" she teased.

He wondered when in the past two days they had become so comfortable with each other. "Complete with long horns to pick my teeth with afterward," he replied and was rewarded by the melodic sound of her laughter.

It was only after she'd finished her chicken salad sandwich and he'd eaten his double burger that he moved to her side of the booth and she pulled her laptop in front of her.

"I think the first thing we should do is search for the Bar None Ranch in Cody," she said, her fingers dancing nimbly over the keys.

"Sounds like a plan, partner." He leaned closer. The search engine did its job and a link popped up for the ranch in question.

"Well, at least we know the place exists," Gray said, as always fighting against a rising desire at her nearness and the additional rush of hunting down concrete answers for Dylan.

"And it is a guest dude ranch." Cath smiled. "At least we know Faye told the truth about the ranch's existence."

"Now all we need is to find out if a John Frick worked there thirty years ago." He moved closer still, his thigh against hers while he viewed the page she'd pulled up. "There's a phone number." Gray pulled a cell phone out of his pocket, but was reluctant to use it inside the coffee shop.

"Thirty years is a long time ago. Hopefully somebody there will remember a John Frick, especially if he died from a fall off a horse at the ranch. I would imagine something like that doesn't happen every day." Cath pulled a spiral-bound notebook from the pocket of the laptop case.

Gray was amused to see that she'd titled the first page Stuck Like Glue Private Investigations. He sipped

his coffee and watched her write down the name of the
ranch, the website location and the contact information;
both an email address and a phone number were listed.

"I'll try to call when we get outside," he said. Although there was an afternoon lull in the coffee shop
and Cody, Wyoming, was a long ways from where they
sat, he didn't want to have a conversation about John
Frick with other people around. A little dose of paranoia was a good thing.

"I'll type in John Frick and see if anything interesting pops up," she replied. Once again her dainty fingers
moved and then a list of John Fricks filled the screen.
"A doctor in Texas, an orthodontist in Maine, a musi-
cian in Mississippi, but no cowboy working in Wyoming and no old news reports of his death," Cath said
as she studied the screen.

"I'm not really surprised. It was a long time ago and
there would be no reason for his information to be out
there on the internet."

"So, our next move is to call the ranch and find out
if anyone remembers him," Cath said, powering down
her computer and packing it in her pink carrying case.
When she'd finished she looked at Gray. "I hope somebody at the ranch remembers him. I hope that everything Faye told Dylan about herself and his father and
Dylan's birth was true." She picked up the notebook
she'd left out where she'd written the contact information for the Bar None Ranch.

"That makes two of us," Gray replied. The warmth
of her thigh against his, the dizzying scent of her that
wrapped around him forced him up and out of the

booth. "Are we ready?" He'd make the phone calls to the Bar None Ranch from his truck and hope that somebody could answer his questions about the mysterious John Frick.

When they settled in the truck, Cath read the number for the ranch from her notebook and Gray punched it into his cell phone. After two rings he connected with a woman named Sally. She was obviously a receptionist eager to make reservations for a visit to their working dude ranch, complete with fun activities for both children and adults.

Gray waited patiently for her to give her spiel and then told her that he needed to know about the employment records from thirty years ago. "Is the owner around?" he asked.

"I'm not sure he could help you even if he was here. The original owner of the ranch sold out ten years ago. The new owner lives in California and only comes here to check in a couple times a year," Sally explained.

Gray withheld a sigh. "Is there anyone at the ranch who might have been working there thirty years ago, anyone who might remember a particular wrangler who was there at the time?"

"Mule. He's our foreman and he's been around forever. His real name is Mike Lawlor, but he's always been known around here by the name of Mule."

"Could I speak to him?"

"He's someplace outside. I'd have to give you his cell number. Who are you and why do you need information about somebody who worked here thirty years ago?" A hint of suspicion had entered her voice.

Gray looked at Cath, who had been watching him with an air of expectancy. She shrugged, as if to tell him she didn't know what story he should tell the woman. Gray opted for a half truth.

"I'm a private investigator and I've been hired by John Frick's son. The son was separated from his father by his mother when he was a baby. His mother has recently died and John's son is desperate to connect with his father who we believe worked there at one time. We're hoping this is at least a starting point for us to reunite a father and son."

Apparently, Sally had a soft heart. As she reeled off Mule's phone number, Cath wrote it down in her notebook.

Gray disconnected from Sally and gazed at the woman next to him.

"Shouldn't there be employment records kept?" she asked.

"Probably, but you have to remember we're talking about thirty years ago. I know how many wranglers we have coming and going at the Dead River Ranch and I imagine it was the same for the Bar None over the years. Half of our records are probably shoved someplace in a rotting cardboard box. It's only been in the past three years that we've started keeping records with a computer."

"So, we're left with a man named Mule to answer our questions," Cath replied.

"I'd trust an old man named Mule to remember past employees before I'd count on an owner who lives out of state and only visits a couple times a year." Gray punched in Mule's phone number.

A deep, smoky voice answered. "Mule here. What do you want?"

Gray went through his story of being a private investigator seeking John Frick who was last known to be working as a wrangler on the Bar None ranch and who had died from a fall off a horse.

"Nobody named John Frick ever worked at this Bar None Ranch," Mule replied with certainty. "And we sure as hell have never had a man die from falling off a horse on this property. You've got the wrong Bar None, buddy."

"You're positive there was never a man named John Frick working there?" Gray pressed.

"As positive as I am that by the end of the day my old bones and arthritis will make me want to cry like a girl," Mule replied. "I've been foreman here for forty years, and I remember every cowboy who has ever worked for me, and somebody named John Frick never worked here." Before Gray could respond, Mule disconnected.

"Do you believe him?" Cath asked.

Gray nodded. "Unfortunately I do. My father was a Mule. When he was foreman at Dead River Ranch he could name all the men who had ever drifted through and worked for him, whether it had been for hours or for years."

Cath's features displayed her dismay. "So, right now we have to go on the possibility that Faye lied about a John Frick."

"At least she lied about what he did and where he worked," Gray agreed.

"Then what's our next move?"

Gray frowned thoughtfully. "We need to check out the validity of that marriage and birth certificate, but short of taking the ride to Cody, I'm not sure how we accomplish that." Cody would be a long ride, requiring a day of travel, an overnight and then another day to travel home. "And I'm not even sure we'd be allowed to access any records of another person."

"I think I know somebody who could help us with that," Cath said.

"Who?"

She shook her head with an air of mystery. "Let me talk to her and see if she's willing to help out and then I'll tell you who and where."

"Partners aren't supposed to have secrets from each other, especially married ones," Gray said in a teasing voice.

"You can't use that argument effectively against me," she replied, her eyes a shade darker than they'd been a moment before. "We both know this is nothing like a real marriage and this partnership will dissolve the minute any danger to me has passed."

"You're right," he agreed, surprised that he managed an even tone at the same time a tinge of anger welled up inside him. He started the truck engine and cursed himself because for just a little while as they'd enjoyed the ride together, as they'd sat side by side in the booth, he'd almost believed that they were real, that he'd be in her life forever.

Her words had simply slammed reality back into his head, reminding him that this marriage was nothing more than a temporary solution to a problem that would hopefully go away soon.

Chapter 12

It took Catherine two days to connect with her friend Jewel Dempsy and ask for her help concerning the validation of Faye's marriage license and Dylan's birth certificate. During those two days Gray had been quiet. He had retreated into the cool indifference she'd suffered from him for the four years before he'd come to her rescue with this marriage of sorts.

Although Gray's mood had changed, their routine hadn't. They slept together, spent the days together and ate meals together and with the rest of the family in the evenings. They'd spent one afternoon getting a tux for Gray to wear the following night to the charity event in Cheyenne, which Cath had already agreed to attend.

The difference in Gray was that she felt as if a switch had been snapped off inside him. The shine in his eyes was gone, there was no attempt to connect to her with any humor. He was just doing his job of being her bodyguard and nothing more. No matter how many times she told herself this was the way it should be, she missed the Gray who had been with her for the first couple of days before their trip into Laramie.

He now stood at the window in the suite, his broad back straight and tension wafting from him like a physical entity in the air.

Catherine had just disconnected with Jewel on the phone. "We have an appointment tonight at nine o'clock with my friend."

He turned from the window, his features set in stone, his eyes flat and dark brown with no hint of sparkling depths. "And what is your friend's name?"

"Jewel Dempsy." She looked at him expectantly, sure that he would recognize the name, but his blank stare told her otherwise. "She's a fairly famous sculptor and painter here in the northwest. Maybe you know her by her professional name...Jewel Dee?"

"Sorry, dusty cowboys like me rarely get a chance to study art or know people in the art world."

A rising irritation filled Cath. "What's your problem, Gray? You've had a chip on your shoulder since we left Laramie. It's not a big deal if you don't know who Jewel is. I don't care what you know or don't know about the art world."

"I don't know anything about art, or fashion or how to act at a cocktail party."

"You signed up for this duty. If you want out just say the word," she snapped.

His eyes remained dark and unreadable. "I didn't say I wanted out."

"You've been cranky and difficult for the past couple of days. That's supposed to be my job. I'm the one who is pregnant and having hormonal changes. As a matter of fact, I'm going to take a nap. That way I don't have to talk to you and you don't have to talk to me."

She didn't wait for his response, but got up from her chair and went into the bedroom area where she curled up on her side facing the wall away from the doorway. She heard him move from the window and grab one of the books he'd brought from his staff room on the second floor, a room he'd kept despite their "marriage."

A grunt told her he was attempting to find a comfortable position on the chaise to read and although she had no intention of taking a nap, her eyes closed and she drifted off.

Gray's voice awoke her, telling her it was time to get ready to go to dinner. His mood didn't appear improved and therefore hers wasn't either.

It was with a cool distance that they walked together to the dining room where the rest of the family was gathered for the evening meal.

"Looks like the honeymoon is over," Darla said snidely, obviously noticing the tension between Gray and Cath as the meal was underway.

Cath poked at the smothered pork chop on her plate. "Don't be ridiculous. I'm just not feeling very well tonight." She wasn't about to allow Darla to start a new round of gossip speculating on the status of the newlyweds relationship.

"Are you getting enough rest?" Amanda asked, her concern evident in her voice. "You know how important it is to make sure you're getting plenty of sleep."

"She's a newlywed," Tawny chirped with a sly grin. "I doubt if she's getting that much sleep."

"I'm sleeping just fine," Cath said, sorry she'd mentioned anything at all.

"At least everything has been fairly peaceful around here the past couple of weeks," Gabby said.

"Boring is more like it," Trip replied.

"There's nothing wrong with boring," Trevor said.

Trip snorted. "I'll take boring when I'm dead."

Thankfully that ended anyone's desire to continue with the conversation and the rest of the meal was finished in relative silence.

Eating hadn't seemed to change Gray's mood, nor had it lightened Cath's. She didn't know what Gray's problem was, but the idea of day after day of his current mood irritated her.

"How long before we need to leave here for the appointment with your friend?" Gray asked once they were back in the suite that now felt far too small for the two of them.

"It will only take us about fifteen minutes to get to her place so we have about an hour to kill before leaving." Cath sank down in her chair and stared out the window, refusing to look at Gray, who paced the room like a caged tiger.

She finally could stand it no longer and turned her gaze to him. "Did I say something? Did I do or say something that has made you angry with me?"

He stopped pacing and stared at her. For a long moment he said nothing. Finally he released a deep sigh and raked a hand through his thick sandy brown hair as he cast his gaze away from her. "No, you didn't do anything wrong. I guess I've just been worried about Dylan and what we're going to find out, and I've been taking out all my frustrations on you."

"Then stop it," she replied.

"Is this our first fight?" he asked, a forced smile curving his lips.

She eyed him seriously, remembering the time they'd spent together as a couple so many years ago. "No, you never fight, Gray. You get cold, you get distant and you withdraw, but you never confront and fight."

He shrugged. "I guess that just makes me a lover, not a fighter."

"When we were younger and you refused to fight with me, it always made me feel like I just wasn't worth the effort." She stood from her chair. "I'm going to freshen up a bit before we head out to Jewel's place." Before he could say anything else she disappeared into the bathroom and closed the door behind her.

She lowered herself to the dainty chair in front of the dresser and mirrors, the place she usually sat to put on her makeup or fix her hair. She stared at her reflection without seeing it, instead seeing a vision of Gray there.

What she'd said to him was true; he wasn't given to arguing or fussing. Whenever he'd been hurt or angry, he'd retreated and sometimes that had driven Cath crazy. She'd wanted him to yell at her if she was wrong, and she'd wanted to yell back at him, to vent frustration instead of swallowing it.

She wasn't sure if she believed what he'd said about his current mood relating completely to concern for Dylan, but she knew no matter how hard she pushed him, he wasn't going to share whatever was eating at him.

She couldn't fix what she didn't know was wrong and she just had to accept that. She stood and brushed her hair, then refreshed her lipstick. It was time to head to Jewel's place.

If the truth was that Gray was concerned about what they might find out about Dylan's mother's past, then it was possible Jewel would have some answers. Whether those answers would ease Gray's concerns or make them worse was yet to be seen.

Gray knew he'd been moody and distant since their trip to Laramie, and he knew the exact reason for it, although he would never admit it to Cath.

He was falling in love with her all over again. When he'd initiated this insane marriage agreement to play full-time bodyguard to her, he'd truly believed himself immune from ever loving her again.

He'd been wrong.

He knew at the end of this protection gig his job was to walk away and let her find a future with somebody else. He'd known that from the beginning, but now he already felt the ache in his heart, the pain of her loss yet again.

All he could do was see this through to the end and

never let her know that she'd gained his heart once more. All he could do was remind himself again and again that this was a job he'd actively signed up for and it was a temporary stint as a pretend husband.

When she came out of the bathroom, he couldn't help the genuine smile that curved his lips. She was right, he'd been a jerk the past couple of days and it was his problem, not hers. It wasn't fair for him to passively punish her for being the woman he loved.

"Stuck Like Glue Private Investigations ready to spring into action again," he said, hoping to see her return his smile. She did. It was one of the things he loved about her, the fact that she had never been able to hold a grudge for any length of time.

As usual, before they opened the door to the suite to exit Gray had his gun in hand. He was wary at every closed door in the house even though there had been no hint of a threat toward Cath in the past week.

He had no idea where or when danger might come. The perp had already tried to get her twice and had shown a willingness to murder. Gray had a feeling a husband wouldn't detour him from his ultimate goal of getting to Cath. Gray was determined that wouldn't happen, but that meant he had to stay wary and alert at all times.

Once they were in Gray's truck, Cath directed him to drive to the small town of Dead. "I'm not sure I understand how an artist is going to be able to help us," he said as he navigated the narrow dark road toward town. He glanced in the rearview mirror often to make sure they hadn't been followed by anyone on the ranch.

"You'll see when we get there," Cath replied mysteriously.

"Why would a well-known artist want to live in Dead?"

"Jewel is a bit eccentric and she likes her privacy. She's originally from Cheyenne. She and I met at one of her showings and instantly bonded. She's beautiful and talented, but something of a recluse when she isn't on display at one of her showings."

"And she's going to sculpt us some answers to our questions?" Gray asked wryly.

"Something like that, just wait and see," Cath replied with another mysterious smile.

It didn't take long for them to enter the edges of Dead, Wyoming. The little town, population four thousand, was aptly named for it appeared to be grasping on to its last gasp of life. Main Street was a mere two blocks long, with the requisite grocery store, bank and general store, along with a diner and a fairly decent restaurant.

At the other end of the small town was a raucous bar that Gray had frequented on occasion as it was the nearest place to get a cold beer away from the ranch.

"Turn here," Cath directed as they came to a street on the right that veered off the main drag.

"Are you sure you know where we're going?" Gray asked with concern. This area of Dead definitely lived up to its name with the only businesses on the shady side of legal. A tattoo parlor nestled next to a convenience store where several thugs lingered near the door with a proprietary air.

"Just keep going," Cath replied. "And when you come to the next left take it and then take an immediate left again."

Gray did as she instructed. Within minutes, they were in a thick stand of woods, and nestled in those woods was a huge dark building that appeared to be a warehouse.

"This is Jewel's place," she said as he came to a stop in front of the building. There were no windows and the place appeared deserted.

"It doesn't look like anyone is home," he said but at that moment a door opened and a woman's figure was silhouetted in the doorway.

Cath jumped out of the passenger side of the truck and raced to her. The two women embraced as Gray got out of the truck and headed toward them. They disappeared through the opened door, and Gray followed after them. He took two steps inside and then halted, stunned by his surroundings. What looked like an abandoned warehouse on the outside was anything but on the inside.

One half of the large area was obviously a studio with large skylights built into the roof and big and small sculptures in various stages of development. Easels were scattered around the area holding partially finished paintings. The atmosphere was one of barely controlled artistic chaos.

"I'm Jewel," the dark-haired woman said to Gray with an outstretched hand. "And I understand you're Cath's new hubby, Gray."

Her hand held the strength of a man's, although she

was petite and exotic-looking. With her porcelain skin, dazzling slightly slanted green eyes and winged black brows, she looked like an attractive creature from another planet.

"Excuse my mess," she said as she released his hand and gave a sweeping wave to her work area. "I suffer a bit from hyperactivity and manic energy and tend to get distracted easily so I always have a ton of things in flux." She pointed to a door. "Come on in where things are a bit more normal."

Cath smiled at Gray as the two of them followed Jewel through the doorway that led to living quarters luxurious enough to rival Cath's suite. Gray recognized that Jewel wasn't just an eccentric artist struggling to make a living and achieving moderate success.

She obviously had money, had come from money and it showed in the tasteful elegance of her living quarters. Gray was struck with the feeling of a fish out of water, a cowboy in a china shop who was afraid of breaking something or committing an unforgiveable faux pas.

She gestured the two of them onto the cushions of a buttery leather sofa, then sank down in the chair opposite them. Jewel and Cath small-talked for a few minutes and then Jewel brought up the reason for their visit. "So, Cath, you mentioned you had a little work for me to do."

Cath pulled from her oversize purse the copies of Faye Frick's marriage certificate and Dylan's birth certificate that Dylan had given them. "We just want to authenticate these and we'd like to do it as quickly and quietly as possible."

Cath exchanged a quick glance with Gray and then

continued, "We know we could send away for certified copies of the originals, but that could take weeks and we'd rather have answers sooner than later."

It was at that moment Gray noticed the large, state-of-the-art computer in a corner of the room, and it was also at that moment that he knew what Cath was asking Jewel to do for them…hack into the Cody, Wyoming, system of records.

He realized Jewel was watching him, as if gauging his reaction to the idea. "I never use my skills for the dark side," she said with a gamin smile. "I can be in and out of their system without them ever knowing I was there."

"Jewel is a computer hacking genius," Cath said.

"It's a little work I do on the side, mostly for the purposes of battered women, lost children and hunting money that parties attempt to hide from rightful owners." She shrugged. "What can I say? It's a gift, like my sculpting and painting."

Gray tried to find a moral button to tell her he didn't want her hacking into any system illegally, but then he thought of his friend and everything that had happened at the ranch. He realized he just wanted answers, and she appeared to be the correct tool to get them.

"If you can help us, we'd appreciate it," he finally replied.

"Great. Before I get started can I get you something to drink, a glass of wine perhaps or some coffee?"

Both Gray and Cath declined the offer of refreshments, and Jewel moved to the chair in front of her computer. Gray found all of this surreal…the surroundings…and the oddly beautiful artist hacker. As he remained seated on the sofa, Cath got up to stand just behind Jewel, watching her over her shoulder. Jewel's long bloodred fingernails clicked across the keyboard.

"This is going to be easy," she said. "Vital statistic stuff isn't usually overly secured unless you're getting into the social security program. It's just a matter of finding a back door, and most of these programs are written with one easily found if you know where to look."

Her fingernails continued to click and an edge of anxiety gnawed at Gray's belly. He hoped she discovered that everything Faye had ever told Dylan was the truth, that the only thing his mother had gotten wrong was the name of the ranch his father had worked at when they'd been together.

Dylan had adored his mother, and he'd mourned deeply at her death, still mourned for her, as did Gray and so many people at the ranch.

Faye had been like a second mother to Gray, chastising him along with Dylan whenever the two found trouble, forcing mittens on his hands when it was cold and occasionally kissing him on the forehead just like Gray's own mother might have done had she stuck around long enough.

Gray realized he didn't want Faye to be exactly who she'd said she was just for Dylan's sake. He wanted to believe in her for himself, as well.

"I'm in," Jewel said, her voice pulling Gray from his thoughts. "And now it's just a matter of checking the marriage licenses issued for the day in question."

The knot in Gray's stomach tightened and Cath moved closer to Jewel. He watched Cath's face as Jewel began to scroll through documents. The anxiety that rode inside his stomach was on Cath's features.

She understood how devastating it would be to Dylan to find out that his mother had lied about everything, that his entire history was bogus.

"Well, the marriage certificate is a fake," Jewel announced.

"Are you sure?" Gray asked, a lead weight landing in the pit of his stomach.

Jewel grinned at him wryly. "This isn't my first rodeo, cowboy. There's no official copy on record. That means what you all have in your hand is a fake. A good one, but definitely fake."

"Maybe Faye was a single mother and she didn't want Dylan to know he was born out of wedlock," Cath said. She touched her stomach and then reached up and began to twirl a strand of her hair. "I can understand a woman doing that, making up a father who died to explain the absence of that man in a little boy's life."

Is that what she was going to do when she and Gray parted? Would she tell her daughter or son that their father had died in a car accident, or maybe overseas in the war? Would she build the fantasy and make up a man who would have loved and devoted himself to her and her child if only he had lived?

"Okay, so Faye wasn't married to a man named John Frick," Gray said aloud. "What about the birth certificate?"

Jewel returned her attention to the computer, typing

in whatever she needed to access filed birth certificates for the date of Dylan's birth.

Minutes crept by in agonizing slowness and Gray found himself holding his breath as Jewel cyber searched to confirm that Dylan Frick had been born at the Cody Memorial Hospital on the date listed on the certificate and by the doctor who had administered the live birth.

"Let me check one more place," Jewel said, her gaze focused on the screen in front of her.

Cath came back to the sofa and sat down next to Gray, both of them united in their concern for their friend. He reached up and captured the hand that was twirling her hair and held it tight in his.

"Not only is this birth certificate a fake, the doctor named on the document doesn't even exist," Jewel finally said.

Gray looked at Cath in stunned surprise. "Then who in the hell is Dylan Frick?" His question hung in the air without an answer.

Chapter 13

The hotel ballroom in the Cheyenne Howard Hotel was already brimming with women in designer gowns and men in high-end tuxedos when Gray and Cath joined the fracas. Cath and her sisters had bought one of the tables at an exorbitant price, knowing that the charity was for children with cancer.

Every time she looked at Gray he nearly stole her breath away. She loved him in his jeans and shirts, but the man was born to wear a black tux.

It had been a somber day and, unfortunately, Gray had been unable to connect with Dylan to let him know what they'd found out. Dylan had left that morning to meet a rancher with a horse who was having behavioral issues.

He hadn't returned to the ranch by the time Gray and Cath had left for the evening festivities. On the drive to

Cheyenne, they both had agreed to set the Dylan issue aside for the night and just enjoy themselves. Tomorrow they'd deal with breaking Dylan with their news that everything he knew about his mother, his father and himself was a lie.

"Cath, it's so nice to see you." Mrs. Wellingford, the wealthy, matronly woman who was giving the event that evening, greeted them at the ballroom doorway. "Your sisters have already arrived and I understand congratulations are in order." She smiled at Gray. "I hope the two of you will enjoy marital bliss for many years to come."

Cath was warmed by Gray's arm pulling her close to his side. "That's definitely our plan," he replied, playing the game to perfection.

"Please, enjoy the cocktails, and dinner will be served in about an hour. After that we have dancing, so don't be in a big rush out of here." With that Mrs. Wellingford moved to greet the next couple coming into the ballroom.

"Let's find your table and then I'll get us something to drink," Gray suggested. She assumed he'd be comfortable turning his back on her for a few minutes if she were surrounded by her sisters and Trevor.

As they wound their way through the white-dressed tables with centerpieces of crystal and orchids, Cath greeted people she knew and paused to introduce Gray. Gray acted like he had attended events like this all his life, with a friendly smile and an aura of being at ease. But Cath knew his tux jacket hid his gun and she felt his tension as he held on to her elbow and they wove through the crowd. His gaze never stopped moving until he spied Gabby and Amanda waving from one of the tables.

"There you are," Gabby said.

"Are Levi and Katie here?" Cath asked, taking the chair next to Gabby.

"They aren't going to make it," Amanda replied. "To be honest I think they accepted just so that Darla wouldn't think there would be room at our table, but they never intended to come."

"Is Darla here?" Cath asked. Gray sat in the chair next to her and groaned.

"Please don't tell me we have to share this meal with her," he said.

"Just shoot me now," Trevor replied dryly.

"Actually, I don't believe Darla and her children were able to pony up the money to attend," Amanda said with just a hint of smugness in her voice. "I'm sure we'll all miss their company this evening."

Cath laughed. "Like I'd miss the flu."

"Can I get you something to drink?" Gray asked Cath. He pointed toward a long bar located across the room. "I'm sure they'll have some soda or iced tea."

"Iced tea would be nice," she replied and then watched him make his way across the room.

"He is a hunk in that tux," Gabby said as if reading Cath's thoughts.

"He's a hunk when he's not wearing a tux," Cath replied with a sigh. It was becoming more and more difficult to be in bed with him each night and not touch him, not want him to touch her.

"He's a good man," Trevor said.

"I know." Cath watched him at the bar get their drinks and then begin the winding route back to their table. "A peach tea for the lady and a light Scotch and soda for me." He sat next to Cath.

"I didn't know I'd married a hard-drinking man," she teased.

"There's not enough Scotch in this glass to make a hummingbird drunk. I like a drink now and then but I like to keep my wits about me, too."

Cath knew the last thing he would do was take her out for an evening in a crowd of people and then proceed to get drunk. She could tell by the way he moved his chair that he watched the crowd, always alert and ready to handle any danger that might come their way.

"Cath, you look gorgeous tonight. I love the way you've got your hair, and that blue dress really pops the color of your eyes, and that necklace," Gabby said.

Cath reached up and touched the aquamarine that hadn't left her neck since the night Gray had reclasped it around her after the attack on her.

Her hair had been braided and then twisted into a crown on top of her head. There would be no hair twirling tonight. The strapless dress hugged her bodice and then had a sleek skirt that fell to the floor. It wouldn't be long and she wouldn't be able to wear such form-fitting clothing.

Although Gray hadn't complimented her out loud, when she'd stepped out of the bathroom ready to go, his gaze had lavished her, beginning at the top of her head and trailing downward with fiery heat.

She didn't need his words to confirm what she knew.

In his gaze she'd known she looked beautiful and sexy and that was enough for her.

For the next hour, the conversation around the table remained pleasant. People stopped by to say hello and the three sisters shared thoughts about particular gowns, the décor and noted the shoes that women wore.

Trevor exchanged a grin with Gray. "It's what they do when they get together in places like this, they look at other women. It's a girl thing."

"At least they aren't looking at other men," Gray replied.

Cath and Gabby laughed. "Why would we do that when we have the best-looking men in the room right here at our table," Gabby said.

By the time dinner was served, the mood at the table was mellow and Cath was enjoying Gray's company. He was funny and charming to her and her sisters and he and Trevor got along well.

When dinner was over, a four-piece band began to play softly and several couples took to the polished dance floor next to where the tables had been set up.

Trevor and Gabby hit the dance floor and Amanda left the table to visit with some friends, leaving Gray and Cath alone. "I never told you how positively stunning you look tonight," he said.

She smiled, warming with pleasure. "And I never told you what a dashing figure you cut in that tux."

"I feel like I'm trussed up in a monkey suit and can't wait to rip this tie off and unfasten a couple of buttons on this shirt."

Her smile turned into a small burst of laughter. "You

and every man in this room. Men just wear tuxes to please their women. It isn't an outfit they would pick to wear on their own."

"You've got that right," he agreed.

Her eyes moved beyond Gray's broad shoulder and a sick feeling swept through her. Dirk Sinclair was heading in their direction.

"Uh-oh, Dirk is headed our way," she said to Gray. "I doubt if he intends to have a pleasant conversation with me."

Gray reached across the top of the table and took her hand in his, then gifted her with a reassuring smile. "Don't worry. We're in a public place. How nasty could things get?"

"You don't know Dirk," she said below her breath.

Gray's smile never wavered. "I guess I'm going to get to know him very quickly."

At that moment Dirk stepped up to the table, his upper lip twisted into a slight sneer. He ignored Gray and looked pointedly at the ring on Cath's finger.

"So, it's true. You're married," he said. For the first time Cath noticed how small Dirk looked, even with his chest puffed out in macho outrage.

Gray didn't bother to stand, as if the man wasn't worth the effort. "Gray Stark. I'm Cath's husband."

Dirk looked at Gray as if he were a piece of manure that had suddenly formed in front of him. "You're the ranch foreman," he replied, the sneer on his face more pronounced.

He looked back at Cath. "You were obviously seeing him while we were dating and I believe that makes you a two-timing whore."

Cath gasped and Gray rose to his feet, the pleasant smile never leaving his face as he not only stood toe-to-toe with Dirk, but towered over the man.

"Gray," Cath whispered, afraid of what he might do, afraid of the flat, dark danger she saw in his eyes despite the smile that curved his lips.

"I won't let anyone talk to my wife that way," Gray said, his voice with a steely edge. "I know that underneath that expensive tux you're nothing but a mama's boy sucking off your father's money and looking for a wealthy woman to keep you doing nothing for the rest of your life.

"I just want you to understand that beneath my tux is a rough and tumble cowboy who will kick your ever-loving ass to hell and back if you ever talk about my wife in derogatory terms again."

Cath's heart swelled, not just because Gray was defending her honor, but also because he was doing it in the middle of a crowd and drawing no attention from anyone in the room.

The only indication that the conversation between the two men might not be pleasant was that Dirk's features went white and he took two steps backward from Gray.

"You're a Neanderthal," Dirk exclaimed.

"And he's my Neanderthal," Cath said firmly.

Dirk whirled on the heels of his Italian dress shoes and quickly disappeared into the crowd. Gray sat back down and smiled at Cath. "See, I told you it wouldn't be unpleasant. The fact that he thinks you were two-timing him works in your favor. Now you can easily play off the baby as mine."

How she wished the baby was his. She knew Gray would make a wonderful father, that he'd had a wonderful role model in his own life.

Gabby and Trevor returned to the table, faces flushed and smiles on their faces. "This is such fun," Gabby said as she picked up her water glass. "We're just here to rest and then we're going to hit that dance floor again."

Trevor didn't even try to hide his groan. "She'll have me dancing so long tonight I won't be able to put my shoes on tomorrow."

Gray laughed and then turned to Cath. "How about we do a little twirl around the dance floor?"

She was shocked by the offer and immediately rose to her feet. She didn't know if Gray could dance or not, but she knew when they hit the dance floor she would be in his arms, and right now she couldn't think of any other place she'd rather be.

Dancing with Cath was like taking a dip into Heaven and yet held all the temptations of the devil. As the soft music began to play, he pulled her into his arms, her body melding against his and her bare shoulders begging for his lips to press against the sweet-smelling skin.

She tucked her head into the hollow of his throat, as if she belonged there. Gray had never considered himself a particularly graceful man, but with her in his arms they glided smoothly around the floor. It felt like they had been dancing together forever.

Gray was aroused and he wanted the dance to never end yet felt that each chord of the music and her curves in his arms were exquisite forms of torture. He wanted the torture to end yet he never wanted to let her go.

However, he did release her when the music finished and he led her off the dance floor. He was grateful when she told him she was tired and ready to call it a night. He was more than ready to get back to the quiet of her suite and perhaps punish himself with yet another cold shower before crawling into bed next to her.

As he drove them back to the ranch, his overwhelming desire to make love to her rode like a third passenger. After a few minutes of small talk they fell into silence.

He wondered if in that room of wealthy, influential men Cath's next husband had been present. He believed she would marry again. She was a woman who loved too easily, who needed to be loved, and he was certain that when he left she wouldn't face a future alone with only her child.

He gripped the steering wheel more tightly, suddenly depressed and wishing he'd never suggested this torturous marriage to Cath. He should have encouraged her to hire a full-time bodyguard, like Amanda had done for Cheyenne.

But he'd wanted to be a hero. He'd wanted to be Cath's hero, and at this moment in time he wasn't sure if he'd done the right thing or not. He only knew for certain that the idea of sleeping in the bed next to her tonight and not taking possession of her might just drive him completely out of his mind.

By the time they reached the suite Gray had taken off his tie and unfastened three buttons on his shirt. As Cath disappeared into the bathroom to get ready for bed, he threw off his jacket, placed his gun on his nightstand and tried to walk off the simmering desire that had risen with the passing of every moment.

He had to get hold of this hunger for her before she came out of the bathroom. He had to remember the deal they had struck, the job he was assigned to do, and nothing in his job description said anything about making wild, passionate love to Cath.

She stepped out of the bathroom, face scrubbed clean, hair loose around her shoulders and clad in a short silk peach-colored nightgown. Gray stared at her, remembering the feel of her, the smell of her as they'd moved across the dance floor. Even though the nightgown was far less sexy than what she'd worn to the dinner, his desire spiraled even higher.

She froze, like a deer in the headlights of his desire-darkened eyes. Her breasts rose and fell with quickened breaths and Gray's knees threatened to buckle with his aching need for her.

"Gray?" His name was a mere whisper falling from her lips.

"I can't crawl into that bed with you tonight, Cath," he said, his voice husky with barely suppressed emotion. "I can't smell your scent for another night and not want to take you into my arms. I can't feel your body heat and not want to drown myself in it."

He expected her to back away from him in horror, to somehow express her utter disgust at his obvious lack of control. Instead she walked toward him and stopped when she was mere inches in front of him.

She reached out and unfastened one of the buttons on his shirt, dampening her lips with the tip of her tongue. Gray froze, afraid to move, afraid that somehow this was all a dream and if he even drew a single breath he might awaken and she'd be gone.

As the last button was unfastened and his shirt hung open, she leaned forward and pressed her warm lips against his chest. He grabbed her by the shoulders and she looked up at him, her eyes a blend of both innocence and desire. A small smile danced on her lips.

"Cath, do you have any idea what you're doing?" he asked breathlessly as she pulled his shirt off his shoulders and allowed it to fall to the floor behind him.

"No," she admitted. "I only know for sure that tonight I want to be in your arms. Tonight I want you to kiss me until I'm mindless and weak. I want to be seventeen again and tonight I want you to make love to me."

It's all he'd been able to think about since the moment he'd moved in here with her. The idea of making love to her again had muddied his thoughts, kept him awake at nights and had kept his blood at a simmering boil for so long.

Now an unexpected hesitation whirled through him. "Is this because I threatened to take Dirk outside and give him a thrashing?"

She laughed, a low, throaty sound that only increased his need to throw her down on the bed and take possession of every inch of her body. "Of course not, although that was a memory that will warm my heart for a very long time."

Her smile faded and her eyes darkened. "I want you, Gray. It's as simple as that. I don't want to change our agreement, I don't want to bind you to me, I just want you to make love to me tonight, no strings attached."

She raised up on her toes, obviously seeking his mouth with hers, and he couldn't help himself. He could wrestle a steer to the ground, he could ride a bucking bull to win a trophy, but he had no strength at all when it came to denying his need for Cath.

He captured her lips with his as his arms wound tightly around her. Her mouth opened to his, allowing a deep kiss with their tongues dancing against each other in a prelude to something more.

He tangled his hands in her silky hair, the tactile pleasure arousing him. She was all flames and he knew he was about to fall into her fire. Someplace in the back of his mind he knew this wasn't a good idea, that it would only make it more difficult when it came time for him to tell her goodbye. But that didn't matter now, what mattered was she wanted him…and oh, how he wanted her. Nothing was going to stop them both from getting what they wanted tonight.

Chapter 14

Cath had known the moment Gray had taken her into his arms to dance earlier in the evening that the night wouldn't pass without her enjoying the pleasure of his lovemaking.

She had known he was aroused as they'd danced together. She'd felt it when he'd pulled her close against him. The fact that he wanted her had made her embrace how desperately she wanted him, had wanted him for years.

She now stepped back from him and got beneath the sheet on the bed. With only the glow of the dim lamp on the nightstand she watched breathlessly as he undressed, enjoying the symmetry of his wide shoulders and slim waist.

The faint lamplight loved his sun-bronzed skin, and

when he was clad only in his boxers he slid beneath the sheets and drew her back into his arms.

As his mouth hungrily plundered hers she felt like a seventeen-year-old again. Gray was the sun, the moon and the entire universe to her. He tasted of fiery heat and a hint of Scotch.

His hands slid down her back, warming her silk nightgown as if to memorize the curve of her spine, each delicate bone beneath her skin.

The kiss continued with his hands moving slowly around her body to cup her full breasts through the slick material. Her nipples rose in response, aching with the pleasure of his touch. She'd thought she'd forgotten him. She'd believed she'd moved past him, but she now realized that for nine long years she'd secretly yearned for him, that her body had really never forgotten his sweet, familiar touch.

She didn't fool herself that what they were doing had anything to do with love. It was lust, pure and simple, and that was fine with her. She'd be satisfied with his lust to sate her own.

His lips moved from hers, kissing and nipping down the side of her throat, finding each and every spot that sent a shiver of delight up and down her spine.

It didn't take long for him to become impeded and frustrated by her nightgown. She sat up and pulled it over her head, leaving her naked except for a tiny pair of panties.

Now it wasn't his hands on her breasts, but rather his mouth, first nipping and licking one nipple and then moving to the other. She tangled her hands in his thick hair, shuddering with the pleasure that swirled in her stomach, fluttered down her thighs and pooled in the very center of her.

His mouth moved down the middle of her stomach, trailing kisses until he reached her lower stomach. He kissed her once there and stroked a hand across it as if to caress the tiny life she carried.

The gesture brought unexpected tears to blur her vision, but then his fingers moved downward, making her gasp as he pulled her panties off and found the spot where all her pleasure was located.

He moved his fingers slowly at first and a massive storm began to rise inside her. She arched her back against his hand, wanting…needing the storm to sweep over her, she wanted to ride the waves that would take her out to sea.

All rational thought left her as she gave in to the mindlessness of pure sensation, of wanton sexual pleasure. His fingers moved faster against her and then the storm was upon her, washing over her. She gasped for air and cried out his name.

"You are so beautiful," he said as she remained boneless. When the power of her climax slowly ebbed away, she reached down and encircled her hand around his hard length, surprised to discover that his boxers were gone.

He hissed his pleasure as she languidly moved her hand up and down on him. She stroked him and her head filled with the scent of hay and the memory of all the nights that they had made love in the stables.

On hot summer nights his body had been slick and

fevered against hers and on cold wintry nights they had cuddled beneath an old blanket, his body warming her like a heater.

She consciously forced the memories of that simple time out of her mind, not wanting to think about yesterday or tomorrow. She just wanted to be here now with him. As she moved her hand against his velvety skin a little faster he grabbed hold of her wrist to stop her, his eyes glittering like a wild animal.

"Not yet," he said, letting her know he was precariously close to the edge. "I want slow. I want to savor every moment of this night…of you."

It was as if he knew what she did, that this night might never be repeated again, that this was potentially a moment of temporary insanity shared between them and dawn would return them both back to sanity.

With slow caresses and long, soulful kisses, Gray took complete control and Cath allowed him to, reveling in the simple joy of being the center of his attention.

As much as she wanted this to last all night long, she wanted…needed him to take her completely, to possess her entirely.

Impatiently, she took hold of his hardness once again. "Take me, Gray. Please don't make me wait any longer."

She didn't have to ask him twice. He rolled over and poised between her thighs, the bulk of his weight on his elbows on either side of her. He gazed at her, as if peering into the very depths of her and then eased into her smoothly, filling her up, body, heart and soul.

"Cath." He groaned her name against her hair and began to shift his hips. He stroked in and out of her in slow sweet movements, creating mindless pleasure that swept through her.

As he stroked more rapidly she looked up at him, loving the play of the nearby lamp on his rigid, rugged features, the corded muscles in his neck and the single focus of his gaze on her.

She saw his imminent release in the glowing depths of his eyes and it shoved her over the edge into a climax that sucked the air out of her body. At the same time he reached his own climax and the world stopped.

He hovered above her for endless seconds, their gazes connected as their bodies joined. He finally stirred, rolling next to her on his back as his ragged breathing mingled with her own. "We always were great together," he said. He propped himself up on one elbow, the lazy smile of a satisfied man curving his lips as one hand toyed with the ends of her hair.

"I lusted after you as a teenage girl and I guess I never quite outgrew it," she replied. This feeling she had for him had to be lust, a powerful emotion that she refused to identify as anything close to love.

"There's nothing wrong with a healthy dose of lust," he said. He tapped the end of her nose with his index finger and then moved out of the bed and disappeared into the bathroom.

Cath remained on her back, staring up at the ceiling, her body still warmed by what she had just shared with Gray. Although she had told herself she'd have no regrets if they made love again, she'd been wrong.

Already the regrets were whispering through her, telling her that this night had been a major mistake, that she'd been stupid to change the rules of their marriage of protection.

Maybe she'd hoped that by making love to him tonight she would banish the magic of those old memories and would realize that what they'd shared years ago hadn't been that special after all.

But if that had been her subconscious plan it had backfired big-time. Making love with Gray tonight had only confirmed to her that there was magic between them, at least on a physical level. That hadn't been enough to keep him by her side years ago and she knew the only reason he was here with her now was because somebody wanted to kidnap her and he'd proclaimed himself her personal bodyguard.

She couldn't forget that he'd disappeared from her life once before without even a goodbye. She'd be a fool to believe that their marriage was anything but a brief contract with a dose of lust thrown in as a complication.

It was predawn when Gray awakened and quietly slid from the bed. He padded into the bathroom, took a quick shower and then dressed in his worn jeans and flannel shirt.

Cath slept peacefully and didn't stir as he left the bathroom. He went into the sitting room, eased down on the chaise and turned on the nearby lamp. He tried not to look in her direction. With the bedroom door open and from his vantage point he could see her in the shadows of the room. Hours could be lost just watching her sleep, especially after last night. Making love to Cath was a habit he could get used to if he allowed himself, but he wouldn't. Last night had been an anomaly and they'd both be fools to repeat it.

He tore his gaze from Cath's direction and instead focused on the folder in front of him. It contained the notes Cath had made concerning what they'd found out from her friend Jewel about Dylan's mother's marriage certificate and his birth certificate. Not only had Jewel discerned that the birth certificate was bogus, she'd also clicked her way into the information that there had been no boys born on the date listed as Dylan's birth date and time at the Cody Memorial Hospital.

Sometime today Gray had to tell this information to Dylan, and he dreaded when that moment came, for he knew he'd be shattering not just Dylan's memories of his mother, but also Dylan's own identity.

Gray not only had the notes Cath had taken from Jewel, but also some of the notes that Mia and Jagger had left behind when they'd done a little investigation of their own into the kidnapping of Cole Colton. He read over their notes, but found himself distracted again and again by Cath as the dawn crept into the window to paint her sleeping figure in shades of pale gold.

Although Dirk Sinclair came from her same social circle, he wasn't good enough to wipe her feet. Gray wasn't sorry that the man had the impression that Cath had been two-timing him. Hopefully by the time the baby arrived Dirk and all the rest of the world would just assume it was Gray's.

He found himself embracing the thought. When the danger to Cath passed and they divorced, the baby would still need a father figure in his or her life.

He was surprised to realize he wouldn't mind being that man, although he recognized that Cath might have a problem with it.

Besides, even with a baby in tow, he knew it wouldn't take long for appropriate suitors to come calling on her. Aside from her money, she was beautiful and kind, smart and funny. She'd move on and so would he.

He got up and moved to the window and stared out where the ranch hands were just beginning to start their daily chores. It felt odd not to be out there with them and it was equally odd that he didn't miss it at all.

All personal feelings aside, he liked the idea that he was keeping Cath safe. He even liked the idea of further investigating Cole Colton's kidnapping from so many years ago and the more recent mystery of Faye Frick and Dylan.

His father had always told him he was born to be a wrangler and for years Gray had believed that was who he was supposed to be. Gray had never thought about being anything else until now.

He returned to the chaise and tried to stay focused on reading and rereading the notes they'd taken, attempting to put together a puzzle despite its missing pieces.

The sun had marched above the horizon and still Cath slept. Gray leaned back against the chaise and allowed his mind free rein.

He thought about the night before and the charity event and he couldn't help but think about Dirk Sinclair. He hadn't liked the idea of Cath dating him at all, but it hadn't been his place to offer his opinion to her.

Dirk Sinclair came from wealth, but he'd done nothing with his life to build any kind of future for himself. Rumor had it that his parents had tired of financing Dirk's playboy ways and had been pressuring him to settle down with a good woman and a job in the family business.

Obviously Dirk had declined the position in the family business and had decided to go heiress-hunting instead. Gray frowned and once again cast his gaze toward the sleeping pregnant woman.

She'd told Gray that Dirk had broken up with her when he'd discovered that she wouldn't get her inheritance for another four years. Was it possible he'd come up with another idea for making money off Cath? Was it conceivable that Dirk had been the kidnapper, attempting to get a ransom payday from the woman he'd been dating?

He made a mental note to himself to have a visit with Chief Peters and let him know that Gray wanted Dirk's alibis checked for the nights of the two kidnapping attempts.

His thoughts scattered once again as he continued to look at Cath. He had no idea what to expect from her this morning. Would she be happy that they'd made love or would regrets shine in the depths of her blue eyes?

He wouldn't allow himself to feel guilty about what had happened. She had been the aggressor, not he. He'd given her an opportunity to change her mind, to think about what she was doing as she'd unfastened his buttons, but she hadn't hesitated.

He suddenly realized her eyes were open and she was gazing at him. "Good morning," he said.

She shoved strands of shiny hair from the side of her face and rose up on one elbow as she huddled beneath the sheet to hide her nakedness. "What time is it?"

"Almost eight and I don't know about you, but I could use a cup of coffee and some breakfast." He watched her closely, trying to discern her mood.

"If you'd grab my robe and bring it to me I'll get dressed so we can get downstairs and get some breakfast and coffee."

Gray relaxed a bit, bringing her the robe. She pulled it around her and then quickly disappeared into the bathroom. It took her only minutes to dress in a pair of black slacks, a black-and-gray lightweight sweater and reappear ready to go to the dining room.

As they walked down the hallway toward the dining room, it was obvious that she had no intention of mentioning what had happened between them the night before.

"I hope the charity took in lots of money last night," she said. "The room certainly was set up beautifully." He didn't reply and she continued talking about the decorations and the people they'd seen.

Her monologue had the flavor of somebody afraid that a topic might arise and she was determined to guide the conversation where she wanted it to go. That was fine with him. His head was jumbled with enough unsettling issues that he didn't mind if they didn't speak of what had happened between them last night.

Most of the family was at the table when they entered the dining room. Gray sat next to Cath and prepared himself for the usual tense unpleasantness of a family gathering.

The first person Cath spoke to was Levi. "Any change in Daddy?" she asked, a question that was common from Cath to Levi.

Levi shook his head. "He's stable but remains in the coma."

Gray felt Cath's pain radiating from her. "At least he's stable," he said to her softly.

She nodded. "I just want him to wake up."

"You and me both," Darla said from across the table.

"Mother is worried about what provisions Jethro has made for us upon his death," Trip said, ignoring Darla's pointed glare at him. "She's afraid if the old man dies we'll be out on the street and she won't be able to afford her designer shoes and Botox treatments."

"Trip, that's enough," Darla said sharply.

Tawny sat between her mother and brother, a small smile curving her lips as if she were pleased that it was her brother at the receiving end of Darla's aggravation for a change.

"Why don't we talk about something more pleasant," Gabby suggested.

"Like those creepy kids that you work with?" Tawny replied.

"They aren't creepy," Gabby replied coolly.

"I guess it's impossible to have a pleasant meal here unless you're eating alone," Amanda said dryly.

This pronouncement was followed by the usual tense silence that accompanied so many meals. "It's a wonder you don't have morning sickness after eating with your family," Gray said as they left the dining room.

Cath smiled at him. "Thank goodness I haven't had a touch of it yet." She patted the small pooch of her tummy. "The bean is being nice to me."

"Speaking of the bean," Gray said as they reached her suite. He waited until she sat in her chair and then he took a place on the chaise. "I was thinking this morning while you were asleep that if you decide to remain single after our time together is over, the bean won't have any kind of a father figure in his or her life."

She looked at him wordlessly and he drew a deep breath and continued, "I just wanted you to know that as far as the world is concerned I'm the bean's father and if you want me to remain a part of his or her life after we split up, I'm more than willing to do that."

Her eyes filled with tears that quickly tracked down her cheeks. Gray was appalled. "I mean, if you don't want me to, then I won't," he quickly exclaimed.

She shook her head and swiped at the tears. "These aren't sad tears," she said as the tears finally halted. "I don't know what to say. That's the most generous offer you could have ever made to me and to the bean."

She turned her head to gaze out the window for several moments, and then looked back at him. "I think the best thing we can do right now is just take it all one day at a time."

Gray nodded agreeably, but inside he was stunned to realize how much he'd wanted her to offer him an official place in the baby's life.

Chapter 15

Cath sat in the passenger seat of Gray's truck as they drove the fifteen miles to the town of Dead to speak with Chief Peters.

When Gray had mentioned to her that he wanted Dirk Sinclair checked out, she'd been stunned at the very idea. As she'd thought about it longer, she'd remembered the anger that had twisted Dirk's features when he'd realized she had no inheritance but rather lived on an allowance and wouldn't see any real money for another four years. Without any other suspects lining up she wasn't going to protest Gray and the officials taking a close look at Dirk.

They'd worked together to take care of her morning chores at the petting barn, then had greeted Dylan and made arrangements for him to meet them in Cath's suite around three that afternoon.

"You must be dreading talking to Dylan," she said, breaking the silence that had settled between them since they'd gotten into his truck.

He'd been unusually quiet since he'd offered to be there for her baby when this was all over and she'd not jumped at the offer. She hadn't meant to hurt his feelings, but she didn't want to bind him to her in any way when this was all over. There was no certainty that he would even remain at the Dead River Ranch after they divorced.

"I can't tell you how much I'm dreading it," he replied. "Our information virtually steals his identity from him, leaving so many more questions for him to have to figure out." He checked the rearview mirror. "I'm thinking about asking Peters if I can get a copy of the original file from Cole's kidnapping and all the murders that have taken place over the past couple of months at the ranch."

"Why would you want to do that?" she asked curiously.

"I've realized over the past week that I like trying to solve puzzles." He glanced in the rearview mirror again and frowned. "And right now I'd like to know who has been following us since we left the ranch."

Cath turned back to see a black pickup truck behind them. As Gray sped up, the truck paced them. When he slowed down to allow it to pass, the truck behind them slowed, as well. "I don't recognize the truck," she said, anxiety starting a breathless twist in her stomach. "But half the workers on the ranch and in the area drive black pickup trucks."

"True, but I don't like this one," Gray replied. He kept one hand on the steering wheel and with the other pulled his gun out of his waistband. "I don't like them behind us at all."

Cath had almost forgotten about the threat to her and now her head exploded with visions of Allison Murray dead on her floor, with the horror of a man's hand smashed hard against her mouth as he tried to drag her away from safety.

"Hang on." Gray's terse warning came an instant before he took a quick right-hand turn onto a narrow road. They went up over a hill and then their tires rattled over metal cattle guards set in the ground.

Cath squeaked in heart-thumping terror as Gray maneuvered a U-turn that had them facing the cattle guard they'd just driven over. He threw the truck in Park, rolled down his window and held his gun, ready for anything that might come over the hill toward them.

Neither of them said a word. Cath had a feeling she couldn't have spoken if her very life depended on it. Her throat had closed up the moment he'd made the unexpected turn. She reached up and grabbed hold of the aquamarine stone of her necklace, as if it were a magic talisman that would ward off danger.

Seconds ticked by. Gray was like a statue, eyes dark and narrowed in concentration, his gun arm sure and steady out the driver window. She knew without a doubt if he thought she was in danger he'd shoot first and ask questions later.

More seconds passed and Cath could swear her heart wasn't beating, that she wasn't breathing at all as they waited to see if the suspicious truck would appear over the rise.

After what felt like an eternity, Gray put his truck in gear and began to creep forward, his arm still extended out the window.

Cath didn't breathe again until they reached the main road and saw no other vehicles in sight. Gray set his gun on the seat between them and turned toward Dead once again.

"Maybe we're both a little paranoid," she finally said.

He flashed a tight grin. "A little paranoid is good when somebody is really after you."

"It was probably just some eighty-year-old rancher driving into town," she replied, trying to diminish her tense fear.

"Probably," Gray agreed, although she wasn't sure he believed it.

Cath continued to grasp her necklace, realizing how easy it would have been for that truck to have crashed into them, for Gray to have been hurt and for her to have been dragged from the wreckage.

"You know you're risking your life for mine," she said.

"I know," he replied, never taking his gaze off the road. "I'm thinking about making protecting people my business."

She stared at him in confusion. "You're going to start a bodyguard business?"

"No, I'm thinking about maybe going to the police academy in Cheyenne when this is all over."

She was stunned. "You want to be a policeman? But

what about the ranch? What about your job as foreman?"

"I've been burned out on ranch work for a long time now and just haven't acknowledged it to myself. The Coltons can always find another ranch foreman, but for the first time in years I'm stoked about going in a new direction with my life."

"Would you work on the police force in Dead?" she asked. Even though she knew he was hers only temporarily, she couldn't imagine once this was all over that she'd never see him again.

"I'd go wherever I was needed."

She was glad he didn't look in her direction for she felt a ridiculous burn of tears at her eyes. Drat her pregnancy hormones. She swallowed hard to suppress her unexpected rise of emotion. "Hopefully this all will be over soon and you can get on with pursuing your future," she said, grateful that her voice betrayed nothing of her thoughts.

"The future will wait for me as long as necessary. In the meantime my most important job here is to keep you and the bean safe from harm."

He pulled up in front of the Dead Police Station and that was the end of their discussion.

When they entered the small building Gray asked for Chief Peters, who immediately greeted them and took them into a small private office.

He gestured them into two chairs and then sat behind his desk and gazed at them curiously. "What brings the two of you here?"

"The idea of a potential suspect in the two kidnapping attempts on Cath," Gray said.

Harry leaned forward. "Tell me more."

As Gray laid out his thoughts about Dirk Sinclair, he was pleased that Peters listened with interest and then wrote a couple of notes on a pad in front of him. "We'll definitely check him out."

"I was also wondering if it would be possible for me to get copies of the files on all the murders that have taken place on the ranch in the past couple of months as well as the file on the cold case of the kidnapping of Cole Colton," Gray said.

Peters leaned back in his chair and looked at him in surprise. "Are you looking to take over my job?"

Gray smiled. "I might be looking for a job on the force someday in the future. Right now I've got Cath's safety to worry about and I thought in my spare time I'd go over the files and see if I can put anything together that makes sense."

"I could get you copies of the files, but they're active right now and in any case they wouldn't do you any good. Hank Drucker was the most corrupt officer of the law I've ever seen and what he left behind in those files can't be trusted. I have my men reworking everything and so I can't release anything to you because they're all ongoing investigations."

Peters leaned forward again and shook his head. "I don't like speaking ill of the dead, but Drucker left behind a mess…potential witnesses that were never interviewed, copies of interviews that never took place. I've got ballistic test results that I'm not sure ever came from a lab or the specifics of where the bullets were found." He threw up his hands in frustration.

"No offense, but he wasn't the first dirty cop who's ever been caught," Gray said.

"True," Peters agreed, but a deep frown cut across his forehead. "What bothers me is that there's usually a reason a cop goes bad and in Drucker's case I haven't been able to find one. His reporting of the usual crimes that have taken place over the years in Dead seems pretty much all right. It's the ones that deal with anything concerning the Dead River Ranch that are dummied up."

"We've always believed somebody at the ranch is the head of the snake who is behind everything that's happened there. Unfortunately we can't figure out exactly who it might be," Gray replied.

"I'm determined to figure it out," Peters said firmly.

"That makes two of us," Gray replied. He met Cath's gaze and saw the shiver of apprehension that swept over her. How he wished he could take away any fear she might feel, but until they figured out who the true evil was at Dead River Ranch, there was no way he could ease her fears.

After they left the police station, they decided to grab a late breakfast at the diner in town. Gray watched in amusement as Cath ordered eggs and bacon and a side of pancakes. She caught his amused gaze as the waitress left with her order.

"I definitely feel like I'm eating for two this morning," she said. "I'm ravenous."

"Are you going to have the doctor tell you if it's a

boy or a girl?" he asked as he settled back in the cheap plastic of the booth they shared.

She took a sip of her orange juice before replying. "I haven't decided yet. I guess it would be practical to know the sex of the baby ahead of time so I could start buying the appropriate clothes and such. But there's a part of me that would like to be surprised."

"What would you prefer? A boy or a girl?"

"Oh, I don't care. As long as he or she is healthy I'll be happy." She looked at him curiously. "Do you want children of your own? You used to talk about it when we were young."

"We used to talk about a lot of things when we were young," he countered. "Right now I don't think about having kids much. I just want to make sure you and yours are safe."

As they ate their breakfast Gray tried not to think about the dreams he'd once shared with the woman across from him. They talked about the ranch, bandied around the names of potential suspects and then talked about their upcoming meeting with Dylan.

"I wish we didn't have to tell him anything we found out," Cath said as she finished the last bite of her stack of pancakes. "I wish Mia and Jagger hadn't set in motion the questions that they did about Faye and her past."

"I agree, but as hard as it's going to be on Dylan, he has a right to try to find out the truth about his mother and himself."

"If he had no birth certificate then how did he get a social security card?" she asked.

"Who knows? I imagine whatever social security

number he has belongs to some baby that died at birth and somehow Faye managed to snag the number for Dylan," Gray replied.

Cath sighed. "It seems like every question brings up another question."

"The real question right now, Mrs. Eating for Two, is if you're finished with your breakfast?" he asked teasingly. Her plate was completely empty.

She looked down and then back at him, her eyes glittering with humor. "I guess I'm finished unless I intend to eat the plate itself."

"That probably wouldn't be a good idea."

"No, I don't think so."

Together they left the café and headed back to the ranch to wait for the time that Dylan would come to Cath's suite. Cath decided to take a short nap and Gray paced the sitting-room floor, dreading the conversation with the man he considered a brother.

As he paced he thought about the question Cath had asked him over breakfast. Would he like to have kids of his own someday? Hypothetically yes, but he only wanted children if he were in a marriage of love, where those children would be raised in an intact family.

If and when the time came for Gray to find a wife, he certainly intended to be picky about who he chose. She would have to be as committed as him to a lifetime together. He didn't want to pick a woman like his mother had been, a weak woman who had decided she didn't want to be a wife or mother. Nor did he want to make the mistake of marrying somebody like Cath's mother, who had found the allure of a sexy rodeo cowboy far stronger than being a wife and mother.

He wanted to marry somebody who wanted, who needed, to be a wife and mother. He shook his head ruefully as he stood at the window and stared outside. He wanted to marry somebody just like Cath.

How ironic was it that he'd left Dead River Ranch years ago because he'd realized he'd never be good enough to marry a Colton heir and now he was her husband…at least for now.

But now would end and he'd be back on his own. The idea of heading off to the police academy appealed to him, and once the drama and danger in this house and to Cath was resolved, he knew his days here were limited.

Eventually they'd both move on with their lives but he had a feeling even if he met and married another woman, even if he had a houseful of kids, there would still be quiet moments when his thoughts would drift back to his first love. He would wonder if Cath was doing okay, if she had found happiness with another man and how tall the bean had grown.

He turned away from the window and sat on the chaise with the notebook that held the notes Cath had taken, along with the few notes he'd gotten from Jagger before he and Mia had left town.

He could ask Mathilda to see Faye's employment application, but he had a feeling it would list the same information that Faye had told her son.

Fifteen minutes before Dylan was due to arrive, Gray went into the bedroom to awaken Cath. She slept on her side facing him as he entered the room. Her beautiful features were softened with sleep and beckoned him closer.

She made his heart ache. He crouched down by the side of the bed and gently ran his fingers over the side of her face. How he would have loved to crawl into the bed next to her and wake her with kisses and caresses that would lead to another bout of lovemaking. He pulled his hand back from her.

"Cath," he said softly.

Her eyes fluttered and then opened fully. Her drowsy smile further ignited the fire inside him. He rose from the side of the bed and stepped backward. "Dylan will be here in about fifteen minutes."

With the message delivered he returned to the sitting room, wishing his body wouldn't respond so automatically to hers, wishing he could turn off any and all emotion where she was concerned.

Within minutes she came out of the bedroom, her hair brushed and looking ready to face the difficult meeting with Dylan.

She sat next to him on the chaise, her scent attempting to muddy his senses, but he refused to allow it to happen. He needed his wits about him when Dylan arrived.

"Are you ready for this?" she asked.

"Not at all," he replied honestly.

At that moment a knock sounded at the door. Gray grabbed his gun and opened the door to admit Dylan. The smile he gave them was terse as he sat in the chair where Cath so often sat.

"I'm assuming you have some information for me, otherwise you wouldn't have called me here," he said.

"And you're not going to like what we found out," Gray warned him.

Dylan nodded and gripped the ends of the armchair as if steeling himself for whatever might come. "Let me have it."

"First of all, we determined that a John Frick never worked at a ranch called the Bar None in Cody," Gray began. "In fact we could find no evidence of a John Frick anywhere."

Dylan's jaw tightened. "And the marriage certificate?" Even though he asked the question Gray knew he already suspected the answer.

"Was a fake," Gray replied.

Dylan's eyes darkened as he slouched back into the chair. "So, my mother made up a father and a marriage. Somehow in the back of my mind I always figured there was no John Frick. She was just too vague about him whenever I asked her questions."

"There's more," Cath said in a gentle tone as she gazed sympathetically at Dylan.

"More? You mean it isn't enough that my mother lied for all these years about being a widow?" Dylan frowned, his gaze going first to Cath and then to Gray.

"Your birth certificate is a fake, too," Gray said, pulling no punches and he saw the punch as if it were a physical one to the center of Dylan's gut.

A gasp whooshed out of him as he stared first at Cath and then back at Gray. "What do you mean, it's a fake?"

"You weren't born at the Cody Memorial Hospital

on the date listed on the certificate and the doctor listed on the certificate not only never worked at that hospital, but also doesn't exist anywhere that we could find," Cath said.

Stunned disbelief worried Dylan's features. He looked at them as if waiting for a laugh, a punch line to let him know this was all just a tasteless joke. When no laughter or smiles were forthcoming, he sat forward. "How do you know all this?" he asked, his voice husky with emotion.

"Cath has a friend who does a little computer hacking," Gray replied, his heart hurting for his friend. "We saw the Cody official records, Dylan." He opened up the folder on the table before him and pulled out both the marriage and the birth certificates. "These aren't real. None of the information on them is real."

"Then I'm not real," Dylan said. Now his gaze darted frantically between them. "Then who am I? Where was I born? Where did I come from?"

"I've been going over all the notes I managed to get and trying to remember everything Mia and Jagger told me after they took a trip Jackson," Gray said. "And I have a theory, although at this point it's just a theory."

"I'm all ears," Dylan replied.

Gray was aware of Cath's curious gaze on him as well. This was something he hadn't shared with her. "Mia and Jagger were looking for clues to Cole's kidnapping, but I think they may have stumbled on to something concerning you."

Dylan frowned. "Like what?"

"We know that after Cole was kidnapped Jethro's

sister-in-law, Desiree Beal, was rumored to be in Jackson with a baby and working at a greasy spoon diner. I'm not sure that anyone caught the fact that Desiree's boss at the diner was named Faye Donner. Then months after Desiree's murder, a Faye Frick shows up here with a year-old baby boy and Faye Donner has disappeared from the diner in Jackson."

Dylan stared at Gray. "So, what are you saying? That my mother murdered Desiree, who had kidnapped Cole, and that I'm the missing heir?" Dylan released a humorless laugh. "I already went through all this with Mia and Jagger. They thought it was possible that Desiree kidnapped Cole, then my mother kidnapped Cole from her and I'm Cole Colton, but how much sense does that make, that my mother would bring me back here to the ranch to raise and never tell anyone who I was. That makes no sense whatsoever."

"It doesn't," Gray agreed.

"Maybe you should take a DNA test just to exclude the possibility," Cath suggested.

Dylan shrugged. "I don't see the point but I'll do it if it shuts the door on people suspecting that's who I am."

Cath shook her head. "You're right, it just doesn't make sense, but I still think you should get a DNA test done and take that off the table altogether."

Gray knew she had a reason for requesting the DNA test…just in case Dylan might be Cole and might possibly be a donor match for Jethro.

"I'll call Chief Peters tomorrow and see what I need to do to get the test done." He stood, appearing smaller than he had when he'd first entered the room. "You both have done enough for me and I thank you. I think now I need to figure out what I can about Faye Donner and maybe in her past I can find out exactly where I belong."

Gray stood and walked his friend to the door. He clapped Dylan on the back. "No matter what you find out, Dylan. You know you belong here."

"And you can never question how much Faye loved you," Cath added.

"I know," he replied. "That's the only thing I'm certain of right now." He pulled open the suite door and a folded piece of paper was taped to the outside. "It looks like somebody left you a note." He pulled the paper off the door and handed it to Gray.

Gray didn't open it, rather he pulled his friend into a quick embrace. "Let us know if you want us to dig further or if we can do anything for you. You know we're here for you."

"I know." With a wave at Cath and a nod to Gray, Dylan left the suite. Gray closed and locked the door behind him.

"That was hard," Cath said and patted the chaise next to her. "He looked so shell-shocked."

"I think he had a suspicion for a long time that his mother had never married and that the story of his wrangler father was fantasy. But I think the birth certificate threw him for a real loop."

"So, who left us a note on the door?" Cath asked.

"Oh." Gray realized he still held the folded piece of paper in his hand. He opened it and his blood iced in his veins. As Cath gasped, he grabbed her hand and held tight, knowing she could see the big black block letters on the paper.

STOP PUTTING YOUR NOSE WHERE IT DOESN'T BELONG OR YOUR NEW WIFE WILL END UP DEAD.

Chapter 16

"We've obviously stirred up somebody," Gray said as he remained holding Cath's ice-cold hand. "What I can't figure out is how anyone knew we've been asking questions about anything. We've been so careful to take it all away from the ranch."

"Maybe somebody overheard you and Dylan talking in the stables when he first asked you for help finding out about his mother." The iciness in her hand apparently had travelled up her arm and through her body for her voice quivered as if she were standing naked in the middle of a snowstorm.

"Maybe," he replied. He scooted closer to her and wrapped his arm around her shoulder. "This doesn't change anything," he said as he wadded up the note and tossed it onto the coffee table. "This is just the work of a coward. If somebody really intended to kill you, a note of warning wouldn't have been delivered. It's just an empty threat, Cath, taped to the door to freak us out."

"I have to admit, the tactic worked. I am more than a little freaked out." She curled into him, as if seeking his strength and the warmth of his body. "Before now I was just being threatened with kidnapping. Now somebody is threatening to kill me."

He tightened his grip around her. "And I have no intention of allowing either of those things to happen to you. I just wish I knew who left the note. Who had the nerve to walk right up to your suite door and leave it behind?"

"It will soon be time for dinner. Maybe somebody saw someone pass by my suite door."

"Yeah, and maybe the moon really is made of green cheese," he replied dryly. He doubted that whoever had left that note had been seen by anyone. The person behind all this was cunning and insidious, clinging to shadows and never showing a hint of identity.

Some of the bad guys had already been caught or killed, names had been on and then off an ever-changing suspect list. On the surface it would be easy to write off each of the crimes and deaths as isolated incidences, but Gray knew in his gut it was more, far more. There was somebody in this house behind it all, somebody pulling strings like a Machiavellian puppet master.

"Don't worry, Cath." He focused his attention back to the woman curled into him, her face pressed into the crook of his neck. He stoked her shoulder and then squeezed her tightly against him. "You and me, kid. I've got your back." And it was definitely a beautiful back.

"Stuck like glue," she said softly and then turned her face up to look at him. "Tell me again why you left here nine years ago," she said. "I don't feel like I really got the whole story from you before. Tell me why you never even took the time to tell me goodbye."

He was shocked by the sudden change of conversation and by the expectation that gleamed from her eyes. She wanted answers, real answers, not the flimsy excuse he'd offered her before when she'd asked.

He frowned thoughtfully. "That last night we spent together you had a friend come over and the two of you sat on the front porch and talked. Do you remember that?"

She looked puzzled and then nodded and sat up. "Sunny King. She was my very best friend at the time, although her family moved away the following year." Her frown deepened. "What does she have to do with anything?"

"The two of you were talking very loudly and I was just outside of the stables working so I could hear most of your conversation." As always, when he thought of that particular night a tight knot formed in his chest, right in the center of his heart.

"I don't understand. What were we talking about that would make you leave the ranch the next morning?"

"Marriage," he replied without hesitation.

"We talked about marriage a lot when we were together. She was going to be my maid of honor and I was going to be hers. We talked about color schemes and styles of dresses." She frowned. "But why would that conversation have made you decide to pick up and leave here?" *Leave me?* Although she didn't say those two words aloud he heard them ringing in her voice.

"I heard you tell your friend that your father would expect you to marry some rich, connected man and I suddenly realized I could never be that man. I ran into the stables and my father could tell I was upset. He's the one who told me that carrying on with you was nothing but foolishness, that not in a million years would a Colton be interested in marrying a ranch hand. He reminded me that you were young and carefree at that time, but soon the responsibilities of your station in life would be the end of us anyway."

His words tumbled over themselves, the hurt of that night and what he'd overheard her say trapped for so long and now loosened in a way he couldn't halt.

"Deep in my heart I knew Dad was right, so he hooked me up with the job with his friend in Montana and the next morning at dawn I left. I figured I was getting out of your way so you could grow up and find the kind of man who fit into your family, a man who would please your father."

She stared at him for several long moments, her eyes holding a well of sadness that resonated inside him. "Oh, Gray, you should have stuck around for the rest of that conversation. You should have heard the part where I told Sunny I didn't care what my father wanted for me. You should have heard me tell her that I knew what I wanted and that was you and a little ranch where we'd live together and raise cattle and babies."

The sadness inside him grew exponentially with each word she spoke. He thought of time lost, of passions denied because he'd heard half a conversation and run off half-cocked. And yet another part of him recognized that even if he'd stuck around it didn't mean a guarantee that there would have ever been any future for them together.

He raced a hand through his hair and released a deep sigh. "I guess at this point it doesn't make any difference. The past is the past and we can't go back and change it. Besides, we were so young. I seriously doubt that we would have gone the distance even if I'd stayed here." He needed to believe that, because he still believed her future didn't lie with a ranch hand.

"Probably not," she agreed with a faint cool edge to her voice, an edge that let him know his words had emotionally distanced her from him and that's exactly what he'd intended. "But you still owed me a goodbye," she added.

"You're right. I should have told you goodbye." He got up from the chaise, needing to physically distance himself from her. "But I didn't and that was then and this is now."

There was no way he would tell her now that he couldn't have told her goodbye, that he'd known if he'd seen her or talked to her one more time he wouldn't have been able to leave her.

"So, where do we go from here?" she asked. Her gaze fell on the note he'd wadded up and tossed in the center of the coffee table.

"We do the same thing we've been doing. Stuck like glue. I told you that I'm here to protect you from anything bad happening to you and nothing has changed that." He turned away from her, unable to look at her without fearing he'd fall into the depths of her eyes and do something stupid...like tell her he was sorry he'd left, that he'd never stopped loving her. "We should probably start getting ready for dinner," he said.

She rose from the chaise and disappeared into the bathroom where he knew she'd probably change her clothes and freshen up her makeup.

He sank down on the chaise once again and picked up the wadded piece of paper. Spreading it out and reading the words once again, an unexpected chill slowly walked up his spine.

Although he'd tried to downplay the note to Cath, the truth was it scared the hell out of him. A kidnapping for ransom would require that Cath be kept alive, otherwise nobody would ever pay for her return.

This note threatened death and there was no way for him to guess if it was an empty threat or not. He had to take it seriously and he had to wonder what questions he and Cath had asked that had made somebody uncomfortable enough to threaten to kill her?

Who was Faye Donner? And what role did she—even after death—have in what was happening at the Dead River Ranch? What secrets had she taken to her grave and who did those secrets worry?

The only thing he knew for certain was that as he stared at the note in his hand he felt a fear for Cath that he'd never felt before. For the first time since their marriage he hoped and prayed that he was the right man and would be in the right place to save her when danger reared its ugly head again.

And he knew it wasn't over. The note had raised the stakes in this deadly game somebody was playing. He mentally cursed himself for wadding up the note and allowing Dylan to touch it. What he needed to do was get this note to Chief Peters and see if he could pull some fingerprints off it, somehow identify something about the paper and the writing that might point to a perpetrator.

The stakes had been raised and in the meantime he had one job to do, to keep Cath alive and well.

Over the next three days life continued as usual, but an anxiety deep in Cath's heart simmered and never went away. The note they'd received had shaken her up more than she'd expressed to Gray. Somehow, someway, by digging into Faye's past she and Gray had attracted the attention of somebody who obviously didn't want anyone asking questions.

And if that particular issue wasn't enough, there was Gray. Constantly by her side whether they were inside the house or out, he'd continued to show all the characteristics that had made her love him years ago.

In spite of the note and an increased sense of wariness and distrust emanating from him toward everyone else, he kept things light and fun between them. He appeared to be going out of his way to make her happy, to keep her smiling and while she was grateful for his efforts, she never forgot that this all was going to end in a new heartache for her.

She found it tragic that he'd left the ranch so many years ago because he'd believed he wasn't good enough for her, that somehow she'd stop loving him and find some dandy to marry. She found it heartbreaking that he'd written off those days and nights of love as nothing more than youth and hadn't believed in the lasting power of that love.

Maybe on his part that was true. He made her believe that he'd moved on from her long ago, that he'd managed to put her where she belonged…in his past. Until now, until danger had circled around her. He'd given no indication that he had any desire to continue their marriage once things were settled and she was safe again.

In fact, he was making plans to move on with his future. He'd already written to the police academy and training center in Cheyenne to get information about becoming a police officer. He was planning a future without her as he should be, and yet she certainly wasn't ready to let him go now and wasn't sure she'd ever want him to leave her again.

He now sat on the chaise, reading one of his mysteries, and she was the one who paced the sitting room with restless energy. In a few minutes they would go to dinner, and after that they'd once again lie in bed side by side, careful not to touch until their bodies found each other's in slumber.

"You're wearing a rut," he said, not looking up from the book he held in his hands.

"I know." She perched on the edge of her chair and wondered why she felt as if a bomb was going to explode at any moment.

It would be Halloween in a week, but nobody in the house had ever done much to celebrate the night. Their ranch was too isolated for trick-or-treaters. Besides, she had a feeling there were already too many ghouls and goblins in the house to suit her.

She released a deep sigh and Gray looked up at her. "What's wrong? You've been on edge all day."

"I know and I don't know what's wrong. I just feel like there's the portent of a bomb about to explode in the air."

He smiled at her. "That's the way I always feel before we go to dinner with your family."

She returned his smile, acknowledging that dinners were never particularly pleasant. "I hope Agnes cooked something especially good tonight. It feels like it's been days since lunch."

Gray laughed. "Your appetite has definitely grown over the past couple of days."

"It's the bean," she replied. "I've never been so hungry in my life. I finish one meal and am already looking forward to the next."

"You must be carrying a boy," he replied. "Maybe instead of calling it the bean we should start calling it Big Bruiser."

A giggle escaped her. "That would be a terrible thing if it is a dainty little girl." Her giggle died as she realized he'd neatly turned the conversation from her anxiety to thoughts of the baby. "Nice work," she said knowingly. "You managed to calm my nerves."

He nodded, his features showing his pleasure. "Then my job is done." He closed the book and set it on the nearby end table. "And now we'd better head to dinner. We wouldn't want to miss a single snipe from Darla or a whine from Tawny or Trip's amazing speeches about his sexual prowess."

Once again Cath laughed, and her love for him expanded her chest a little fuller. She would always remember how easily he'd made her laugh when she'd been tense or anxious just like she would always remember the early mornings when she awakened with their bodies tangled warmly together.

He held on to her elbow as they left the suite and went down the long hallway toward the dining room. Mathilda greeted them before they entered, nodding her head and smiling at the two she still considered newlyweds.

Trevor and Gabby were already seated at the table. Amanda was missing as were Levi and Katie. "Is it just going to be us tonight?" Cath asked as she sat in her chair and Gray eased down next to her.

"I know Amanda got called out for a sick cow. I'm not sure about Levi and Katie, but Darla and her darling children should be showing up anytime," Gabby said.

"And here I was hoping to eat without indigestion tonight," Gray replied under his breath. He whooshed out air as Cath elbowed him in the ribs.

"Be nice," she said. "I'm hungry and I just want to enjoy a peaceful meal."

At that moment any peace in the room was destroyed as Darla, Tawny and Trip came into the room. Darla took her seat and looked at Cath. "Has there been any change in Jethro?"

"When I spoke to Levi at noon today there had been no change," Cath replied.

Darla scowled. "You'd think with all his money he could just buy a donor who could give him what he needs to beat this cancer."

"Don't forget he was refusing any treatment at all before Levi got here," Gabby said. "At least Levi managed to talk him into some drug therapy."

"If we could just find Cole," Cath said. "Not only would it rally Dad's spirits, but Cole also might be a perfect match as a donor."

"For all we know the old man is brain-dead by now," Trip said. The others at the table gasped. Trip shrugged as if surprised that anyone would find his words shocking. "Come on, he's been in a coma for a month. Do you really believe that finding his long-lost son is going to make him wake up and jump out of that bed with joy?"

"Jethro isn't that old," Trevor said. "He should still have a lot of fight left in him."

"And I've heard that people in comas sometimes hear the people around them talking. Maybe the sound of Cole's voice will call him out of the coma," Gray added, making Cath want to jump out of her chair and give him a hug.

Thankfully Gabby took over the conversation, talking about her work with her kids, the renovations in the big red barn and the lunch she and Trevor had shared the day before at a new restaurant in Laramie.

As the meal was served, Agnes stood in the doorway, her arms folded over her ample bosom and a critical eye on the servers. The only person who terrified the staff more than this short, plump red-haired cook was Bernice with her milky eye whose domain was in the bowels of the house.

Cath smiled at Agnes, seeing that the woman had prepared one of her favorite meals, roasted chicken with crisp cooked carrots and new potatoes. Agnes nodded, then whirled on her tiny feet and disappeared back into the kitchen.

"That woman gives me the creeps," Tawny said. "She's like a troll who lives under a bridge and jumps out at you when you least expect it."

"I went into the kitchen late one night to get a tea bag, and I thought she was going to hit me over the head with a rolling pin," Darla replied.

Gabby grinned despite Tawny's less than kind description. "She is very territorial about the kitchen."

"But nobody can master the art of her roasted chicken," Cath said, digging into the dish with relish.

"I think that's the one thing we can all agree on," Trevor said.

Surprisingly, the dinner remained pleasant, the conversation devoted to favorite foods and Agnes's specialties. Even Trip stayed on his best behavior and joined in the discussion by praising Agnes's beef Wellington.

They finished eating and Cath and Gray returned to their suite where Cath sank down on the chaise and released a sigh of contentment. "So, this is the way it's supposed to feel like after a nice dinner with no stress," she said.

"Amazing, isn't it," Gray agreed as he sank down next to her.

She could tell he was relaxed and she fought the desire to lean into him, to snuggle against him as if their marriage was real and forever, like he would never, ever want to leave her.

He seemed to read her mind and threw an arm across her shoulder, pulling her closer to him. "It's been nice the past couple of days."

"It has been nice," she replied, drinking in the scent of his familiar cologne, the warmth of his body against hers. They were no closer to knowing who wanted her kidnapped or who might have been stirred up by their questions about Faye. At the moment, none of that mattered because, as always, she felt safe and secure in Gray's arms.

She wanted him again. She wanted him to make love to her again. He'd reawakened the need she'd once had for him, and now she felt as if she couldn't get enough.

But he hadn't made a move on her since that night they'd shared making love. He'd been affectionate and caring, and although she'd swear there were moments when she thought his eyes glowed with desire for her, he hadn't approached her in any sexual way.

She should be glad that, other than that one night, he was adhering to the rules they had set in place when she'd agreed to this marriage of protection, but she wasn't.

She didn't know what might come first, another attack on her or the time when this arrangement with Gray would become too emotionally painful and she'd ask for a divorce despite any danger that might arise?

Chapter 17

Cath had woke up on the wrong side of the bed. Gray could tell the minute she opened her eyes that she was cranky and it was probably going to be a long day.

Without acknowledging his presence she stomped into the bathroom and a moment later he heard the water running and knew she was taking a shower.

Maybe a nice dunk under the water would wash away whatever was wrong with her. She'd slept later than usual. It was just after nine. He could have awakened her earlier to go down to breakfast, but mindful of her condition he'd decided to let her sleep. Gabby kept telling Cath that she needed extra rest and with death threats and kidnapping attempts he figured he should let her sleep whenever possible.

The water ran for several minutes and when it shut off a cabinet slammed. Gray winced. She was definitely in rare form. Probably those pregnancy hormones flaring up.

He sighed, walked to the window and stared outside. He tensed as he saw Jared Hansen and Cal Clark standing in the distance, talking. There was no reason for any anxiety to worry him at the sight of two wranglers having a conversation except the fact that he didn't trust either of the two men.

They spoke together for only a couple of minutes and then headed in different directions. At that moment Cath came out of the bathroom. She looked stunning, with her hair clean and shiny and her face wearing a minimum of makeup. She was clad in a pair of jeans and a denim-blue sweatshirt that emphasized the unusual blue of her eyes.

"Feel better?" he asked cautiously.

"I didn't feel bad," she replied. "I know we missed breakfast but I'm starving and then I need to get out to the petting barn."

"Let's go get some breakfast and then we'll head outside," he said. He grabbed his gun and ushered her out the door. "Did you sleep well?" he asked as they walked down the long hallway toward the dining room.

"Actually, I didn't. I had bad dreams all night."

"Bad dreams?" He took hold of her elbow in an effort to comfort her.

She looked up at him, her gaze holding a hint of irritation. "I dreamed that somebody came up behind me and grabbed me. They were carrying me off and you just stood there and watched."

"You know that would never happen," he replied. So,

this was the root of her bad mood. "Are you cranky and punishing me for what happened in a dream?"

Her eyes flashed with a hint of guilt. "Maybe," she admitted.

"Just so I know," he replied. By that time they had reached the empty dining room. As if possessing a sixth sense, Agnes came in from the kitchen and greeted them while they sat at the table.

"I'm sorry, Agnes, I overslept breakfast. Would it be possible to just get some juice and toast for me?" Cath said and then looked at Gray.

"Just coffee," he replied. "I'll eat a big lunch later."

With a nod, Agnes disappeared like an elfish ghost back into the kitchen. It was only minutes later that Lucinda delivered their food.

"Do you intend to punish me all day because of your bad dream?" Gray asked once Lucinda had left the room.

"Maybe," Cath said, but there was a glint of humor in her eyes.

Gray grinned at her. He knew she wouldn't be able to sustain a bad mood, not his Cath. She was sunshine, rarely clouds. As he sipped his coffee, once again he was struck by the depth of his love for her, a love that had never died despite distance and time.

She'd owned his heart since he was a boy and she owned it still, but as a man, he was afraid to speak the words of love that had fallen so easily from his lips years ago.

He wanted this marriage to be real. He wanted to be the man who stood in the delivery room when the bean was born, the man who shared laughter and love with her for the rest of their lives. But she'd given no indication that she felt the same way, that she had any interest in transforming this marriage of protection into a real marriage of love.

He took another sip of his coffee and realized that if he dwelled on these kinds of thoughts he would be in a foul mood instead of her.

It didn't take her long to eat her toast and drink her juice. Once she was finished they left the dining room to head outside.

It was an unusually mild day for late October. The sun was bright overhead, as if expending the last of its heat before the cold of winter moved in.

They stopped in the stable where Dylan was brushing down a horse. "Anything new?" Gray asked him, knowing that since he and Cath had told Dylan about his mother's marriage certificate and his own birth certificate being bogus, Dylan had intended to ferret out the truth.

"Nothing much," Dylan replied. "I talked to Mathilda but she only confirmed that the story my mother told me was the same story mom had told her when she'd first applied for a job."

"What about the DNA test?" Cath asked.

"Got swabbed yesterday at the police station," he replied. "Chief Peters says it will take a while to get the results back."

"Are you doing okay?" Gray asked in concern.

Dylan offered them a faint smile. "I'm getting through it all as best as I can."

"You know where to find us if you just need to talk," Cath said.

Dylan flashed a genuine smile. "I do. Thanks, Cath."

After a few more minutes of conversation about the workers and the ranch, Gray and Cath continued toward the petting barn. "I hope he figures things out in a way that can give him peace," Cath said as they walked side by side.

"Yeah, me, too. He's one of the good guys," Gray replied. As always, his hand was on the butt of his gun and his gaze swept the area for potential signs of trouble, but he saw nothing and nobody to concern him.

He did notice the large tractor mower pulled up nearby with a wooden four-sided trailer attached and vaguely wondered who had left it unattended. Probably one of the men had brought it out to carry off some of the foul hay that Cath piled behind the petting barn. This was a task that was done a couple of times a week by different men.

Whoever had been assigned the task today had probably decided to wait until he and Cath were finished out here and then he'd return to load up the old hay and carry it off to one of the distant pastures.

"Maybe I should do the mucking today," Gray suggested, thinking about her condition. The idea of her lifting shovels full of hay didn't sit well with him.

"I'll take care of it," she replied. "I'm not an invalid yet. Besides, I'd much rather you hang out at the fence and keep an eye on things while I work in the barn."

"Okay, you're the boss. Just don't do any straining. If something is too heavy, call for my help." He opened the fence and she entered to the bleating, hee-hawing and happy snorting of her beloved pets.

Gray stood at the fence and watched her as she laughed at the enthusiasm of the animals. "I never know if they really love me or just get excited to see me because I represent food." Her eyes sparkled and Gray's love for her pressed tight against his chest, threatening to spill from his mouth.

She disappeared into the barn and he listened as she greeted the ducks, the ferrets and the bunnies, her voice light as air and with the melodic tones of happiness.

He needed to tell her how he felt, but he didn't want to do it here, not out in the open while she was doing her morning chores. He wanted to take her back to their suite, pull her into his arms and tell her that he wanted this marriage to be real, to be the forever kind of love.

He knew he would be taking a chance. If she didn't feel the same way he did then things could get very awkward between them as they continued this crazy relationship.

But he had to take that chance. If he didn't speak to her of his feelings he felt as if he would explode. Maybe this was the way fate had intended it all along for the two of them.

Maybe it would be better if he had the conversation with her away from the house, away from the ranch altogether. "What do you think about maybe driving into Laramie tonight for dinner? We can try out that new restaurant that Gabby and Trevor told us about," he said, his voice raised so she could hear him inside the barn.

"Sounds good to me. I'd never turn down dinner away from here." Her disembodied voice drifted out.

Gray's heart tightened as he realized that tonight he intended to tell her that he loved her and that he wanted to be with her and her child for the rest of their lives.

He heard a faint footfall behind him and before he could turn, before he had time to react, something hard crashed down on his head. He fell to his knees as the world spun and sheer panic washed over him at the same time he fell into darkness.

"What time do you want to plan to drive into Laramie?" Cath asked as she leaned over to pet a couple of the rabbits in their pen. She straightened and waited for an answer. "Gray?" She raised her voice in case he hadn't been able to hear her.

He appeared before her, the man dressed all in black, with a ski mask covering his features, making it impossible for her to identify him. He carried with him a horse blanket and the glittering dark eyes of determination.

The shock of his presence froze her in place and sent her mind reeling in a hundred directions. Gray! What had he done to Gray? Oh, God, please not Gray.

Trapped. Her head spun to her own situation. She was trapped unless she could get out the small back door where she'd been shoveling out old hay. Those miniscule seconds of inertia worked against her. Before she could move he was on her. Before she could scream he'd slapped a wide band of duct tape across her mouth and threw the blanket over her head.

Panic screamed inside her as he grabbed her, pinning

her arms to her sides beneath the blanket. He lifted her
as if she were a sack of potatoes.

With the tape across her mouth and the blanket so
tight around her she was disoriented, terrified and ut-
terly helpless to fight back.

She had no idea where he carried her, but groaned
as he dumped her body into something, and then the
sound of a tractor mower revved up. She knew...she
was in the wooden trailer that was used to transport hay.

She tried to fight her way out of the blanket, but it
had been tucked around her like a tight shroud. *Gray,
where are you?* Her heart cried out for him...for somebody to come to her rescue.

Her heart stopped as the tractor came to a halt and
the engine shut off. Strong arms picked her up once
again and in the process she managed to get one arm up
to grasp her necklace. But this time the feel of the stone
brought no pleasure, no hope. It felt cold and alien, as
if all hope had been sucked out.

Although she twisted her body, trying to get free,
it did no good. His hold on her was too strong and the
blanket too tight. Emotion welled up, but she shoved it
away, knowing that if she began to cry she could stran-
gle herself because of the duct tape across her mouth.

She had no idea where she was being taken. Although she heard sounds, a door closing softly, another
one squeaking open, she couldn't guess where she was
being taken. In one final act of desperation she ripped
the necklace from around her throat and fought to get
her hand out of the blanket.

She wasn't sure her hand was free of the material or

not when she dropped the necklace, praying that somebody would see it and it would provide a clue as to her whereabouts.

The man who carried her never said a word, but she smelled his sweat. She had the sensation of going down. Stairs? Was she in somebody's home? It had to be somewhere nearby as they hadn't travelled that long in the tractor.

The Blacks' house?

One of the outbuildings?

A new smell mingled with the odor of the man, the scent of dank earth. Her heart slammed against her ribs. Was she going to be buried? Why would somebody do that to her? Who was it behind all this?

Once again tears threatened and she screamed over and over again, but with the duct tape so firmly across her mouth her screams sounded like nothing more than the squeaking of a mouse.

He walked for what seemed like forever and not only was she filled with fear for her own life, but also for Gray. What had the man done to Gray? Was he dead? That could be the only reason for this happening.

She should have told him that she loved him. She should have told him that she'd never stopped loving him. In the near month that they'd shared she believed more than ever that they belonged together.

And now it was too late.

Finally, after what seemed like forever, he placed her on her feet and pulled off the blanket. While she was still disoriented, he whirled her around and efficiently bound her wrists together behind her back.

When he turned her around she realized three things...they were in a dimly lit tunnel with a small room in front of them and they were not alone.

As the man shoved Cath into the small room, he turned to speak to the other figure, also dressed all in black and wearing a ski mask. Cath had the impression that it was a woman and there was something hauntingly familiar about her.

She stared at the figure, trying to identify who it was behind the mask, who appeared to be in charge of her kidnapping.

The eyes behind the woman's mask met hers, although Cath couldn't discern the color of the eyes. Those evil eyes narrowed, as if she didn't like Cath looking at her.

In a sudden rush of movement, the woman raced toward her, punched her in the face and then shoved her hard. Cath reeled from the unexpected blow and her head collided into the room's wall.

Pain crashed through her head. Stars exploded, blinding her as she slid down the wall and knew no more.

"Gray? Gray, wake up."

The familiar deep voice slivered faintly through the darkness but didn't pull him out of the abyss where he'd fallen.

"Gray. Dammit, open your eyes."

This time the voice sliced through the dark and Gray opened his eyes to find Dylan crouched down next to him. Dylan's expression was dark with worry as he helped Gray to a sitting position.

"What happened?" Dylan asked.

Gray, completely disoriented, stared at him and attempted to fight past the shattering pain in the back of his head. He continued to stare dully at Dylan. He raised a hand to the back of his head where a lump the size of Montana rose up to greet him. One touch of the lump and any lingering darkness or disorientation that had plagued him instantly vanished.

"Cath," he said, the single word holding all the panic that scorched through him.

He struggled to his feet with Dylan's help, horror coupled with urgency as he started toward the barn. She wouldn't be there. Even as he raced to the fence he knew she was no longer inside the structure.

Gone.

She was gone.

He'd been so busy, so distracted thinking about his love for her that somebody had managed to slam him over the head and get to her. He'd let down his guard and now she was gone.

He turned to Dylan. "She was working here and somebody came up behind me, knocked me out and took her. We've got to find her, Dylan." Pain centered in his stomach and seared through his chest, making it feel as if he was on the verge of a heart attack.

The tractor with the wagon that had been parked on the side of the petting barn was gone, as well. Where was the tractor? Had that been how the kidnapper had carried her away?

How long had he been unconscious? A glance at his

watch let him estimate that he'd only been out for maybe ten or fifteen minutes.

"There was a lawn tractor here with a wagon. We need to find that tractor because I think it was used to carry Cath away from here." He grabbed Dylan by the shoulders. "We've got to find her. She's in trouble."

Dylan nodded, his gaze steady as if in an attempt to calm Gray. Nothing would calm Gray except having Cath back in his arms. "We'll start by looking for that tractor. You take the east outbuilding and I'll take the west ones. We'll meet up back here after all the outbuildings have been cleared."

Gray took off running, grateful that Dylan had a plan, for Gray's head felt jumbled, filled with both physical pain and mental anguish.

The first building he reached was a small storage shed that held a variety of gardening tools. What it didn't contain was Cath.

Somewhere in the back of his mind he knew he should call for help, rouse every cowboy and house staff available to search, but somebody had smashed him over the head and he didn't know if raising an alarm might put Cath in even more danger.

He and Dylan knew this land, knew this place better than anyone on staff. They'd grown up here, explored every nook and cranny. If Cath was still on the property they'd find her. He didn't even want to think that she might have already been moved off the property.

He ran from the gardening shed to one of the old barns that populated the grounds. "Cath!" He cried her name again and again, hoping against all reason for a reply.

There was none.

Chapter 18

Cath regained consciousness slowly, her first sensation of coming out of the darkness the scent of earth
filling her nose and the hardness of the ground beneath
her body.

She lay facedown, where she must have finally come
to rest after hitting her head so hard she'd been ren-
dered unconscious. Her wrists were still bound behind
her back, her shoulders screaming at the strain of the
unnatural position.

The duct tape remained intact and smothered her
mouth, making it impossible for her even to move her
lips beneath the thick, silver tape.

She felt the trickle of blood running down the side
of her face and could only guess that the fist that had
connected with her face had split the skin someplace

around her eyebrow, for that area throbbed with unrelenting pain.

She rolled over on her back and sat up, grateful for the single light bulb that dangled overhead in the small room where she was held captive. Had she awakened to the utter darkness of a tomb, she might have lost her mind completely.

All four walls and the floor of the room were earthen, letting her know that she was someplace underground. But where? It hadn't felt as if they'd traveled that far with her in the bottom of the wagon, but shock might have altered her ability to judge time and distance.

The only break in the dirt was the wooden door that she'd been shoved through. She stared at the door, as if she could magically open it by the very will of her being.

Only one way in and one way out, and that was the door. But before she could even think about somehow breaking down a door, she had to stand up, not an easy feat with her hands bound behind her back and her face and head begging her not to move.

It took her three attempts before she finally managed to maneuver herself up to a standing position. Although her head ached and terror ruled the rhythm of her heartbeat, she advanced on the door.

She had no illusion that it was unlocked, but she also didn't know how thick it might be. She walked over to it, turned and knocked her knuckles against it. Solid, with a steel-like ring. Definitely far too solid for her body to attempt to break through.

Besides, she wouldn't do anything physical enough

to harm the baby inside her. If it were possible she would have released a burst of hysterical laughter. She was the perfect victim…afraid to fight back because of her condition and now silenced from calling for help by a simple strip of strong tape.

She walked back to the wall opposite the door and slid down to sit on her rear. There was nothing she could do but sit and wait to see what happened next.

She kept her mind off thoughts of Gray, knowing that if she lingered there she would definitely lose her mind. She had to be strong for the bean. Her baby. She couldn't even place a hand on her tummy to caress the life inside her, to somehow assure herself and the bean that everything would be okay.

Instead of speculating on what happened to Gray or the baby, she thought about both the man who had taken her and the figure he'd met here in the bowels of the earth, a figure she thought might be a woman.

Why had she seemed so familiar? Had it been Tawny hiding beneath the black clothes and ski mask? Or maybe Darla? Had they become so worried that her father would die and leave them out in the cold that they'd kidnapped Cath for the ransom she would bring?

It would be a ransom that would give them enough money to get out of the house and live in the same kind of luxury after Jethro's death. Had the man who had attacked her been Trip or somebody they had hired? Was it a family affair of deception?

Or had the woman been one of the maids and the man one of the ranch workers? She couldn't begin to guess who might be behind it, but whoever it was, was guilty of Allison's murder.

Were the same people also responsible for Jenny Burke's murder? Or was there more than one strain of evil that had taken control of the Dead River Ranch?

"Cath! Cath, are you here?"

Gray! Her heart expanded. He was alive! He was here! Still, the voice was so faint Cath didn't know if it was real or simply her intense desire to hear Gray's voice one last time, the need for him to rescue her so she could tell him she loved him, that she'd always and forever love him.

"Cath?"

Not knowing if his cry was real or imagined, she screamed his name against the tape that kept her mute. She struggled to her feet and slammed her shoulder over and over again into the door, hoping that the sound would travel to wherever he was, hoping that he would hear the noise and come to get her out of this hellhole.

Tears streamed down her cheeks as she held her breath and listened for his voice once again. *Please, Gray. Find me. Save me.*

Nothing. She heard nothing.

She remained by the door for what felt like an eternity, hoping, praying to hear him call to her once again. He was gone, if he'd ever been nearby in the first place.

Maybe she'd heard him calling her from the beyond. Maybe he was telling her that soon they would all be together in death.

On shaking legs, with her shoulder aching from the contact with the door, she stumbled back to the wall

and slid down to sit, once again watching the door...
waiting to find out what happened next.

She was tired, so tired, and as she watched, as she
waited, her eyes drifted closed and she fell back into
the darkness.

Gray's headache had abated, usurped by the panic
that tightened his throat and burned in his chest. As he
raced back toward the petting barn, having checked out
all of the outbuilding, he was dismayed to see Dylan
waiting for him there, shaking his head negatively to
indicate he'd found no sign of Cath.

"The tractor and wagon were in the shed, but there
was no sign of who might have been driving it or of
Cath," he said as Gray stopped in front of him. "And
I'm assuming you found nothing."

Gray shook his head, the panic rising up the back of
his throat, nearing cutting off his ability to draw air. He
looked at Dylan helplessly. "Where could he have taken
her? I can't believe I wasn't unconscious that long...
maybe ten minutes or so."

Together they both gazed toward the mansion. "It's
the only place we haven't checked," Dylan said.

"And there are plenty of nooks and crannies, rooms
and closets." Gray took off at a run toward the house,
aware of Dylan following closely behind him.

They burst through the front door, encountering
Mathilda in the hallway. "Dylan...Mr. Gray," she exclaimed in surprise.

"Cath is missing," Gray said as Mathilda gasped.
"We're going to search this house from top to bottom."

"I'll gather the house staff to help," Mathilda replied.

"No," Gray said quickly. There was no way he would trust the word of anyone in this house where a search for Cath was concerned. He was aware that with each minute that passed he was gambling with Cath's life.

What he hoped was that she'd been kidnapped for ransom and whoever held her wouldn't harm her. But he couldn't be sure of that after the note they had received threatening her life.

What he did know was that potentially the person holding Cath might be a member of the staff, who could lie about checking rooms and closets and keep her whereabouts in the house hidden from them.

"Dylan and I will search, Mathilda. You keep this to yourself," Gray said. "It's possible the guilty party is a member of the staff."

Mathilda wrung her hands together, tears appearing in her eyes. "I hope that's not true," she said in a mere whisper. "Because if that's the case then I hired whoever has taken her."

Gray put a hand on Mathilda's shoulder. "Just go about your business as usual. We're going to start in the basement." He nodded for Dylan to follow him to the door that led downstairs.

As they raced down the steps the scent of laundry soap and the heat of constantly running dryers greeted them. Bernice Black's domain was a steamy pit of industrial-size equipment that kept the family in clean sheets, towels and clothing.

At this time in the afternoon the laundress was in full work mode, bent over a washing machine as Dylan and Gray appeared at the base of the stairs. She rose up with a surprised squeal, her eyes widened by the invasion into her area.

"We need to look around down here," Gray said, already moving to check behind machines as Dylan searched the rest of the area.

"What are you looking for?" Bernice asked, her milky eye appearing more opaque than usual.

"Has anyone else been down here this afternoon?" Gray asked as Dylan returned to his side with a negative shake of his head.

"No, people don't like to come down here unless it's absolutely necessary," she replied.

"Have you been here all day?" Once again Gray felt the pound of urgency racing his heartbeat.

"Since just after dawn," she replied. "And nobody else has been down here today.

"Come on, Gray, there's nothing here." Dylan touched Gray's shoulder and the two men moved back upstairs where Mathilda stood looking at them anxiously.

"I want to check out every room on the male staff floor," he said to the housekeeper. "You have keys to everyone's rooms. I want those rooms opened right now." If it had been the male who'd attempted to take her twice before who had succeeded this time, it was possible that she'd been taken to one of these staff rooms and was being held behind a locked door.

Mathilda followed Gray and Dylan up the stairs to where the male staff lived. Her fingers trembled as she began to unlock doors and Gray and Dylan checked each one of the rooms.

It didn't take long to clear each room. A simple check in the closets as that was the only place somebody could stash a woman. Door after door was unlocked, closet after closet was checked and still no Cath.

Gray felt perilously close to coming undone by the time they'd checked the last room. Dylan placed his hand on Gray's shoulder, his brown eyes sympathetic. "Okay, so we go down a level and check the great room, Jethro's and Cath's suites, the dining room and the kitchen."

They searched methodically, opening closets, checking behind furniture and pulling open cabinets that were big enough to hold a body. They worked in silence, quickly and efficiently but all the while Gray wanted to scream in agony.

Where was she? Who had taken her? If she'd been taken off the property, then he feared they would never find her. They'd just have to wait to see if a ransom note showed up. He refused to consider that it might be her body that was found.

After checking in Cath's and Jethro's suites, the great room and dining room, they finally moved to the kitchen, where Agnes eyed them with a narrowed gaze.

"What are the two of you doing in here?" she demanded. "You know I don't like anyone in here except my kitchen staff."

"Have you been in here all afternoon?" Gray asked as he opened a broom closet and then closed it.

Agnes's eyes narrowed further. "I stepped out for a

little fresh air earlier. I'm not chained to this room. I do my job, everyone gets fed."

"I don't give a damn if you take rumba lessons every afternoon," Gray said impatiently. "I just need to know if it's possible somebody came in here and you weren't here to see them."

"I suppose it's possible," she said grudgingly, her back stiffened defensively.

Gray opened up the pantry door, once again wanting to scream in frustration, in fear as he saw only shelves of canned goods and food products.

He felt as if they were running out of time. It had been over an hour and a half since Dylan had pulled him from unconsciousness and they'd begun their search. He started to slam the pantry door when he stopped, his gaze drifting to the floor of the shelves directly in front of him.

Something sparkled…a piece of gold chain. He leaned down to pick it up but couldn't as it was caught on something. He tugged again, his heart stepping up a new beat, one of adrenaline, of sudden discovery.

"Dylan, get in here," he said urgently. "I think there's something behind this back wall."

"What are you talking about?" Agnes asked as she moved closer to the pantry door.

Both Dylan and Gray ignored her as Gray remained crouched down holding on to the length of gold and Dylan began to press and prod along the sides of wooden shelves.

"I've got something," he said, excitement lacing his voice. "It's a lever." He did something and the wall swung outward, displaying the sloping earth that led to what appeared to be a tunnel.

"I'll be damned," Dylan said in stunned surprise.

It was as the door swung fully open that Gray pulled the length of delicate chain from where it had been on the floor. At the end of it was the aquamarine stone Cath had worn around her neck.

He rose to his feet, the necklace warm in his hand as he showed it to Dylan. "Agnes, we need a flashlight," Dylan said.

The short, plump woman reached beneath the kitchen sink and withdrew a high-power flashlight. Dylan grabbed the light and held it out to Gray, but Gray shook his head and instead pulled his gun from his holster.

"She's someplace down there, Dylan," Gray said as he slipped the necklace into his pocket and turned on the flashlight.

Now all they had to do was find her and hope that she was still alive.

"Call Chief Peters and get him and his men here. Tell him it's an emergency." Dylan said to Agnes as he and Gray started down the steep sloping dirt that led down...down, the only light the beam from the flashlight in Dylan's hand.

"How did we not know about this?" Dylan marveled in a hushed voice. They advanced slowly, unsure what awaited them in the darkness just beyond the flashlight's beam. "I thought we know everything there was to know about this ranch."

"The big question is who does know about it?" Gray replied, tightening his grip on his gun.

The two men fell silent and they baby-stepped through the semidarkness. Gray's heartbeat thundered erratically and Cath's necklace burned in his pocket. He wanted to run ahead, get to the end of wherever the tunnel led, but he feared making too much noise, of making a fatal mistake. Slow and steady was better than fast and furious.

Who had built this tunnel and why? Where did it go? Was Cath down here someplace or were they racing toward a dead end? The air was cool and smelled of the packed earth that surrounded them.

They heard nothing as they continued forward side by side. It was like being in a grave and Gray fought the illusion that the walls were closing in on them. He battled a claustrophobia he'd never experienced before.

He wondered if Dylan felt the same way. A glance at the man next to him showed only his friend's features taut with tension and ghostly pale in the residual spill of the flashlight that barely pierced the darkness ahead of them.

Seconds crept by, their footsteps faint as they inched forward. How long could this tunnel go on? Gray tried to discern the direction they traveled, the distance they had gone. They had to be in the middle of the area between the house and one of the barns Gray had checked earlier.

Had he missed something there? A secret door? A hidden panel? Damn, had he missed something that would have led to Cath sooner?

What worried him more than anything was the memory of the note that had been taped to her suite door.

Had the person who had taken her kidnapped her for ransom or had he taken her to follow through on the promise that she would die because of the questions they'd been asking.

He would never be able to live with himself if she'd been killed. He was supposed to be her protector. He'd wanted, no needed to be her hero, and he feared it was already too late.

The man appeared before them in Dylan's beam of light. In filthy clothes, he was somebody Gray had never seen before. Gray's first instinct was to shoot, but he was afraid that if he killed the man he'd never find out where Cath had been taken.

He expected the man to turn and run from the two figures in the tunnel, but to Gray's shock he barreled toward them, Dylan's light catching the gleam of a knife in the man's hand.

Gray's gun clattered to the ground. Dylan stepped backward and Gray stepped forward to meet the attacker. The man grunted and slashed the knife in the air as if wanting to use it across Gray's throat.

While Gray maintained a healthy respect for the weapon, there was no way this man was getting past him and no way Gray wanted him dead unless it came to a him or Gray situation.

The filthy man and the knife upped Gray's fear for Cath. If he found out this man had used his knife on her, Gray would see to it that the man died a slow and painful death.

In the meantime Gray sidestepped another slash of

the knife in the air, and as the man was partially turned with the motion, Gray slammed into him.

They hit the tunnel wall with a force that whooshed the air out of the man, but he held to the knife. Gray pinned his wrist against the earth in an attempt to keep the weapon out of play.

At the same time he raised his knee to slam the man in his groin. There was no such thing as a fair fight when it came to fighting for your life. The man anticipated Gray's move, and Gray's knee slammed into the dirt next to his body. "Where is she?" Gray demanded, keeping his body against the man who was fighting to get free, fighting to unpin his hand with the knife from Gray's grip.

He might look and smell like nothing more than a tramp, but he was strong and Gray was determined. It was a standoff with both struggling for dominance.

Dylan trained the light on the man, as if attempting to blind him with the high-beam glare, but although he winced, it didn't appear to weaken him in any way.

Gray threw several punches at his face, punches that the attacker blocked with his free hand. Gray's arm muscles began to shake as he desperately tried to keep the knife out of the picture.

Without warning the man twisted, his hand slipped from beneath Gray's and the knife sliced across Gray's arm. The burning pain, coupled with the feel of blood flowing, renewed the fight in Gray.

He slammed his hand into the man's nose, this time connecting. He followed that punch with another to the side of the man's head. With a faint sigh of stale breath, the man's eyes fluttered and he slid down the floor and landed on his face.

Gray picked up his gun and picked up the knife by its steely point, hoping the handle would hold fingerprints that might identify the assailant.

He stuffed the knife in his pocket, noted the blood that soaked his shirtsleeve and then looked at Dylan. "Thanks for the help," he whispered dryly.

"I knew you could take him."

Gray heard rather than saw Dylan's smile. Gray leaned down to check the unconscious man's pulse. "He's alive, but completely out." Gray picked up his gun from nearby, straightened and pointed forward. "Come on. Let's see what we find at the end of this tunnel."

They left the unconscious man and moved forward. "We've got to be under one of the barns," Dylan whispered. Gray nodded his agreement.

He couldn't imagine why this tunnel had been created in the first place or who might have been responsible for its presence. He only prayed that somewhere in the darkness ahead Cath was alive and well.

After several more minutes of walking, they came to a wooden structure built into the tunnel. Gray's blood pressure spiked and his heart beat so rapidly he felt light-headed as he saw the heavy steel door with the rasp and padlock.

"What the hell?" Dylan muttered, his beam focused on the padlock.

Gray tugged on the lock, finding it heavy-duty and impossible to break. He knew with every instinct he owned that Cath was just beyond that lock. What he didn't know was if they would find her dead or alive.

"There's no way we can break through that door," Dylan said.

"I'll have to shoot off the lock," Gray replied as he pulled his gun. If he shot it sideways then the bullet would hopefully shatter the lock and travel on into the earth on the other side of the tunnel. "Get back," he said to Dylan, hoping that by some crazy horror of fate the bullet wouldn't ricochet around in the tunnel and wind up killing them both.

Dylan did as he was told, taking several steps backward, the beam of the light steady on the lock. Gray took his position and pointed his gun.

The explosion of the gun could possibly deafen them both in these close quarters, but Gray would risk a lifetime of deafness to get to Cath. One look at Dylan's face let him know his friend felt the same way.

Gray pointed the gun and his hand shook with the stress that nearly consumed him. He closed his eyes, imagined Cath's beautiful face and drew a deep breath. When he opened his eyes again his aim was sure and steady.

The blast and the flash occurred almost simultaneously, both deafening and blinding Gray for several seconds. He waited for his hearing and sight to return, then hurried toward the lock, pleased to see it shattered and hanging open. Ignoring the pain in his arm, he worked the last of the lock off and then crashed open the door.

"Cath!" He reeled toward her prone figure on the floor, his heart drowning in unshed tears of uncertainty.

"Cath," he cried again as he crashed down to his knees next to her.

He gasped in relief, tears blurring his vision as she opened her eyes. "Gray. Oh, Gray, I thought you were dead." Tears misted her eyes, as well.

"Let's get her out of here before somebody else shows up," Dylan said.

Despite the searing pain in his arm, Gray leaned down and scooped Cath up in his embrace, anger mingling with unimagined relief as he saw the blood that trekked down her face from a split and swollen eyebrow. There was no question that she'd been hit and hit hard. Somehow, someway, if he found the person who'd done that he'd kill them without blinking an eye.

She wrapped her arms around his neck and buried her face in the front of his shirt and they started back the way they had come.

Nobody spoke as they moved silently back through the dark tomblike tunnel. It was enough for now that Gray held Cath in his arms and that her breath warmed his collarbones.

They came to the man in the tunnel and stepped over him. Dylan kept the light away from him so Cath wouldn't get a glance at the man who must have attacked her.

In the distance, Gray could hear the sound of Harry Peters and his men, and he and Dylan picked up their pace and met the chief in the kitchen.

"I'm taking Cath to the hospital," Gray said by way of greeting the police official. "Dylan can fill you in on everything that's happened."

Gray didn't wait for a response, but carried Cath through the kitchen, out the back door and to his truck. It was only when she was buckled in to his passenger seat and he was behind the wheel that she spoke for the first time.

"I was so afraid that you were dead, and I was afraid I was going to die, too." She began to weep and she continued to cry as he drove them to the small urgent care center in Dead.

Chapter 19

Cath was whisked away from Gray and taken into one of the examining rooms in the small urgent care center that attended to the people in the immediate area.

The doctors and nurses who worked here were accustomed to dealing with sniffles and colds, with flu and an occasional broken bone. Dr. Ralph Anderson cleaned up her face, checked the cut in her brow and took her vitals, and then asked her questions about her head wound, most of which she couldn't answer.

No, she didn't know how long she'd been unconscious, although she didn't think it had been that long. No, she wasn't aware of hitting anything else and had not received any hits or kicks to the stomach. She didn't have any dizziness or nausea, although she did have a small lump that was tender to the touch. Still, the doctor didn't believe she'd suffered a concussion.

Unfortunately the urgent care center didn't have the appropriate equipment to perform an ultrasound. He suggested she rest, put some ice on her swollen eyebrow and check in with her obstetrician as soon as possible.

Throughout her time of talking and being treated by the doctor all Cath could think about was Gray, who'd looked as if he'd been to hell and back as he'd driven her here. She could only imagine the panic he must have felt when he awoke and found her gone from the petting zoo.

Outside the window dusk had fallen, which meant Gray had been searching for her for the whole afternoon. If anyone needed to be checked for a concussion it was probably him. He'd been hit far harder over the head than her reeling into a wall and hitting her head.

When she was released from the doctor she returned to the waiting room with the intention of making sure Gray was checked out, as well. To her surprise he wasn't in the waiting room and a nurse let her know he was in an examining room getting stitches to the wound in his arm.

Distraught, Cath sank down in a chair to wait for him. She hadn't even known he was wounded. He'd lifted her up and carried her all the way out of the tunnel, all the way through the house and had gotten her here, never indicating that he was hurt in any way.

When he finally came into the waiting room, his shirt sleeve had been cut off and he sported a long wrap of bandaging. She jumped out of her chair and ran to him, tears once again spilling down her face.

"You didn't tell me you were hurt," she said through the tears.

"It was nothing, just a little cut that required a few stitches." He pulled her into his arms.

She looked up at him. "How many stitches?"

"Fourteen," he admitted.

She gasped and the tears raced faster. "Hey," he said softly as he swiped at her cheeks. "It's all good. We're both safe and sound and we left the bad guy unconscious in the tunnel so hopefully by now Chief Peters will have him in custody and have some answers for us."

"Then we should get back to the ranch," she said.

"And tomorrow I'll take you to see the bean doctor just to put our minds at rest," he replied. They stepped out into the night and got into his pickup.

"I'm sure the baby is fine, but it wouldn't hurt to confirm that all is well," she replied.

He started the engine and then turned and looked at her, his eyes dark and glittering in the illumination from the dashboard lights. "Cath, I'm sorry. I'm so very sorry that I let you down."

"Please stop. I don't want to hear any talk like that," she exclaimed. "You didn't let me down. I'm here, I'm safe and I know it's because of your unrelenting search for me."

"It definitely helped that you dropped this." He dug in his pocket and pulled out her necklace. The sight of it brought tears to her eyes once again as he handed it to her. "If I hadn't seen that in the bottom of the pantry, we wouldn't have known where to begin looking for you."

"I dropped it hoping somebody would see it, hoping it would provide a clue, but I wasn't sure where it landed or if I'd ever see it again." She clutched it tightly in her hand.

"The clasp is broken. While we're in Laramie seeing your doctor tomorrow, we'll stop by a jeweler's and have a stronger clasp put on it." He pulled out of the parking lot and headed back to the ranch house.

"I thought I'd never see you again," he said, his voice sounding full and huskier than usual. "I've never been so afraid in my life. What happened after I was knocked out?"

She told him about the man taping her mouth and binding her in a blanket, then the ride in the wagon and after that the man carrying her through the tunnel to the small room.

She explained that there had been somebody there waiting for them and she had the distinct impression that it was a female, although the figure had been clothed all in black and had worn a mask.

By the time she'd given him that much information, they'd arrived back at the ranch where three police vehicles were parked and lights shone from every window of the mansion.

They found Peters and his two officers, Mike Harriman and Patrick Carter, with most of the staff gathered in the great room.

As they hesitated at the threshold of the room, Peters approached them, his features tortured with concern and questions. "Are you both okay?" His gaze went to Cath, who nodded.

"We're both fine now," she replied, grateful for Gray's arm around her shoulder.

"Did Dylan fill you in on what happened?" Gray asked.

Peters nodded. "He told me what happened from the moment he saw you unconscious out by the petting barn until the two of you found Cath in that room at the end of the tunnel. What I need to know is which one of you put the bullet into the chest of the man down there? A man, by the way, nobody seems to be able to identify."

Gray gasped and pulled Cath closer against him, as if to shield her from any ugliness. "Neither of us."

"That's what Dylan said," Peters replied.

"I'll take credit for beating the hell out of him and knocking him unconscious but not before he cut me with a knife."

Gray released his hold on Cath and turned sideways. "If you'll grab a pair of gloves and reach into my pocket, you'll find the knife he used. I didn't touch the handle so maybe you can pull some prints. You can take my gun, too. I only fired one shot down there and it was to blow off the lock on the door."

"So, if nobody knows who the man is that took me, then nobody knows who the other person was who met him down there," Cath said. "And if he's dead there's no way he can tell us."

"What other person?" Peters asked.

Once again Cath explained about the figure who had met them by the hidden room. "I think it was a woman and there was something familiar about her but I can't figure out exactly what."

By that time Gabby and Amanda were at Cath's side and Peters motioned Gray to follow him into the kitchen. Gabby led Cath to a chair where she collapsed, exhausted and slightly traumatized by all the events that had occurred.

"Are you sure you're okay?" Amanda asked worriedly. "Can we get you anything? Do anything for you?"

"I'll get a cold cloth for your eye." Gabby's eyes filled with tears. "Oh, Cath, I can't imagine what you've been through."

As she left to get a cold cloth, Amanda leaned down to give Cath a hug. Cath's love for her sisters and her love for Gray filled her to the brim. In the time she'd spent in that tiny room, not knowing what the future held, not knowing if she had a future, all she'd been able to think about was her family, her baby and Gray.

Gabby returned with a cold damp washcloth and gently placed it on Cath's eyebrow. Cath caught her sister's hand and squeezed it. "I just want you to know how much I love you, Gabby and Amanda. I was so afraid I'd never have the chance to tell you again."

Mathilda walked over to Cath and lightly touched her on the shoulder, her features twisted in agony. "I feel so horrible. I'm responsible for all this. The police chief feels certain that this was an inside job and that means whoever did this to you was hired by me. Despite my love for this family, I'm terrified that I've made a deadly mistake in hiring somebody. I can't tell the good people from the bad."

She spoke quickly, her hands once again wringing

as she gazed at the three sisters. "I need to leave here and let you hire somebody who does a better job than I have."

"Mathilda, don't talk crazy," Amanda said.

"We need you here," Gabby added.

Cath reached out and took the older woman's hand in hers and squeezed it gently. "Mathilda, this isn't your fault. You can't take the blame for any of this. Sometimes evil hides so well nobody can see it until it explodes. You've been a valuable member of this household for years, and I won't stand for any talk of you leaving us now." She released Mathilda's hand, as if the subject was closed.

Mathilda wiped the tears from her eyes. "I can't imagine not being here with the family, but if it's best that I leave, then I'll go."

"And we can't imagine this house, this family functioning without you," Gabby replied. "Now, no more nonsense talk about you leaving us."

Mathilda nodded gratefully and moved to the opposite side of the room where most of the maids who worked directly under her supervision were gathered together.

Apparently the kitchen staff was gathered in the kitchen or in the employee's dining room, for none of them was present in the great room.

What she wanted more than anything was to tell Gray how much she loved him, to tell him that she was tired of pretending she would be ready to let him go when this was all over. She wanted him forever. She just wasn't sure that he wanted her forever, too.

* * *

The kitchen staff was in the employee dining room as Gray followed Harry Peters into kitchen. The door to the pantry stood open and the shelving unit remained aside to display the entry to the tunnel.

"If you or Dylan didn't kill the man down there, then who did?" Peters asked—a rhetorical question since it was already established that Gray didn't know the answer.

"Somebody had to have gone down there after we carried Cath upstairs or they shot him while we were in the room with Cath and used a silencer. I honestly can't tell you if he was dead or alive when we left the tunnel. I just assumed he was still alive but unconscious."

"And neither you nor Dylan recognized him?"

"I've never seen him before in my life," Gray replied.

"As far as we can tell this is the only way in or out of the tunnel. I've got some men checking in the barn where we believe this leads. They'll see if there's a trapdoor in the floor or some other way to enter that room other than through the tunnel."

Gray sighed in frustration. "So, the answers lie with a dead man in a tunnel."

"Not necessarily," Peters replied and gazed through the doorway that led to the employee's dining room. "I've questioned all the kitchen staff. Of course nobody admitted to knowing anything about the tunnel. But Agnes told me that at the time all of this was going down she was in the storage shed just outside. She said that one of the maids, Misty Mayhew, saw her out there and that the two had a brief conversation, but when I questioned Misty she denied that happened."

Gray frowned. "This kitchen has been Agnes's domain for years. She's always been very territorial about it. She's probably in and out of this pantry a hundred times a day. It's hard to believe she didn't know about the pantry shelves hiding a secret tunnel."

"My thoughts exactly," Peters replied. "Maybe a couple of nights in lockup will get some real information out of her."

While Gray found it hard to believe that the short, red-haired, ill-tempered woman could have anything to do with what had been happening around the ranch and specifically with Cath's kidnapping, he also couldn't discount the fact that she was the most logical person to have known about the tunnel's existence.

"Fine by me," Gray replied. "I'm all for anything that might get us some answers as to who the bad guys are around here."

Peters nodded and stepped into the employee dining room and motioned for Agnes to come into the kitchen. Peters pulled his cuffs from his belt. "Agnes Barlow, you're under arrest for conspiracy to commit kidnapping."

Agnes's green eyes nearly bulged out of her plump face. "No, you're making a mistake here." Her gaze darted around the kitchen, as if seeking a rolling pin or an iron skillet she could use to pop Chief Peters over the top of his head. But he twirled her around and cuffed her wrists behind her back as he gave her the Miranda rights.

"I'm going to take her down to the station," Peters said to Gray. "My men will stay and continue to process both the scene in the petting barn and the tunnel and secret room. I've got the coroner coming to take out the body. I'm sure there will be more questions for you and Catherine and Dylan in the morning."

Gray nodded, grateful that he wasn't being asked to hand over his gun…at least not yet. Just because they'd found Cath and a man was dead, there were still no answers as to who might be the mastermind. Until this question was answered, the danger to Cath was still very much alive.

It was hours later that Cath and Gray finally found themselves alone in her suite. Gray sat on the chaise lounge and pulled Cath into his arms.

"Maybe Agnes will break after she's been locked up for a while," he said.

"Agnes?" She raised up and looked at him in surprise.

"Peters took her in to the station. She's the most logical person to have known about the tunnel's existence. She was probably the female you saw with the man who abducted you."

She frowned and began to shake her head. "No, it wasn't Agnes down there. The woman was taller, leaner…built more like Darla and Tawny. You need to let Chief Peters know that she wasn't the person in the tunnel."

He pulled her back in his arms. "I'll let him know in the morning. It won't hurt Agnes to spend a night as a guest of Peters. Maybe the time behind bars will force her to admit to knowing something. We'll also let Peters know that the woman was a different shape than Agnes."

"First thing in the morning we'll straighten it out," she murmured. She leaned her head against his shoulder. For a long time they simply remained in the embrace, not speaking but just existing in the pleasure of each other's presence.

"I got hit over the head because I was distracted," he finally said with a heavy sigh. "I was distracted by wondering if maybe fate had intended us to be together all along. I got lost in thinking that maybe we were supposed to part as young teenagers so we could grow up apart and then come together as two adults ready to love each other again."

She raised her head to gaze at him and he continued, his gut suddenly tight as his heart beat a little faster. "You're right, Cath. I didn't fight for you years ago. I left here with a heart broken and a bitterness against you I thought would never end. I didn't believe I was good enough for you. I believed that eventually you'd recognize that fact, too. I was just a ranch hand and you were a Colton. That really hasn't changed, but the difference between then and now is that I intend to fight for you now."

Her eyes flared with an emotion he couldn't read and he wondered if he was about to bare his soul to a woman who no longer cared. "I love you, Cath. I never stopped loving you and I don't want this marriage to ever end." He held his breath as she moved out of his arms to sit up straight.

Tears misted her eyes and she released a small laugh and swiped them away. "Darned pregnancy hormones seem to have me crying all the time."

Gray's heart sank. "I don't want to make you cry, Cath. I just want to love you and the bean for the rest of my life."

Her eyes shimmered with the indigo-blue color that he knew he'd never forget for the rest of his life. "I've been trying to get up the nerve to tell you how much I love you, Gray. I don't care about the Colton money. I've never cared about anything but you. I want you to be my husband forever. I want you to be the father to all my children...all of our children. Gray, I..."

She got no other words out of her mouth as he pulled her to him and kissed her with all the heart, all the soul he possessed inside.

The kiss finally ended, and he gazed at her with all the love he had in his heart. "I want to be that man in your life, Cath. I want to be your lover, your friend and the man who is beside you for the rest of your life, but I have a plan for us that I'm not sure you're going to like."

She frowned and once again leaned away from him. "What kind of a plan?"

Throughout the long evening a plan for their future had been formulating in his head, the only plan he thought made sense under the current circumstances, but he knew it was possible that she would never agree to it.

He reached out and took her hand in his. Her delicate fingers twined with his and again his love for her nearly overwhelmed him.

"If today has taught me anything, it's shown me that no matter how hard I try, no matter what measures we take, I can't guarantee your safety, at least not here at the ranch." She started to pull her hand from his, but he held tight and continued. "Cath, we still don't know who the bad guys are. We still don't know who has been behind these kidnapping attempts on you. That woman you saw could be Tawny or Darla, or it could have been any one of the female staff members. There is danger here that we can't avoid."

She nodded slowly. "So, what's your plan?"

He drew a deep breath, grateful that at least she was willing to listen. "We leave here for a while. We remove you from the danger. I won't take you far. We'll get a little apartment in Cheyenne with plenty of security. I'll go through the police academy and you go through your pregnancy without having to be scared, without having to constantly look over your shoulder."

He'd expected her to instantly reject the idea and was surprised when she gazed at him thoughtfully. "Cheyenne isn't so far away," she said slowly.

"I wouldn't want anyone here to know exactly where we go, but we can get you throwaway phones so that you can stay in touch with your sisters. If there's a change in your father's condition, we can be back here within an hour. Wherever we choose to live I'll invest in the best security system money can buy."

"Okay," she said.

He looked at her in stunned surprise. "Really?"

"Really." She reached out and placed a palm against his cheek, her eyes holding a wealth of emotion. "I realized today that the danger here just didn't pertain to me, but also my baby and to you. In those long hours of being in that little room and believing you were dead, my heart hurt like I hope it never hurts again. I'll go to Cheyenne with you, Gray. Eventually, I'd like to come back here and raise my kids here, but I'll do it your way for as long as we need to."

Once again Gray pulled her into his arms. Her agreeing to leave Dead River Ranch with him spoke more of her love for him than any other words she could say, anything else she could do.

He kissed her deep and long, knowing that this was the right way for them to truly begin their life together as a loving, rightfully married couple.

When the danger here was gone they'd return and he'd abide by her wishes to raise their children here and hopefully he could get a job as a police officer on the Dead police force.

Once they pulled apart, she leaned against his chest where she obviously felt as if she belonged. "I just have one final request," she said.

"What's that?"

She raised her head to gaze at him and a wealth of emotions shone from her eyes…love and desire and the faintest hint of humor. "It's not bean anymore. It's a baby, and I insist we come up with names so that we stop calling it a bean."

Gray laughed and pulled her closer to him. "I think we can manage that."

In fact, he was certain they could manage anything together. They would live a temporary future in Cheyenne while he went through the police academy and assured her safety, and then whatever she wanted he would provide.

There were still deadly secrets here at the ranch, but they were secrets somebody else would have to figure out. Gray was removing himself and the woman and baby he loved from the picture. He just prayed that when all the secrets were uncovered there was somebody still standing here at the ranch.

Shoving these worrisome thoughts aside, he once again pulled Cath closer, and as he kissed her, his hand caressed the baby he'd claimed as his own.

His woman.

His family.

His happily-ever-after.

* * * * *

Don't miss the next story in
THE COLTONS OF WYOMING:
THE COLTON HEIR
by Colleen Thompson, available November 2013
from Harlequin Romantic Suspense!

REQUEST YOUR FREE BOOKS!
2 FREE NOVELS PLUS 2 FREE GIFTS!

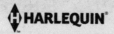

ROMANTIC suspense

Sparked by danger, fueled by passion

YES! Please send me 2 FREE Harlequin® Romantic Suspense novels and my 2 FREE gifts (gifts are worth about $10). After receiving them, if I don't wish to receive any more books, I can return the shipping statement marked "cancel." If I don't cancel, I will receive 4 brand-new novels every month and be billed just $4.74 per book in the U.S. or $5.24 per book in Canada. That's a savings of at least 14% off the cover price! It's quite a bargain! Shipping and handling is just 50¢ per book in the U.S. and 75¢ per book in Canada.* I understand that accepting the 2 free books and gifts places me under no obligation to buy anything. I can always return a shipment and cancel at any time. Even if I never buy another book, the two free books and gifts are mine to keep forever.

240/340 HDN F45N

Name	(PLEASE PRINT)
Address	Apt. #
City	State/Prov.	Zip/Postal Code

Signature (if under 18, a parent or guardian must sign)

Mail to the Harlequin® Reader Service:
IN U.S.A.: P.O. Box 1867, Buffalo, NY 14240-1867
IN CANADA: P.O. Box 609, Fort Erie, Ontario L2A 5X3

Want to try two free books from another line?
Call 1-800-873-8635 or visit www.ReaderService.com.

* Terms and prices subject to change without notice. Prices do not include applicable taxes. Sales tax applicable in N.Y. Canadian residents will be charged applicable taxes. Offer not valid in Quebec. This offer is limited to one order per household. Not valid for current subscribers to Harlequin Romantic Suspense books. All orders subject to credit approval. Credit or debit balances in a customer's account(s) may be offset by any other outstanding balance owed by or to the customer. Please allow 4 to 6 weeks for delivery. Offer available while quantities last.

Your Privacy—The Harlequin® Reader Service is committed to protecting your privacy. Our Privacy Policy is available online at www.ReaderService.com or upon request from the Harlequin Reader Service.

We make a portion of our mailing list available to reputable third parties that offer products we believe may interest you. If you prefer that we not exchange your name with third parties, or if you wish to clarify or modify your communication preferences, please visit us at www.ReaderService.com/consumerschoice or write to us at Harlequin Reader Service Preference Service, P.O. Box 9062, Buffalo, NY 14269. Include your complete name and address.

HRS13R

"What are you doing?" Laila asked, taking his arm.

Harris stared at her. "Why didn't you go with your family?"

"And leave you here alone?" Laila asked.

He didn't want Laila in the thick of this. An attempt had
been made on her life in America and he didn't know if she
had been one of the targets of the bombing here. "You need
to be somewhere safe."

She gripped his arm harder. "I am safest with you."

Another explosion boomed through the air. Harris grabbed
Laila and shielded her with his body, pulling them to the
ground. Was the sound a building collapsing from the damage
or another bomb? Harris guessed another bomb. Laila was
shaking in his arms. Harris waited for the noise around him to
quiet and concentrated on listening for the rat-tat-tat of gun
shots or another bomb.

His protective instincts roared louder. He wouldn't let any-thing happen to Laila. "I'm going to help where I can."

Her eyes widened with fear. "What if there is another bomb—"

He had some basic first-aid training and he'd been a marine. Dealing with difficult situations had been part of his training. "There might be another one. There's no time to wait for help."

"I can help, too," Laila said, lifting her chin.

"You aren't trained for this," he said.

"No, but I'm capable and smart. I will be useful. Don't treat me like a crystal vase."

Laila wouldn't back down. She wouldn't leave the scene, not when her countrymen needed help. Arguing wouldn't get him anywhere. He'd seen her strength many times before. She might act like a shrinking violet in front of her brother or other males, but she had an iron core. "You're stubborn when you want something."

"So are you," Laila said, giving him a small smile.

**Don't miss
PROTECTING HIS PRINCESS
by C.J. Miller,
available November 2013 from
Harlequin® Romantic Suspense.**

HARLEQUIN®

ROMANTIC suspense

THE COLTON HEIR

Ranch hand Dylan Frick threatens to turn
in a gorgeous intruder, but Hope begs him
to keep her deadly secret. She isn't the only
one whose identity is under wraps.
Will the truth set them free?

Look for the next installment of the
Coltons of Wyoming miniseries
next month from Colleen Thompson.

Only from Harlequin® Romantic Suspense!

Wherever books and ebooks are sold.

Heart-racing romance, high-stakes suspense!

HRS27846